ALSO BY OMAR TYREE

Leslie

Just Say No!

For the Love of Money

Sweet St. Louis

Single Mom

A Do Right Man

Flyy Girl

Books by the Urban Griot

College Boy

Diary of a Groupie

A Novel

Omar Tyree

Simon & Schuster
New York • London • Toronto • Sydney • Singapore

SIMON & SCHUSTER
Rockefeller Center
1230 Avenue of the Americas
New York, NY 10020

SIMON & SCHUSTER and colophon are registered trademarks
of Simon & Schuster, Inc.

Manufactured in the United States of America

ISBN 0-7432-2867-7

She believed

with all of her *heart*

that it was *real*.

They believed

with all of their *minds*

that it was *not*.

Maybe

they were *all* wrong.

Or maybe

they were all *right*.

Omar Tyree, "Illusions"

Diary of a
Groupie

MGM Grand

Main Street in Las Vegas, Nevada, was the hottest spot for adult fun and games that America had to offer. Every night was a Christmas light show from the biggest front lawns in the neighborhood. Bright lights flickered and enticed the mind in hues of red, pink, yellow, green, purple, blue, white, and orange from every creatively designed building that made up the skyline. "The Strip" was an overdose to the senses, a giant pinball machine of all-night gambling and solicitation. It was a wonder that people ever managed to sleep there. However, they did sleep—they slept on their own realities and became easy prey for those who recognized the value of remaining awake.

"You ready for this, girl? 'Cause if ya' not, then you betta' *get* ready. Ain't nuntin' in this world like Vegas. *Nothin'*."

The girl smiled and kept her cool while sitting inside the white stretch limo with the man. She looked young enough to be his daughter, but she wasn't. That's why the man felt so comfortable when he slid his big right hand over her burnt orange dress and landed it between her legs.

The girl barely noticed his touch. She was too busy being entertained by the bright lights that lit up the Vegas night.

"You need sunglasses out here," she said with a smile.

"Ha, ha, ha!" the man laughed, louder than what was expected. He wasn't even drunk yet.

The girl paid his overreaction no mind.

As the limo came to a complete stop at the curb, she said, "That's a big lion out there."

The man laughed hard again. He said, "Shit, girl, that's the MGM Grand. That's where our fight is tonight."

She nodded to him. "Oh . . . looks like fun."

"Shit yeah, it's fun," he told her.

The limo driver, a small Latino man in a tuxedo, opened the curbside door for his two African-American passengers.

"Here we are, Mr. Bennett. The MGM Grand."

The driver extended his hand to the young lady, who sat at curbside, and helped her out of the limo.

"Thank you," she told him and grinned.

"No problem."

"Hey, no flirtin' with her, Jose," Mr. Bennett joked.

His driver laughed and shook it off.

"You don't have to worry about me. I have a wife and six children at home."

Mr. Bennett climbed out of the limo and stood at the curb, wearing a black tuxedo himself, size extra large.

He towered over Jose. He said, "You got six young'uns and you only twenty-five years old."

The driver grinned and ignored the slander.

He said, "I wish I was twenty-five again."

Mr. Bennett greased his palm with a ten-dollar bill.

"I'll call you when we're ready to go," he told him. He smiled in the direction of his young lady. "Or better yet, *Teresa*'ll call you when we're ready. She'll probably have to drag me outta here anyway."

Teresa took her cue and grinned, right before she locked her arm in his and pulled him toward the casino.

Thousands of well-dressed fight fans headed inside the casino alongside them, with some of them rushing to get to their seats before they missed any of the action.

"You can tell when these motherfuckers never been to a fight before," Mr. Bennett said to his young date. "They act like they in a got'damned track meet."

Teresa smiled at him and squeezed his bulky arm.

"Marvin 'Head Hunter' Bennett!" someone yelled out.

Mr. Bennett turned his freshly shaved head, standing more than six feet tall and leaning slightly to his left. His rugged brown face showed several healed nicks and scars from too many battles won and lost in the boxing ring. Teresa stood beside him with a baby-doll face, shoulder-length hair, and a sultry young body that appeared untouched and docile.

"How you doin'?" the stranger asked Teresa first, ignoring his old friend for the moment.

Marvin "Head Hunter" Bennett was not as easy on the eyes as his young date was.

"She's doin' just *fine*," Mr. Bennett answered for her. "Now back ya' ass up off her."

The two older men scrambled into action and began to spar with each other in their tailored suits, right there in the middle of the casino. His friend was not as big or as dark brown as "Head Hunter," but he appeared a touch quicker and more athletic in his old age.

"What 'chew got? What 'chew got?" Mr. Bennett challenged with out-stretched jabs. "I'll still knock ya' ass out."

Teresa stood off to the side and shook her head. Boys will be boys, even as old men.

After a minute or so, when they had both run out of gas, the old friend looked at Teresa a second time.

He said, "I see *you're* doin' well, Marvin." He was referring more to his friend's healthy choice of a date than his actual physical appearance that night.

Mr. Bennett nodded his head with pride and looked Teresa over for himself.

He said, "Yeah, well . . . some of us *earned* it."

His friend chuckled at his boast, an old, slick chuckle.

"Yeah, I see."

Teresa stopped their idle chatter and asked, "So . . . are we gonna see the fight any time soon?"

"Oh, and she can *talk* too? Well, that's a damn *bonus*," Mr. Bennett's friend joked.

"I can do much *more* than that," Teresa teased him.

She didn't seem offended by his slight at all.

The old man became interested in exploring what more she could do, or *would* do. However, Mr. Bennett cut his plans short.

"Yeah, well, let's get on to this fight," he concluded.

"Aw'ight, I'll see you later on then, Marvin. I got some other people I'm waiting on," his friend told him.

"No you *won't* see me later," Mr. Bennett responded.

His friend looked at Teresa one last time and said, "Yeah . . . I guess not."

Marvin "Head Hunter" Bennett strutted through the casino crowds with his young eye candy on his arm, headed to the fights inside MGM Grand's main arena. All around them superstitious travelers prayed hard to strike it rich over a thousand game tables and slot machines. Occasionally, the money-grubbing machines and card dealers would hemorrhage on a few of the lucky gamblers, just to keep the crowd of sleepwalkers from waking up to the slim chances of actually winning.

"Oh, yeah! I won! I won!"

Ding! Ding! Ding! Ding!

A flashy jackpot spat out silver coins faster than the old white woman could catch with her plastic bucket.

Sshinnk sshinnk sshinnk sshinnk sshinnk!

Mr. Bennett looked her way and sneered. "Lucky old bitch."

Then he bragged at Teresa, "I don't need to win a bucket full of quarters in this damn place. I already *got* money. We 'bout to go where the *real* money is being made, inside that boxing arena."

He said, "You hear me? Ten, twenty *million* in one night! And that's just the *boxers'* share."

With that, he yanked Teresa's hand in his with more urgency to get to the fight.

She complained softly without stopping or slowing them down, "Be gentle with me. I'm coming."

Her old man looked back at her and froze for a minute. "Now that's why I like you so much, girl. You know just how to say shit to an old man," he told her.

Teresa smiled at him and squeezed his arm again to acknowledge his attempt at a compliment. No more words were needed. They had figured out how to bond that night. They would just enjoy themselves.

When they reached the MGM Grand's main arena, Teresa took a deep breath. Roman gladiators went to battle in similar domes of excitement two thousand years ago, and the pandemonium of the crowd had not changed since.

Teresa cupped her ears for a moment to protect them from the deafening roars of boxing fanatics:

"Kick his *ass*!"

"Yeeaaahh!"

"He ain't got nothin' on you! He ain't got *nothin'*!"

"Hit 'em wit' 'da left! Hit 'em wit' 'da *left*!"

The fanatics screamed as if their individual words would be deciphered in a tiny ring of flooded bright lights a football throw away. They screamed, yelled, and hollered all at the same time. It was a wild and spontaneous scene, erupting on Teresa's ears from all angles:

"Yeeaaahh!"

"Fire his ass up!"

"Whhuuuuu-weee!"

"He ain't nothin'! He a *bum*! He don't deserve this fight!"

"Knock his ass out!"

"He don't want it! Who let his ass up in the ring?!"

"This is *it,* girl. This is *it*!" Mr. Bennett exclaimed, as if Teresa had failed to notice.

"Head Hunter" launched into a flashback of his own march into a championship fight some twenty years ago. He began to bounce his head and shoulders left and right as they made their way to their seats near the front.

"You still think you can go a couple of rounds?" Teresa asked him.

She was only teasing, but "Head Hunter" took her seriously. He was a lifelong athlete. His pride overruled the reality of his body.

"You damn right I can still go a few rounds," he answered. "I ain't lost it yet."

Teresa only grinned at him as they found their seats close to ringside.

"Wow, we're up here pretty close," she commented.

Mr. Bennett remained standing at his seat and frowned at her.

"What the hell you think, we were gonna sit up in the nosebleed section wit' 'da nobodies? Shit. I'm a *somebody.* I'm Marvin "Head Hunter" *Bennett* up in here!"

He looked around to make sure no one would deny him his right to history that night. And they didn't. The fight fans sitting around them nodded to him with respect. Mr. Bennett nodded back to them and took his seat with his young lady, feeling satisfied with himself.

Teresa took another breath and tried to become comfortable in her surroundings.

"Yeeaahh, that's how you do 'em!" another fanatic screamed from behind her.

Teresa ducked as if a bullet had shot past her.

"God," she mumbled to herself with bent shoulders.

Mr. Bennett caught her protective lean and laughed at her.

He said. "You betta' get used to that, girl. They gon' be doin' that all night. Especially when the *big* fight comes."

"What's the big fight?" she asked him.

It occurred to her that she had never bothered to ask. She only knew that she had never been to a fight before, so she was honored to accept his offer to accompany him to one that night.

" 'Pretty Boy' Floyd Mayweather Jr.," he answered.

Teresa held back her smile and offered a sedate nod instead. She didn't want to alarm her date with too much of a response. She had heard of "Pretty Boy" Floyd Mayweather Jr. often since she moved to Las Vegas. He was one of the most successful and available young bachelors who had made the city his home. But there were plenty of other bachelors who crossed through Las Vegas, bachelors *and* married men; married men who had left their wives at home.

Teresa looked around and spotted celebrity bachelors and married men who sat in cologne-smelling range. There were actors, singers, rappers, athletes, politicians, comedians, local pimps, and national drug dealers all dressed to the T—and with plenty of money to spend on the Las Vegas playground.

"Good jab, boy! *Work it!*" Mr. Bennett shouted toward the ring.

He snapped his young date out of her daydreaming about the other available men there, who were much younger and attractive. Some of them were also wealthier and still marriageable. Marriage and kids remained a viable option for the young woman.

Mr. Bennett had unknowingly brought the girl into a giant shopping mall of new opportunities. It only took her a few minutes before deciding to shop.

"Umm . . . how long before the main fight?" she asked him innocently.

"As soon as these bums get this shit over with," Mr. Bennett answered. "Why?"

"I have to use the restroom."

"Well, go 'head and do it then. The pre-fight talk takes thirty minutes anyway. So you might as well beat that long-ass line to the women's bathroom now," he joked.

Teresa smiled and stood up at her seat. "I'll be right back."

Mr. Bennett grabbed her arm before she left.

He said, "Look here . . . don't you get lost now."

Teresa paused long enough to set the old man's mind at ease.

She said, "I know my way around."

"Yeah, that's what I'm afraid of," he responded.

She shook her head and grinned at him sheepishly. "I'm coming back. Okay? Now, don't have me stand here and wet my panties. Let me run to the bathroom."

After her fresh-mouthed comment, every set of male eyes in their vicinity locked on the young girl's mug and the burnt orange dress that covered her curves. However, the few women who sat around them *knew* better. It was some good old-fashioned bullshit. Any mention of the word *panties,* especially from the mouth of a young woman, consistently moved a man's thinking to the wrong head. They figured the girl was old enough to know as much herself; otherwise she wouldn't be with a man who was more than twice her age.

Mr. Bennett smiled and started laughing, confirming what the other women already knew.

He said, "Yeah, we can wet them together later on."

Teresa smiled at him with superior patience. She allowed him to let her go before she moved.

"Thank you," she told him.

He responded with a long peek over her ripe body, "Yeah, you just, ah . . . hurry back."

As soon as Teresa made her way to the aisle, her old man looked around and collected the knowing smiles from the other men who envied what he had brought with him to the fight that night, a nice fresh hottie who knew her place.

Mr. Bennett grinned to himself and mumbled out loud, "Shit. I need me a drink. Hey, bring them damn drinks over here!" he hollered in the direction of a beer man who was working the aisles. The old man struggled to negotiate his massive hand into his pants pocket and past his throbbing hard-on to pull out his wad of money. Boy, did that beer taste extra good and cold when it met his lips, creating a foam-filled mustache across his mouth. He just knew he was in for a good night. He had struck the jackpot.

Teresa made her way up the aisle and toward the restroom while watching the eyes that watched her.

"Lookin' good! Lookin' good!" someone yelled.

He was not screaming about the boxers this time.

Teresa kept her groove toward the restroom without missing a beat. She already knew what would happen. She was an attractive female in a dress, invading a male-dominated arena.

"Hey, how you doin'?" her first suitor asked.

He was too short for her type and too eager to have any real money. She passed on him with no more than a look.

"Hey there, gorgeous," went the next suitor.

He was too homely to even look at.

The next man went ahead and grabbed her hand.

"I know you're on your way to the bathroom, but I wanna talk to you as soon as you come out. Okay?"

Teresa stopped and asked him, "And what would my friend say about that?"

"The key word you used is *friend*? So what *can* he say? Whatever happens between me and you *stays* between me and you."

Teresa kept her cool. This guy was too forward and precise with his words, which meant one of two things: He was either a pimp on the prowl for new whores or a professional womanizer. Neither one of those was what she was after. However, assertive men allowed her a chance to set up the type of guys that she was *really* after, the knights in golden armor.

"I don't know if I can do that," she told him. She angled herself toward the restroom without breaking away from his grasp.

Her assertive new suitor said, "Look. I *know* you wanna get away from that old geezer you came in here with. So let's stop the charades right now."

Off to the right, she spotted an extra-tall young man with an entourage of shorter friends who surrounded him. When he momentarily caught her eye, she went into a girlish twirl of her body, as if she lacked the strength needed to break away from the hold the stranger held her in.

"Look, I just can't do that," she whined to the man, while leaning away from him.

She gave her tall friend with the entourage a pleading look to rescue her. And he responded.

"Ay, dog, let her go, man. She ain't try'na hear ya' game."

"Thank you," Teresa responded to him immediately.

Her aggressive suitor noticed when the professional basketball player spoke up, and he got the point. This girl was as crafty as he was. Maybe more so. She was obviously choosing, and she had found a way to use him to do so.

He sneered at her and walked away in a huff.

"Fake-ass bitch," he mumbled to himself out of her earshot. Nevertheless, he understood the rules of the game, so he moved on to score with the next stray kitten.

Teresa looked up to her tall new friend and said, "Aren't you, ah . . ."

"Terrence Matthews," he answered for her.

She snapped her fingers and followed up with more innocence.

"Yeah. And don't you play for, um . . ."

"The Minnesota Timberwolves."

Teresa then took her excited posture down a thousand.

She said, "I hate that I always mix the teams up. That's the team that just moved to Memphis, right?"

Terrence answered, "Naw, the Vancouver Grizzlies moved to Memphis."

The mating game continued on while the baller's entourage of friends read through the continuation of bullshit.

"Here we go again. This shit is groupie heaven out here, man. I *swear*," one of his friends complained.

"Yeah, well, I don't give a fuck. As long as *I* get one or two of them," another member of the entourage countered.

"That's what *I'm* sayin', as long as *I* get one tonight," he was seconded.

Female eye candy was everywhere inside the lobby. They didn't seem to care much about the fight. Their presence only seemed to distract the men who were there.

"So what's your name?" the baller asked Teresa amidst the crowd.

"Toni Karson," she told him. "And that's Karson with a *K*."

"Oh, okay. Well, who you here with?"

"A friend."

"What kind of friend?"

"Somebody who paid my way to the fight."

He chuckled and asked, "That's all he is, hunh, a free ticket to the fight?"

"No, he's more than that, but, you know. We don't have any rings or kids or anything."

The baller nodded his head and got the point. She was free to roam.

"How old are you?" he asked her. She appeared younger than *he* was.

"I'm turning twenty next month," she answered.

"I thought so," he responded with a grin.

"Why, I look that young?"

"In *here* you do. It's a lot of *grown* women up in here. But at a lot of the basketball games and the after parties, you would fit right in."

"You wanna come to our after party tonight?" he asked her.

She paused for a minute. "I don't really do after parties," she told him. "I'm more of a one-on-one person."

She looked into his eyes deeply to let her personal taste sink in on him.

He nodded to her again. "Aw'ight, aw'ight, I feel you on that. So if you call me on my cell phone, I can hook up with you on the private tip." He promptly gave her his cell phone number.

When Teresa finally made it back to her old man after four more offers for her company that night, the main event was just about to begin.

Mr. Bennett was on his way to drunken skunk land.

"You made it back right in time, girl," he told her. " 'Pretty Boy' Floyd 'bout t' come out the tunnel."

Teresa took in his alcohol-laced breath and ignored it.

"I guess I did get back at the right time then," she responded. "I love when they walk out to the ring. I always like to see what they're wearing."

Mr. Bennett looked at her and frowned.

"You like to see what they're *wearin'*. Shit, you sound just like a woman," he snapped at her.

She said, "Well . . . that's what I am, aren't I?"

He looked her over with glassy eyes and said, "Yeah, you sure are. You *all* woman."

When "Pretty Boy" Floyd Mayweather Jr. made his way to the ring, Teresa was forced to duck and cup her ears again.

"Yeeaahh!"

"Bring it on, champ!"

"Show 'em what you got out there, Junior! Show 'em what you got!"

The fight hadn't even started yet. She could only imagine how loud it would get in there once it did.

Floyd Mayweather Jr. wore white sequin trunks with red-and-gold trimming. He was fairly short, like most of the boxers in his lighter weight division, but his lean muscles and definition made him knockout attractive.

"I see you lookin' at him," Mr. Bennett joked to his young date.

"You're lookin' at him, too," she joked back.

"Yeah, but not for the same reason that you're lookin' at him."

"What, I can't be interested in seeing him fight?"

"Shit, you didn't even know who he was. You thought the other guy was Mayweather. And that nigga over there ain't even pretty."

Teresa shook her head and smiled it off.

"Let's get it on!" the fanatics began to yell into the ring.

"Time for the fight!"

"Let's do it! Let's *do it*!"

"Yeeaahh!"

After a while, the poor girl's ears were so damaged from the round-to-round yelling that she became immune to it. By the end of the fight, Floyd Mayweather Jr. had pulled out a unanimous decision, and her date for the night, Marvin "Head Hunter" Bennett, was flat-out drunk as expected.

"You need any help with him?" a handsome man asked as Teresa struggled to guide Mr. Bennett out of the arena and through the post-fight crowd.

"Yeah," she admitted.

Mr. Bennett looked the man over and said, "She don't need your help. She got big muscles."

Nevertheless, he allowed the man to help him out to his limo. He didn't have much of a choice. Teresa could hardly shoulder his drunken load.

After they placed him safely into the car outside the MGM Grand, the handsome man was finally able to ask the questions he wanted to ask her.

"Are you really with him . . . or is this just a thing?"

"A thing?" she quizzed.

"An outing?" he corrected himself.

"Why? Are you interested?"

"That depends."

"On what?"

"On what I would be getting myself in to."

She smirked and said, "I'm not who you think I am."

"Well, who are you?"

The game just never stopped. Teresa left the man hanging.

"What that motherfucker say to you?" Mr. Bennett asked as soon as she joined him inside the limo. He could barely sit up straight inside the car, but he was obviously still able to spit out his venom.

Teresa lied to him, "He said to make sure I got a famous champ like you safe home in bed."

Mr. Bennett looked her hard in the eyes before he began to laugh.

He said, "Shit, girl, you must think I was born yesterday. I know that motherfucker tried to take you away from me."

Teresa smiled and kept her cool.

She said, "I guess he must have failed then."

Mr. Bennett nodded his head and chuckled. He reached out for her leg and nearly missed.

He said, "Girl, that's why I like you. You know just what to say to an old ass man. You know just what to say."

Sweet Dreams

Teresa made it back to the lobby of an extravagant hotel with her old man that night and had a hotel attendant help them up to their room. They arrived at the suite on the eleventh floor and stretched Marvin "Head Hunter" Bennett across the plush, king-size bed covered in burgundy sheets.

"Thank you so much again," she told the hotel attendant and slipped him a considerate tip.

"Oh, no problem. No problem at all," the man responded before he left.

Mr. Bennett leaned up from the bed and told Teresa to bring him the ice bucket from the bathroom. Before she could reach him with it, he leaned over the bed just in time to hurl onto the floor and away from the sheets.

"Uuuuugghhhh! . . . uuuuuugghhhh!"

When it seemed that he was finished, he wiped his mouth with his white dress shirt and looked up to smile.

Teresa smiled back. "You feel better now?"

"Yeah. My system never lets me hold that shit down."

She nodded. "That's a good system. Why would you want to hold those intoxicants inside of you?"

He stared at her for a minute. He was in deep thought about the question.

"That's a good got'damn question," he finally uttered. But he still had no answer for it.

He said, "Uhh . . . I don't know . . . Why do women shop so damn much?" he asked her back.

"We like new clothes," she told him.

Mr. Bennett looked at her and started laughing. She wasted no time with her answer.

He stared at her and asked, "What kind of clothes you got under that dress?"

Teresa stared back at him. "You wanna see?"

"Shit, do I got a dick in my pants? You damn right I wanna see."

She chuckled a minute and began to undo her dress. When the burnt orange dress fell to the floor, she revealed beige panties and a bra that matched the stitching of her dress.

"Well, ain't you all coordinated," Mr. Bennett commented with a grin. "Now come on over here and sit down next to me."

He sat up straight and patted the bed.

Teresa walked over to the bed from the opposite side. She crawled up on the sheets next to him like a kitten.

"Heh, heh, heh," Mr. Bennett snickered. "Now what was all that shit about? I just told you to get up on the bed. I didn't ask for all that."

Teresa paused in her kitten stance on hands and knees. She said, "That's a good question," mocking him.

Mr. Bennett laughed harder.

He said, "Girl, you know what the hell you doin' in here. You try'na give an old man a heart attack?"

She fell down beside him and asked, "Is that what I'm doin'?"

"That's what it looks like to me."

As he spoke, the young woman began to gently massage his tool through his black tuxedo pants.

"I guess it does feel like you're about to have a heart attack . . . down here."

"Ha, ha, ha. You betta' cut it out, girl. He gon' jump up and bite you in a minute."

"Well, I have teeth, too. I'll just bite him back," she told him.

She slid her hand inside his pants.

Mr. Bennett's eyes shut and his mouth popped wide open at the tingling sensation of a young woman's fingers sliding over his erect tool.

"Yeah, you 'bout to send me to heaven," he told her with his eyes still closed.

"Is that a bad thing? I hear that heaven is nice."

"Yeah, it may be nice. I just ain't try'na go t' 'dat motherfucka yet. So you take it easy on me like you did the last time, ya' hear me?"

Teresa began to undo his pants and the rest of his clothes as he spoke.

"I hear you," she said.

She straddled him and undid her bra so Mr. Bennett could caress her ripe young breasts with his big brown hands.

"You wanna take 'em off yourself?" she asked him in reference to her panties.

Mr. Bennett thought about it and said, "Naw. I don't wanna do nothin' but count the spots up on the ceiling."

She inspected the cleanness of his private parts.

"Well, start counting them then," she told him.

She stood up to undress herself fully and walked over to click off the lights.

"Here we go for the ride," the old man said aloud as his young naked date straddled him again.

"Awww, yeeaah," he moaned to her. "Awwww . . ."

Mr. Bennett sounded more like he was getting a life-saving massage than sex.

Teresa smiled and stared down into his tightly shut eyes. She pleased him with a slow rowing of her firm body into his.

The old man reached up with both of his big brown hands and held on to her for the ride.

"Uuuueeww! . . . Yeaaahhh! . . . Awwwww!"

"Is it good?" Teresa asked rhetorically. Of course it was good.

Mr. Bennett confirmed it with a deep groan. "Yeeaaaaahhh!"

"Good. I'm glad you feel better," she told him softly. She continued to move with him.

"Ohh, little momma. Ohh, little momma," the old man began to squeal. His pleasure increased toward a climax.

"You want me faster?" his young date asked him. "Just a little bit?"

The old man was not able to answer with words, only body movements. He tensed up and gripped her body more firmly in his hands.

"Oooohhhhh, momma!" he exclaimed. He released himself into his pretty young host.

Teresa closed her own eyes and felt the warm explosion pulsating into her flush body.

When it was over, Mr. Bennett found himself out of breath and gasping for air.

"Huh, huh, huh," he breathed.

"You okay?" the young woman asked him.

"In a . . . few . . . minutes," he struggled to answer.

Teresa smiled and was satisfied with her body work. She lay beside him on the perspiration-soaked bed. As she stared up at the ceiling herself, she thought about what she would write in her diary once her old man had gone to sleep.

"So . . . I guess you're a little too *pooped* to take me gambling tonight?" she assumed. "I guess I'll just have to try my luck by myself."

Mr. Bennett grinned and didn't budge.

He mumbled, "Shit . . . twenty years ago . . . I could get back up . . . and go gambling. But t'night . . . *shit.*"

His young date smiled and knew it was the truth. Even young men ran out of the needed energy to get back up and go out after a good romp in the bedroom.

She hinted, "Well, I don't wanna spend *too* much out there anyway. I still have plenty of bills to pay this month."

Mr. Bennett paused before he responded to her.

"Are you behind on anything?"

"Nope," she answered quickly. "But the extra always helps to stay ahead."

She got up and walked into the elegant bathroom of eggshell marble with shiny gold trim around the mirrors, sink, and shower knobs.

"I'm gonna take a shower before I go. Okay?" she told the old man.

"Yeah," he grunted to her.

"How much you want me to take with me?" she asked, referring to the wad of money he had stashed that night inside of his suit jacket.

"Ah . . . three hun'net should be good," he answered.

That was the last thing he uttered to her before he slipped off into dream world. Her body work had knocked the old man out harder than a boxing glove ever did.

Teresa grinned across the room at him. She walked back over to kiss him on the forehead as he began to snore with his mouth still open.

"Sweet dreams, Mr. 'Head Hunter,' " she whispered to him, soft enough to be ignored.

She then fetched her carry bag to take it with her.

A Sweet Old Man

Teresa locked the bathroom door with all of her necessities inside and began to run the shower water on warm. Before she stepped inside for her shower, she sat on an outstretched towel that she had placed over the toilet seat. Then she pulled her latest diary book and a pen out of her carry bag to write a new entry:

Saturday, February 16, 2002
Las Vegas, Nevada
Teresa Kelly

I had a great time tonight at the "Pretty Boy" Floyd Mayweather Jr. fight. It was my first fight ever. It was major loud in there with plenty of flirtatious men with money to burn. And boy was I tempted to start a fire.

I went out with Mr. Marvin Bennett again. He's such a sweet old man. There were plenty of sexy guys at the fight who wanted me to ditch my date and go with them, but I stuck to my rule: You never leave your date for another one while you're still on it. That's just not right. Mr. Bennett's such a needful man that I wouldn't feel right about leaving him. He's just trying to hold on to his last days of manhood. I respect that.

I like him. He's honest. He tells you everything you need to know without even asking. I could grow a real liking to him if I don't watch myself. What could be so wrong with having a sweet old man around to keep me company?

The sex? Well, Mr. Bennett doesn't have much energy left for that. I have to take over in that department. Not that he's so old that he can't get it up or anything. He just spends too much of his energy still trying to be a hard-nosed boxer.

I haven't been to any fights before, but I do know that those boxers find it the hardest job to quit. That Holyfield guy in Atlanta just needs to. He needs to quit everything. Find something else to do with your life, for God's sake.

I just like to help people, myself. Marvin needs somebody to care for him. All that his children and ex-wives do is bug him for money. That's sad. I'm not saying that they shouldn't ask for any money if they really need it, but that shouldn't be the only thing you talk to your father or ex-husband about. He has a lot of pride about who he is. I'll make sure to talk to him more about that tomorrow. And we'll see what he says.

When she was finished with her short entry, she closed her diary and slid it with her pen back into her bag of personal things. Then she went ahead and took her shower, while thinking of the men, the shopping, and the excitement that would fill the next pages of her diary.

The Proposition

There was so much action going on in Las Vegas on a Saturday night that it was nearly demented to think about anyone watching you. It could be everyone and no one, depending on your state of mind. But surely, as humans had eyes and curiosity, everyone was being watched that night. Single men were watching for single women, as well as for the call girls who were sprinkled about, for a possible roll in the sack. Single women watched for big-spending men and an opportunity of a lifetime. Married men watched for single women and available call girls themselves, although usually in vain. Married women kept their eyes open to the taste and expense of the clothing and adornment being worn in Las Vegas. And the security cameras that protected the assets of the major hustlers, who owned the city of glitter and fortunes won and lost, watched them all. So why would a lone young black woman think twice about anyone of importance watching for her that night? She was just a speck of sand in the sandbox. Or so she thought. Because eager eyes *were* watching her every move that night.

As she approached the exit door of the hotel casino for a breath of fresh air, it happened so fast it felt as if it were a camera flash. Someone grabbed her quickly from behind and pushed her forward while slapping cold steel around her fragile wrists.

"Ow, what the hell . . ." she protested.

It was no use. Before she could finish her sentence, she found herself being shoved into the back of an unmarked car.

"You're under arrest for false identity, reckless endangerment, and prostitution," a cold woman's voice informed her.

The young woman sat up inside the backseat of the unmarked car and faced her abductor for the first time.

"What?" she responded.

Although she didn't agree with all of the charges, she didn't care to repeat them out loud. Some of the charges sounded arguably truthful.

"I think you heard me," the older black woman responded to her from the front seat. She pulled out a badge in front of the young woman's face to validate her legal authority.

There was an awkward silence for a moment, right up until a young black man jumped into the driver's seat and sped the car away from the curb.

That made the young woman suspicious. It was rare to see two under-cover black officers working together.

"How do I really know you're a cop?" she asked the woman.

Her abductors ignored her.

"Take us back to the parking lot and I'll handle it from there," the black woman officer told her young male driver.

He nodded. "I got'cha."

The young woman watched them in confusion from the backseat.

"Is anyone gonna answer me?" she asked them both.

The woman officer took out a cigarette and began to smoke, while still ignoring the girl. That only served to irritate her.

"What the hell is this? These things hurt. What are you doing to me?" she whined.

The driver began to chuckle before he noticed a cold stare from the senior officer, who continued to blow smoke without comment.

The young woman in the back began to cough.

"Oh, I forgot. You don't like smoke, do you, Tabby?" the woman officer asked her from the front.

The young woman froze at the sound of her real nickname, the name she heard from those who really knew her.

The officer turned without an answer and smiled to the driver.

"She sure likes men, though, I'll tell you that," she said in reference to the girl.

The young woman sat in confusion, busted. She didn't know what to say or what to think.

"Who are you?" she finally asked.

The woman officer blew out another cloud of smoke before she answered without facing the girl.

"The real question here, is who are *you*?" she responded.

The driver spun the car into a dark parking lot a distance away from the flashing lights of The Strip and pulled it to a stop.

"I'll handle it from here," the woman officer told him.

"All right then. Tell me how it went tomorrow," he said as he climbed out of the car and left the keys in the ignition.

The woman officer turned off the car and finished her cigarette before she said another word to her captive. The girl sat bewildered in the back, in cold, steel handcuffs, and continued to cough at the smoke.

The officer finally rolled down the windows to let the smoke out and clear the air in the car for the poor girl.

"You feel better now?"

"No," the young woman snapped at her.

The officer grinned.

"You want me to roll the windows back up?"

The girl looked at her with evil eyes from the backseat, like a caged lioness. She answered, "I want you to tell me what this is about. Now if I'm under arrest for something, then how come you're not taking me to a police station?"

The officer paused for a minute.

"You're not under arrest," she admitted. "I just said that to get you away to where I needed you. And to let you know that *I* know who you are . . . Miss Tabitha Knight. Or should I call you . . ." She picked up her notepad from the front seat and said, "Teresa Kelly? Or Toni Karson? Tamarra King? Or Tonya Kennedy?"

She let the information sink into the young girl's head for a moment.

She said, "Well, at least you kept the initials consistent."

"And I must admit, you look mighty *teenagish* for a twenty-six-year-old," she added. "I guess you figured out that these *child* molesters out here like 'em young. The younger the better, right?"

The young woman sat speechless. She wasn't prepared to be broadsided that night. She was just out to have a good time on the Vegas scene.

She finally asked, "What do you want from me?" She needed to establish some form of direction between them. "And this is a false arrest. I can have *you* arrested now. You got me in handcuffs and everything. Now you're trying to give me cancer in here with your cigarettes."

The woman officer laughed.

"Girl, you've been around plenty of smoke before," she commented. "And I bet some of the men you deal with were smoking a lot more than cigarettes."

After another moment of silence, Tabitha became spiteful.

She spat, "So what? I live my life the way I do and I don't hurt *nobody*."

"Yeah, but you lie to them, Tabby. You tell them all kinds of lies, starting with your name and your age. And I bet you never told them that you grew up in foster homes."

"Why is that any of their business? And why is it *your* business?" she snapped at the woman.

"Because somebody *made it* my business," the officer snapped back at her.

This revelation forced another stale silence between them.

"Who?" the young woman asked, breaking the silence.

"That part is none of *your* business," the officer answered.

"Well, why am I here then? Evidently, it must *be* part of my business."

The woman turned to level with her, "I will tell you this: There's a lot of money involved in it for you. More than I'm comfortable with saying."

"Yeah, well, I don't *do* things for money. So I don't know what you *think,* but you got me all wrong."

The older black woman began to laugh as if she had heard the most ridiculous line in her life. "Is that so?" she asked her young captive.

"Yeah."

"Well, let me ask you something, Tabitha. When was the last time you held a steady job? Because I do believe that you've been turned out by men who *don't* happen to be broke."

"That doesn't mean that I do anything for the money."

"Please, girl, save me the rationalizations because I am *not* here to hear them."

"Well, what are you here to do?"

"I'm here to offer you a business opportunity."

The young woman stared at her.

"To do what?"

The officer took a breath to prepare herself for the full explanation of her business.

She said, "I've been hired to find out whether or not you'd be willing to get close to a man who needs to be brought to justice for his, ah . . . how should I say . . . known fetish for young ladies."

The young woman continued to stare. But instead of responding to the business at hand, she commented, "These things on my wrists are hurting me, just to let you know. So could you take them off, please? Because if you know as much about me as you *think* you do, then you should know that I'm not violent."

The officer nodded in agreement. "Turn around and face them to me."

The young woman turned the handcuffs in her direction and felt the immediate liberation of the cold steel being pulled from her wrists.

"Thank you," she commented while rubbing her sore wrists. "Those things hurt."

"Yeah, well, they weren't made to feel good. They were made to restrain criminals. That's what I'm here to talk to you about. Because it's criminal for these men to prey on young girls, no matter *who* they are," the officer explained.

The young woman began to listen more reasonably now with her freedom restored. However, she still did not want to be there.

"So . . . I'm not saying that I'll do it, but what man are you talking about?" she asked out of curiosity. "Because I don't know what *you* think, but as far as *I* know, I don't deal with any child molesters."

"They are *all* child molesters," the older woman told her. "Do you hear me? But some of them are worse than others, and this one is one of the bad ones."

"Well, what makes you think *I* wanna deal with him, whoever it is?"

The officer paused and contemplated the question.

She said, "How are your foster sisters doing? Are they doing as well as you are? Maybe *they* could use some of this money if *you* can't."

Tabitha looked pissed at more invasion of her privacy.

She said, "You know what, you cops are as slimy as the criminals. It's just like on television and the movies. You're always twisting people's emotions to get what you want. I mean, is that a class that you take in police school or something?"

The officer grinned at her. She responded, "And what about what *you* do in getting close to these men? Did you take a class for that? Don't you twist their emotions? Or I guess you don't see it that way."

"Whatever," the young woman responded tartly.

"Well, getting back to business," the officer said, redirecting their conversation, "you *do* know the man. Maybe not personally, but you have heard of him."

Tabitha stared.

"So who is he?" she asked.

"Isaac Abraham," the officer informed her.

The young woman looked surprised.

"The actor?"

"Yes, the actor."

"Well, I don't know him. I mean, I've *heard* about him like everybody else, but you probably know more about him than I do. I'm not sweating him like that."

"I'm sure I *do* know more about him than you do," the officer admitted. "But what I *can't* do is get close to him like you can."

"And he's supposed to be a *child* molester? He's won awards and stuff," the young woman reasoned.

"Awards don't mean he doesn't break the law."

"But I mean . . . how would that look? You want me to go to court and all that kind of stuff if I actually find out something? I mean, that's crazy. I don't care what kind of money it is. I just won't do that. That's not right." She said, "Let the girls who he really molested take him to court. I'm not some undercover cop. You find somebody else for that."

"A lot of these young girls are not going to court," the officer explained. "Some of the underage women were bought off, some are still in love with him, and a few have even disappeared into hiding."

She continued, "Now let me tell you what *I* understand about this situation. I understand that a lot of young women who haven't had strong father figures are endearing themselves to these older men and being taken advantage of."

The young woman sat in silence. She was forced to reflect deeper on the information.

The older woman looked over her young captive and added, "You haven't had a strong father figure in your own life, you or your foster sisters. And you or one of them has probably been taken advantage of at some point in your own life. So you understand the mind-set of these young girls, and it's time for someone to be brave enough to stand up and admit what's going on out here in this sick world. Only then can we come to grips with trying to solve the problem."

She said, "Now I wouldn't be involved in this case myself if I didn't believe in it. I'm not doing this for the money either. However, the money *is* part of the issue, because it's being offered. Plenty of it."

Instead of asking how much money, the young woman denied the whole proposition. She said, "Are you finished with me now? Because I'm not interested in this."

The officer took a deep breath and nodded her head in submission.

"Okay."

Nevertheless, she took out a card with her name and a phone number on it.

"You call me if you change your mind."

Tabitha took it just to read the name. It said Sylvia Green, private investigator.

"How do you know I won't bring you up for charges for false arrest?" she challenged the woman spitefully.

"I think we both understand that you don't want your personal life exposed, especially if it's not going to benefit you and your loved ones. Sending me to jail for whatever is gonna benefit *who*?" the private investigator asked the young woman.

She had a good point.

"Well, why didn't you just ask me about all of this instead of . . . kidnapping me? That's what this really boils down to," the young woman questioned.

The private investigator answered civilly, "I have my methods just like you have yours. I have to do things a certain way to make sure I get people's attention. And I take my job . . . very seriously."

She stood up out of the car and let the young woman out, offering her a twenty-dollar bill.

"What's that for?"

"A taxi."

Tabitha turned that down as well. "I have my own money," she said.

She began to walk toward the street to flag down a taxi on her own.

The private investigator told her, "You be safe out here. You hear me? There are some very bad men out there. Hopefully, somebody's always watching out for you."

Tabitha ignored her and went on about her business of getting back to her hotel room.

When she arrived back at the room that night, Mr. Bennett was still asleep and snoring. But his date no longer felt like Teresa. She had been busted. The charade was over. So she went back inside the elegant bathroom and took out her diary and pen for another entry.

Saturday, February 16, 2002
After Midnight
Tabby

I went out for a good time in Las Vegas tonight and something real crazy happened to me.

That was all Tabitha bothered to write about it. She kept the rest of the information to herself. She had never written every detail that went on in her life inside of her diaries under *any* name. But she still had the private investigator's phone number with her, which was a compromising thing for her to do. Because as long as she held on to the number . . . she could decide to use it.

Love

Rise and shine, Mister. Breakfast is here. I got you grits, country ham, Belgian waffles, and coffee with plenty of cream, just like you like it." She had cleaned up his vomit from the night before.

Mr. Bennett opened his eyes and grinned. What a surprise it was to see a wide spread of hot food sitting out in front of him before he had even asked for it.

"You gon' feed it to me, too?" he asked.

His young date smiled. She was already dressed and ready to go.

"Baby, I'm sorry, but I have some errands to run this morning. I can put the tray on the bed in front of you and feed you a few bites, but that's about it."

"Well, where you gotta go this morning?" he asked her, protesting it.

"I have family coming to see me today," she whined. "I thought I told you that."

She made sure she smiled real good and rubbed his belly when she said it.

"If you did tell me, I guess I wasn't try'na remember it," he told her.

She said, "I'll make it up to you the next go round." She stood up to leave before he could protest again.

"Well, what am I supposed to do by myself for the rest of the day?"

His young date paused for a moment at the door and thought about it.

"I'll see how fast I can make it back to you. So keep that cell phone on for me. Okay, Mister?"

"Yeah, just for you," he answered.

He leaned up in bed to eat as she opened the door.

He joked, "Just don't have me waitin' *too* long. Or I might have to find me another young girl around here to give me a heart attack."

Tabitha Knight smiled as she finished off her role as Teresa Kelly for the old man. But she damn sure didn't find his comment humorous.

She joked back to him and said, "I guess you wanna see a catfight tonight."

Mr. Bennett caught her hint of violent jealousy and laughed it off.

"Bring it on," he told her. "Let me see what you workin' wit'."

She smiled again. "I've got the punch of a heavyweight."

When Tabitha shut the door to the hotel room that morning, she was more aware that someone, *anyone,* could be watching her. She rode the elevator to the lobby and was suspicious of everyone.

"This is ridiculous," she mumbled.

She had always lived her life with confidence. Now her privacy had been invaded.

She watched everyone who neared her or looked at her too hard. When it was time to walk out of the hotel, she made sure to exit alone, when no one else was around her.

She made it outside the hotel and caught a taxi without being abducted again.

"Southside," she told her driver.

He barked back to her, "Yup," and drove off on Main Street.

Tabitha made it back to her two-bedroom apartment on the south end of Las Vegas. It was a two-story apartment building surrounded by new, bright green grass. She walked into her comfortable place and stared in bewilderment at all of her unpacked boxes of clothing and accessories. It had been three weeks since she moved to Vegas, and she still had not settled down long enough to unpack her things.

The phone rang and broke her from her idle thoughts.

"Shit," she responded, startled by it.

She didn't move to answer it, though. The answering machine did it for her. She waited to listen for a message.

"Yeah, girl, this is Darryl. You know who it is. I just wanted to tell you that you moving out to Las Vegas is perfect for me. Now I can fly out there to see you and treat you to a nice time with no drama. So holla back at me on that. 'Cause I know you miss this. Aw'ight. Holla back."

She didn't respond to the message immediately. First she had to remember who she had been with Darryl.

"Tamarra King," she reminded herself. "But I don't feel like dealing with him right now. He has a major ego problem," she said of the Kansas City Chiefs' football player.

She thought about her assessment for a minute and added, "They *all* do. But that's who I choose to deal with, right? So why complain?"

She began to organize her unpacked things before another call came through.

"Hey, Tabby, it's Patrice. I just remembered to call you back. I've been meaning to for weeks now . . ."

Tabby jumped to grab the phone before the message ended. She was eager to talk to her foster sister from back home in Seattle.

"Hey, girl, I'm here," she answered.

"Screening phone calls again, hunh?"

Tabitha sighed and answered, "Always. But that's the life I live, right?"

"It's better than mine," Patrice responded.

Tabitha paused. "Things aren't getting any better?" she asked. She knew the answer already.

Patrice reminded her anyway. "Nothing I seem to do is good enough. And I keep asking myself, 'Why did he even want to marry me?' He should have just left me with the first baby like so many other guys do."

"That's a real bad attitude to have about men," Tabitha told her. "I mean, he's still doing what he's supposed to as a father."

"Yeah, and he's being an asshole about it every step of the way. I mean, just because he's doing the father thing doesn't mean he has to treat *me* like he does. He treats me like *I'm* one of the kids."

Tabitha left that alone.

She said, "Things could be better, I agree. But they also could be worse."

"Worse like in how?" Patrice asked her.

There was a long silence between them. Tabitha pondered whether she wanted to even finish the dead-end conversation. It wasn't her life to negotiate. Nevertheless, that's what love was for, advice even in vain. So she responded anyway.

"You could've had three kids with three different men, with none of them doing what they're supposed to do, and *all* of them acting like assholes."

Patrice listened to her and laughed.

She said, "You always find a way to make me laugh."

"I'm serious, though," Tabitha told her. "Sometimes you have to flip to the other side of the coin and realize what you *do* have."

"Well, how has your life been lately? Is it all wild nights in Vegas or what?" Patrice asked her.

"Not all wild nights, no. But I went to my first fight out here last night."

"Oh yeah, with who?"

"An old boxer."

"How old?"

"Too old."

They both laughed.

"But he wasn't *that* old, you know," Tabitha stated.

"Sometimes the older ones treat you a lot nicer, don't they?" Patrice assumed.

"Yeah, they do," Tabitha confirmed.

Patrice chuckled and said, "You still tell them you're five and six years younger than you are?"

Tabitha grinned. "Yeah. But . . ."

She stopped mid-sentence and thought about the conversation she'd had with the private investigator the night before.

"But what?" Patrice asked her.

"You think those older guys are like . . . *molesters* or anything?"

Patrice laughed harder.

"Girl, you gon' make me wake the baby."

"I'm serious. Have you ever thought about that?"

Patrice went silent for a moment.

She said real calmly, "There's a lot of things that . . . well, people just don't know everything about each other, Tabby."

"What are you trying to say? Somebody molested you?"

Tabitha wanted to take it back as soon as she said it. It sounded too forward. *Harsh* even.

Patrice responded, "You've always been the happy one. I guess that's your blessing. But the rest of us have always had . . . I guess you can say, family histories.

"I mean, your family just didn't have anyone to take you in," she continued. "But the rest of us had families . . . that were just not good for us to begin with."

Tabitha didn't know what else to say. It seemed that she was always finding out new information from people. She was rarely at a loss for words. Her brain worked fast to regain her bearings.

She said, "So it was a good thing for you to be away from a *bad* family then."

"Yeah, but . . . I still have scars from that, Tabby. I mean, not physical scars, but . . . emotional scars."

Tabitha paused for a second. She asked, "From who?"

Patrice didn't want to go there.

"Some things are better left unsaid, Tabby."

Tabitha thought about all of the complex details she often left out of her diaries and agreed.

"I know what you mean."

"So, anyway," Patrice cheered up, "what have you written recently in that *diary* of yours? You know that's your best friend."

Tabitha smiled at the truth.

"Oh, just a little something."

"Well, let me ask you something. Do these men you go out with know that you keep a diary?" Patrice asked her.

"No. Of course not. I always write it in privacy and keep it with my personal things."

"Well, what do you think would happen if they knew?"

Tabitha thought again about her abduction the night before.

She said, "I don't know. I just know that it's none of their business."

She was becoming defensive about it, in defense of her privacy.

Patrice countered, "It's *not*? But aren't you writing it about *them*?"

"Yeah, but . . . it's not even really me."

"Girl, them damn fake names don't mean anything to them. If anything, that'll make them think *worse* about the situation. Like they were just being played for the *fools* that they are."

"I resent that," Tabitha countered. "I mean. I'm not trying to say that anyone is an angel or whatever, but they deserve to be understood like anyone else. So just like I care about *you* and help you out when I can, why can't I care about *them* the same way?"

"Tabby, no one said anything about you *caring* about these guys. I was just asking you if they knew about your diary."

Tabitha backed off and realized her overreaction.

"I'm sorry. I guess I've been feeling guilty about it lately."

"Yeah, well, it's about *time*," Patrice told her. "I don't know how long you figured you could keep doing this and moving around to different cities and all that without eventually feeling guilty. I mean . . . to be honest with you, Tabby . . . I've always wanted to ask you if you really thought about the life that you're leading?"

As Patrice finished up her sentence, the other line rang on Tabitha's phone.

"Are you gonna get that?" Patrice asked her.

"No. I have a lot of thinking that I want to do right now," Tabitha answered.

"I see. Well, I just wanted to catch up to you and see how things are going. I wanna go ahead and get some sleep now before the baby wakes up."

"Well, kiss all of them for me and tell them that Aunt Tabby loves them, okay?"

"I sure will."

"I'll be back there to see you guys before you know it."

Tabitha hung up the phone and immediately retrieved the message on her unanswered phone call.

"Tabby, this is Mari. I need your help. This motherfuckin' guy is trying to kill me because he thinks I slept with his ugly-ass friend. I don't know who else to turn to but you. I need a plane ticket out of Seattle to come stay with you in Las Vegas for a while before he really tries to kill my ass. He already tried to beat me upside the head today.

"I just don't know if I can take too much more of this shit. So call me back on my pager. He broke my damn cell phone so I'm calling you on one of those long-distance pay phones. It took me an hour to find one.

"Okay? So call me back."

Tabitha hung up the phone and took a breath.

"Here we go," she told herself.

She paged her second foster sister in Seattle.

Marisol called her right back from the pay phone.

"Thank God you got my message in time, girl. So when can you get me out of here?"

"Slow down a minute," Tabitha told her.

"I don't have time to slow down. He's still after me," Marisol responded in haste.

"Well, I can't just call up an airport and get you on a damn plane," Tabitha explained.

Marisol snapped, "Yes you can. How many times have those guys done it for you?"

"Yeah, and it cost them a whole lot of money to do that, too. They're just impulsive people. But I don't *have* money like that."

Mari whined, "Come on, Tabby. I know you got it. I need to get away from here. He's driving me crazy."

"Well, why do you keep going back?"

"Because I don't have charm like you have to switch 'em up every other night."

"You don't need it," Tabitha told her. "You just need to attract less *drama* to your life."

"All right, all right, I see your point. Now can you get me out of here for a weekend or what?"

Tabitha paused. She said, "It's Sunday. By the time you get out here, the weekend will be over."

"Well, you don't have no job, so it's always the weekend for you," Marisol hinted.

"And what about *your* job?"

"To hell with that job, Tabby. I need a break from that, *too*. The manager's always try'na hit on somebody."

Tabitha was still trying to slow the conversation down long enough to reject her.

"Why didn't you call—"

"Treece," Marisol finished for her. "Here we go with that shit again. Look, you know Patrice and I don't see eye to eye on things."

"I don't see eye to eye with you either."

"Yeah, but *you* don't judge me, though. You *can't,* really."

"Why can't I?"

Mari grunted and said, "Shit, you know what you do."

"I'm not a prostitute," Tabitha responded in her own defense.

"Yeah, you're a lot smarter than them, and with no pimp," Mari joked.

Tabitha didn't know how to respond.

She said, "I can't fly you out here," just to see if it would work.

Marisol stopped cold and asked her, "You can't?"

"No," Tabitha stated. "You just have to deal with it."

Marisol huffed, "Okay then, *bitch*! If I die out here it's *your* fuckin' fault!" and she slammed the phone on Tabitha's ear.

Tabitha thought about it for ten seconds before she got on the phone to call an airline.

"Yes, what flights are available today for reservations from Seattle to Las Vegas?"

That's what love was for, unconditional support, even in vain.

Tabitha made the last-minute reservations for her foster sister. Since she had no idea when Marisol would need to fly back to Seattle, she made sure the return ticket was refundable.

When it was all done, she mumbled, "Well, Mr. Head Hunter, I guess I told you the truth. I *do* have family coming to see me today."

The Baller

With Marisol flying into Las Vegas to stay with her for a few days, Tabitha became anxious. Mari was worse than the nicotine in cigarettes and the caffeine in coffee. The girl's poisonous flair was just not good to be around for too long.

"Shit," Tabitha cursed while thinking things over. "I still need to get this apartment in order."

However, with Marisol flying in in five hours, her immediate concern was finding shelter before the storm. Tabitha liked finding shelter with men, the wealthier the better. Why bundle up in a wooden shed if a stone mansion was available? She needed a pick-me-up now, and Mr. Bennett was not the man for the job. The vigorous energy that she desired at the moment was found more in the younger guys.

After a few minutes of thought about her latest prospects, Tabitha settled on the new basketball player she had met at the fight.

"He's probably just waking up from his little party last night," she assumed. If so, what energy would he have left to offer her that morning?

There was only one way to find out.

She found his cell phone number in her bag and dialed him up.

"Toni Karson," she reminded herself before he picked up the line.

Terrence Matthews answered his cell phone with plenty of pep in his voice, "What up?"

He sounded energized that morning.

Tabitha ran with his energy.

"How did your party go last night?"

He stopped and asked, "Who 'dis?"

"Toni Karson from the fight last night. You saved my life from that pressed stalker who had me hemmed up near the restroom. Now you don't even remember me," she told him. "All I wanted to do is call you up and thank you. I guess you must have had a hell of a party."

He laughed. "Naw, I didn't party like that last night. I was tired. I ended up crashin'."

"With who?" she teased him.

"Aw, you reading me all wrong. It's not even like that," he told her.

"How is it then? Are you taken?"

She had no time to waste. Her sister was flying in in *less* than five hours now.

"What do you mean by *'taken'*?" the baller asked her.

She smiled. She could tell just by his spin on the question that he was game.

She answered, "You know, married, fiancée, serious girlfriend . . ."

"None of that," he answered.

She doubted the honesty of his answer, but she didn't expect the truth. The truth was not what she wanted. She wanted his ambitions. All men had ambitions, especially the already successful men. They thrived on new challenges, similar to how she thrived on meeting new men.

"Why not?" she asked her new prospect.

"I mean . . . my life is a little hectic right now. Not hectic where it's *bad* or anything, 'cause I'm lovin' it. But I ain't really got time to be . . . *committin'* to nobody," he explained to her.

"Not even right now?" she quizzed him.

"What?" he asked her. He was slightly stunned by it.

However, pressure was a good thing for the younger guys. They tended to like the game played fast. So she continued to press him.

"I just wanna see you before you leave."

"How you know I'm leavin'?"

"Because it's still basketball season. What do you have, a day off, or two?"

He laughed again.

He said, "I like that. Most women whine about what I gotta do, as if I can sit up around them all day."

"I know you're busy," she told him. "But are you busy right now?"

He paused for a second and got serious.

"Naw. Why, you wanna come over?"

"Are you asking?"

"Did it sound like I just asked?"

"Yes."

After a beat, they laughed together. She had broken down his defenses with too much offense. The poor guy had no idea that he was dealing with a pro.

He backed up and asked her, "So, you live out here?"

"Now I do. But I'll tell you all about it."

She stopped there and waited for his solid invitation.

"So . . . you wanna come over then?" he asked her a second time.

He still sounded uncertain.

She answered, "Nope, I just changed my mind."

"Why?"

"Because you're acting slow, like you don't want my company. I can take a hint when a girl's not wanted."

"Naw, it's not like 'dat. You can come over."

"Are you sure? I mean, I'm not getting in the middle of anything, am I? I don't wanna get you in trouble."

"Get me in trouble from who?"

"From whoever."

"Ain't nobody over here," he told her.

"And you wanna *keep it* that way?"

Words were clever tools when used properly.

Terrence finally understood her underlying message of urgency and gave in.

He said, "I'm at the Mandalay Bay. You know where that is?"

"That's right next to the pyramid one, right?"

"Yeah, that's the Luxor. Mandalay Bay is right behind it in gold mirrored windows."

"Okay. What room?"

Before she left for her morning pick-me-up with the young baller, Tabitha called to check in with Mr. Bennett as Teresa Kelly. But when she called, she got no answer from his hotel room or from his cell phone.

She left him messages on both and went on about her day. Mr. Bennett was a grown-ass man. He'd get over it.

"He's probably in the bathtub recuperating for a couple hours," she told herself with a grin.

She then called for a taxi to drive her back to The Strip.

When she arrived at the Mandalay Bay in the taxi, she still had an uneasiness about someone watching her. People had always watched her before, but now it was different. Someone was taking note of her personal dealings on a morality level.

She walked cautiously through the lobby of the hotel and continued to eye her surroundings for anyone who looked unusual.

"Damn cop got me trippin'," she grumbled under her breath. She had reached the elevators of the hotel. She rode an elevator up alone and was able to relax while ascending to the twenty-first floor, where Terrence Matthews awaited her arrival in a plush suite.

However, he didn't look so pleased to see her when he answered her knock at the door.

Before she could get any words out, he told her, "You fuckin' jinxed me."

She stood frozen at the door before entering. She wore a white buttoned-up shirt and a long dark-brown skirt.

"Someone came?" she whispered up to him.

She was still concerned about his other women, the women that she *knew* he had. That's why she carried a box of condoms with her for needed protection against . . . *whatever.* She was less concerned with protection from Mr. Bennett. He didn't get out much. But a professional basketball player in his prime . . .

"Naw, you can come in. I'm not talking about that. I'm talking about my career," he told her.

Tabitha walked into the spacious hotel room feeling in need of an explanation.

"What do you mean, I jinxed you? What happened?"

He looked down at her from his tall, wiry frame. He was wearing purple shorts and a white tank top.

He answered, "I got fuckin' traded . . . to Memphis."

Tabitha didn't follow enough basketball to know the pros and cons of each team. But she did realize that the Minnesota Timberwolves, with superstar Kevin Garnett, were a lot more popular than the relocated franchise in Memphis. Teams generally didn't relocate when they were doing well.

Terrence told her, "The Grizzlies are never gonna make the fuckin' play-offs. You basically playin' just to stay in shape down there. That team is like the new fuckin' Clippers."

Tabitha was confused for a second. She didn't know how to respond.

How angry was he? How much did he really expect to blame her. It was just a coincidence that she had mentioned the Memphis team. She didn't even know their team name.

"They traded you on a Sunday?" was all that she thought to ask.

"Naw, my agent said it happened Friday before our game in Seattle. But he was trying to convince them not to do it."

"So, he's just telling you now?"

"Yeah, but it ain't shit he could do. So now I gotta report to Memphis by Tuesday."

He sat on his king-size bed and looked glum. Video game joysticks had been stretched to the bed from the television. John Madden's football game was still on the screen.

Tabitha tried to look on the bright side for him. She sat down next to him on the bed and asked, "You don't think that maybe you can make their team better?"

"Fuck no," he answered her sourly. "We gon' need to get a whole new team to make them win."

She had to compose her laugh at his candor.

"Are they really that bad?"

"Yeah."

She began to chuckle anyway.

"I'm sorry," she told him. "I didn't mean to do that."

He looked at her and snapped, "This shit ain't funny. This is my fuckin' *life*! I mean, these motherfuckers just up and trade ya' ass for no good reason. Saving salary caps and shit like that. You fuckin' buying houses and homes, but they don't give a fuck," he ranted. "They just up and move your ass."

Tabitha remained calm. She realized that he needed to vent. She helped him with it.

"It's like a new form of slavery, hunh?"

Terrence looked in her face and was bewildered by her choice of words.

"Yeah," he responded. "That's what it is. It's a new form of slavery."

He said, "Yeah, these old-ass, rich white motherfuckers buy you from college, clap their pink-ass hands while they watch you run up and down the court all night, and then they go and trade ya' ass when they don't want you no more."

He was taking the concept further than she intended. He was getting a bit ahead of himself and a little too militant for his own good.

Tabitha tried to tone him back down.

She said, "Many people would still love to be in your position, though."

She stopped herself there before she allowed herself to bring up the subject of money. Just because he had plenty of moolah didn't mean he was devoid of human emotions. Tabitha knew that fact well. She knew it from the other wealthy men whom she chose to deal with over the years.

Terrence realized the truth of her statement and sat there in silence a few minutes.

"So . . . I guess I just roll with the punches, hunh?" he asked her rhetorically.

"Do you still like to play the game?"

He nodded. "Yeah."

"Do you still like the fans who love to watch the game?"

"Oh, no doubt."

She said, "Well . . . just keep playing for yourself and for them."

He rowed back and forth in his thoughts from his seat on the bed and began to smile.

"So you 'dun jinxed me into gettin' traded, and then you come over here and make me feel better, hunh?" he joked.

She smiled back to him and was more relaxed now.

"That happened before you even met me," she told him. "So I guess that me bringing up Memphis just means that we were supposed to meet each other this way."

He studied her face to see how serious she was.

"You really believe that?"

"What do you believe?" she asked him.

"I still believe that you jinxed me," he insisted.

At least he didn't seem so glum anymore.

"Well, how can I make it up to you then?" she teased him. She was still there for her pick-me-up energy boost, and her time was winding down.

Terrence picked up the joysticks to the video game from the foot of the bed.

"You can play me in a game of John Madden football."

Tabitha looked into his eyes and kept her cool. She didn't come to play any damn video games. But if it meant that much to him . . . then his wish was her command.

"What if I don't know how to play?" she asked him.

"I'll teach you."

She smiled at him.

"Just enough so you can whip me real good, hunh?"

He smiled back and laughed.

"You guys just have to have your egos boosted," she told him.

They didn't get a chance to play the video game for long before Terrence's thoughts about being traded began to overwhelm him.

He slammed the joystick to the floor without notice and grunted, "*Shit!* I can't believe this shit. Just when I start gettin' some fuckin' *time!*"

Tabitha continued to keep her cool and let him get it out of his system.

Terrence stood back up from the bed and told himself, "Aw'ight, aw'ight, they gon' have to play me then. They gon' have to give me twenty minutes a fuckin' game. At *least!*"

Tabitha didn't know if she should make her move to console him or continue to wait for the storm to settle on its own.

She finally said, "I'm here for you, for as long as you need me to be."

The wiry-framed baller looked down at her from his towering stance and snapped, "For what? You hardly fuckin' know me. You just *met* me last night. What, you just came over here to get your shit off?"

Tabitha kept her cool. She knew how emotions worked, especially the emotions of men under stress. Whenever they were hurt, they tended to lash out at anyone or anything that happened to be around them.

She said real calmly, "This is when a person who really cares about you could come in handy. Now since I just met you, like you said, I may not be that person for you. But you need to think about that for next time."

After her logical speech, instead of rushing to make her exit like an amateur would have done, she remained seated and let her words of wisdom sink in. Despite his lack of awareness, she was older than him, in mind, body, and in spirit. He was no more than a child in her hands, like hasty men had been with her before him.

"Yeah, whatever, man," he grumbled to her. But not in her direction. Terrence understood how childish his tantrum was. It would have been much easier for him had she left. He wouldn't be forced to feel guilty about it. However, he had been raised right by his grandparents, and he was forced to respect the truth when revealed to him. So he allowed his useless anger to simmer away in her presence.

"Are you hungry?" she asked him out of the blue.

Terrence looked back at her and began to smile.

He said, "How can you think about food at a time like this?"

As soon as he made his comment, his stomach began to growl, increasing his embarrassment with her.

"Aw, my God," he told himself. "What, are you reading my body now, too?"

She grinned and said, "Whenever a person exerts too much energy on something, they get hungry. And you've been thinking about this trade situation for at least an hour now. You got that phone call before I got here, and I've been here for a while. So I figured that you might be hungry."

What could he say? She was on point. He looked at her and admitted it. "Yeah, I'm hungry. Let's order some room service."

Intimacies

S o what do we do now? We just wait for the food to get here?" Tabitha asked Terrence. She hated to be pushy, but she was running out of time. Sex on a full stomach was not what she had in mind for either one of them.

"Is your full name Antoinette?" he asked her out of the blue.

"No, just Toni."

"Oh, 'cause most people named Toni are really named Antoinette."

"I know, I get that a lot. I guess it's kind of like Terry from Terrence."

"Yeah, well, I don't let people call me that. I don't want them gettin' it fucked up and thinkin' I'm no fag out here."

She shook her head and grinned. "Why are guys always thinking about their sexuality? If you're not gay, why even sweat it?"

"'Cause you don't want nobody gettin' it *wrong*," he huffed at her.

She continued to smile with her own thoughts in mind.

"Well . . . you're not sending the right message with me," she hinted. "You're hungry for food."

He got her point. "Oh, so what are you sayin'?"

She looked away from him. "I'm not saying anything else about it."

Terrence paused for a minute and sized her up.

"I mean . . . you do look *good* up in here."

She said, "I can't tell that you noticed."

"Yeah, I noticed. I noticed that last night."

"Really?"

"Yeah."

"Well, then?" she asked him.

Terrence shook his head. "That don't mean I gotta be all over you," he told her. "That's the problem with girls. When we want it all like that, we get called dogs. But then when we don't, y'all start thinking something's wrong with us. So, in reality, we fucked up either way."

She said, "It's not as if *we* don't get treated the same way. When we give it up, we're sluts and whores, but when we don't, we're snobby bitches."

He broke down and started laughing.

"But sometimes you become marriageable when you hold out."

Tabitha heard him and thought about it. She wanted to hold out sometimes. It would be nice to settle down. Sometimes she hated being so hot. But the heat brought the real closeness that everything else lacked. There were no guarantees in a serious relationship. Those guarantees always seemed to fail her. However, there was always a connection in sex. Bodies and energies met there, especially when it was good.

"So . . . is that what you're trying to do with me?" Tabitha asked him.

Terrence looked her over on his bed and found a hard-on developing.

He answered, "Not exactly. That's not to say that you're not marriageable or anything, but since you keep acting like you want something from me right now, I'm thinking about giving it to you."

She looked up at him with innocent eyes. "You're thinking about giving me what?"

He caressed his hardening crotch and said, "My third leg."

She gave a humorous jab right back to him.

"You mean your third finger."

"Aw, you got jokes."

He walked over to the foot of the bed where she continued to sit. He faced her with his hard-on, which had become increasingly noticeable inside his gym shorts.

"You want this for real? Let me know," he asked her.

"Let me see it," she challenged him.

He paused a minute.

"What, just like that?"

"You wanna do a song and dance first? You got it all up in my face."

She reached out to caress it through his shorts.

He responded to her touch, but then remembered their room service order.

"Aw, shit, now we got this food coming."

"We'll just have to let him wait outside in the hallway," she told him.

Terrence started laughing.

"You wicked. That's some freaky shit right there."

"What, you'd rather let him in?"

All the while, she continued to finger his erection through his shorts.

"I'm just sayin'."

He never got a chance to finish his sentence before she pulled his shorts down.

"Mmm, nice size," she told him.

"What, you thought I was lyin'?"

"Well, it's not exactly *leg* size, but it's nice."

"And what size are you?" he asked her back. "Let me see you pull down your shit."

She smiled at him before she stood up from the bed. She undid the zipper at the back of her skirt and wiggled out of it. Then she slid her fingers inside of her panty line and pulled them down real slowly.

Terrence said, "I like how you doin' that."

"Do you?"

"Yeah, you doin' it like you got no fear."

She looked at him while she undid her bra and blouse. She wore plenty of buttons and zippers just for the tease, all the way down to her tall brown leather boots.

"Should I be afraid of anything?" she asked him.

"Naw. I'm not sadistic. You safe with me."

"Am I?" she questioned. "But I will tell you this, you do need to wear a condom with me."

"That's my rule, too. I feel you," he told her.

She smiled and said, "You're going to."

He stood there with his shorts down, with a full erection, and started laughing before he took his shirt off.

She pulled out a three-pack of condoms and passed it to him football style.

He caught it and said, "Good throw."

She nodded to him and crawled up to the pillows at the head of the bed. She slipped under the sheets while Terrence opened a condom and rolled it down over his erection.

"Aw'ight, here I come," he announced. "Don't make too much noise with me."

"You like it silent?" she questioned.

"Not all the way. But I definitely don't like it loud. It throws off my concentration."

"Really? I thought it added to a guy's ego."

"Not if you already know you good. That's for them guys who always trying to prove it."

"And you don't have to prove it?"

He slid his tall, brown frame under the covers with her. "You'll see."

"I like your confidence," she told him. He slid inside her with no fore-play and stopped. He said, "So . . . you're not gonna complain about the lack of foreplay?"

She grinned up at him.

"I don't want that all the time either. Sometimes you just want to feel what a guy wants to bring to it. And the foreplay . . . I mean, it just gets in the way sometimes. It seems like it stops the rawness."

Terrence smiled. He said, "I feel you on that. The *rawness*. That's a good word for it."

As he spoke, he rammed her, causing her to jerk in response to it.

"Like that, right?" he quizzed her.

She closed her eyes and nodded to him.

"Mmm, hmm."

Young guys were good for rawness. That's what she wanted. She didn't have much time for anything else. Foreplay made the clock run.

Terrence Matthews pushed and pulled her body with urgency as she massaged his long and slender hips and bony back.

"You like it like this?" he asked her.

She ignored him while allowing her mind and body to explore the pleasure and slight pain of intimacy. It was the joy and pain of life. Sexuality brought it all together. There was no lying in sex. It was either good or bad, wet or dry, fast or slow, or various in-betweens that told the truth of physical bonding.

"You like it?" Terrence asked her again.

He was only ruining her groove and concentration.

"Don't talk," she told him. "Just do it."

When he laughed, he made it worse for her. She wanted seriousness. Who could concentrate while laughing?

Bonb, bonb, bonb!

"Room service."

"Aw, shit," Terrence panicked.

Tabitha held him down and whispered to him, "Shhhsh. Don't say anything. Just keep going."

With the waiter at the door, Terrence began to concentrate more himself, like cheating on a math test while the teacher sat and read at her desk in the front of the room. Full concentration was needed now. Someone was listening in on them.

The waiter's intrusion was perfect timing for Tabitha. She was in her el-

ement now, the element of closed-door privacy. People could think whatever they wanted to while locked outside her door. But inside, she could be
as uninhibited as she wanted to be. After all, it was *her* life, and they had their
own lives to live.

Bonb, bonb, bonb!

"Room service," the waiter called again.

Terrence flexed in response to it. Tabitha held on tighter to maintain his
steady flow with her.

Terrence whispered, "Shit, girl. Seem like it feel better wit' that dude
waitin' out there."

She allowed a slight smile to crease her face, while she continued to pull
him into her. She even wrapped her legs tightly in his.

The young baller was inside on the thrill and didn't realize it. Intimacy
was always better while in the middle of commotion. What fun was coming
home at night to the quiet safety of a boyfriend or husband when there were
celebrity superstars waiting across town inside penthouse hotel rooms that
thousands of women *begged* to share with them, if only for one night. It was
an honest little girl's dream that most young ladies had been trained to *lie*
about. So young ladies made their boyfriends and husbands the dream, the
sneaky pleasure of a man who they could share their inner fantasies with.

However, the safety of the committed man had often made nice girls lazy.
The open doors of sexuality were no longer turn ons. The boyfriends and
husbands could no longer bring out the inner dreams of the girls, which eventually served to reduce the girlfriends and wives to coldhearted balls-and-
chains for the little boys who still dreamed of becoming sex conquerors. What
fun was hunting sheep on the prairie for meek plates of rations when there was
still passionate, wild game to be chased and devoured whole in the jungle?

Tabitha understood those fast-paced little boys well. With them, sex was
the best behind locked doors, in foreign beds, in office buildings, in parked
cars, in stairways, and wherever they could find a dark hideaway to turn a
young lady out and make her squeal for more. That's what they wanted, to
make girls squeal with an audience nearby. Guys felt more important when
they did, as if they had scored a winning touchdown in the Super Bowl while
a hundred million people cheered them on. So Tabitha willed herself to become their supportive cheerleader, the one who never turned them down.
Who wanted to be denied a celebration after scoring the winning touchdown? They *deserved* their passions, the passions that too many girlfriends and
wives seemed to forget.

Nevertheless, they were not ruled by passion alone. Those little boys still had *feelings,* and they were sometimes emotional. Common people tended to ignore that part of young men, particularly whenever they became successful, wealthy, and famous. It was as if their personal emotions and opinions were now meaningless, as long as they could continue to produce what had made them successful in the first place. Were the two entities separate, the content of the man versus the product of the man? Or were they a complicated whole that few seemed to fully understand?

Blinnnnggg!

"Shit, now they calling us on the phone," Terrence commented.

Blinnnnggg!

"Don't answer it," Tabitha told him.

"I'm not. This shit feel too damn good for that," he moaned to her.

As the phone continued to ring, the king-size bed began to bounce with the increase of their shared pleasure.

"Oooh, shit!" Terrence moaned.

Tabitha became still and finally let him in on her joy.

"Mmmm, bay-bee. Don't stop 'til you get what you need. Don't stop."

He didn't. He poured it on her from his backbone.

"Like that? Like that?"

"Yeah, yeah," she moaned rapidly.

The two of them became a connected machine for a minute, vibrating with reckless abandon toward a detonation. They were creating the energy of life, the big bang. What bang was bigger? When they reached it, it was the truth, where all darkness became light and stood still for a heated moment of illumination. . . .

"Damn, that was the bomb!" Terrence exclaimed. They were recuperating.

Tabitha was silent. She only smiled. She had gotten what she had come to get, energy. She just didn't realize how much of it he would give to her. Sometimes too much of an adrenaline boost served to tire you, causing you to need a longer recuperation period.

Tabitha rubbed her bare stomach. She said, "Let's call that room service back. I'm hungry now."

Terrence chuckled and agreed.

"Yeah . . . let me do that."

However . . . he found himself too drained at the moment to budge.

Visitations

Funny how time flies, and after they had eaten, time for Mr. Basketball was up. Tabitha had a high-maintenance sister to meet at the Las Vegas airport.

Terrence asked her, "Where are you going?"

Tabitha rushed to re-dress without bothering to answer him.

"I have to meet someone at the airport," she finally told him.

It was always good to let her prospects know she had a life of her own. She thrived on her independence.

"To meet a guy?" Terrence asked her.

She stopped for half a second just to grin at the possibilities. How easy some of them left their noses open.

"No, it's not a guy. I'm pretty satisfied for now. I wouldn't be rushing off for that."

Terrence smiled again. Flattery was a good thing to use against inflated egos.

"Is that right?" he asked, his hand rubbing his tool through the sheets.

"Mmm, hmm," she hummed and smiled back.

"You need a ride?" he asked her next.

That surprised her.

"A ride . . . ? What, you have a limo or something?"

"Naw. I rented a yellow Lamborghini. It has seats and legroom for tall people."

She was at a loss for words.

"Umm . . . what happened to all your friends?"

She had been thinking about that for a few hours. The question served as a perfect diversion from her lack of a response to his Lamborghini offer.

Terrence answered, "Oh, them niggas know how I get when I need my space. I always been that way. So I told them last night, 'Y'all go do y'all thing, and don't bother me 'til tomorrow afternoon sometime.' 'Cause them ma-fuckas can drive you crazy. And ain't none of *them* get traded. You feel me?"

Tabitha nodded. "I know what you mean. I like my space, too. That's why I told you I wasn't into parties like that."

"We just alike then," he told her. "We both like goin' solo."

Time was still ticking. Tabitha looked at the clock.

Terrence asked her again, "So, you want me to drive you to the airport or what?"

She had no more time to waste. What the hell?

"All right. . . . Let's go."

Sometimes the reality of a fantasy can sneak right up on you before you have time to realize it. What happens then? Do you pause with uncertainty and let it slip through your nervous fingers? Or do you grab it in both hands with confidence and reel it in with a kiss?

Tabitha Knight relaxed her head into the sturdy black leather seat of the Lamborghini sports car. She let the dream take her where it would, with her feet dangling in plenty of space on the passenger side.

She jetted through the sunny streets of Las Vegas on her way to the airport with not a care in the world.

"You diggin' the ride?" Terrence asked her, grinning.

Tabitha grinned back to him. "You know it."

They spoke not another word while they continued to smile together, with the wind blowing over their brown faces from the rapid acceleration of luxury. When they arrived at the Las Vegas airport in a flash, they both wished that it had lasted much longer.

"That was some ride," Tabitha expressed to Terrence.

She climbed out and shut the door.

"Yeah, any time," he told her. "You still got that cell phone number, right?"

"Yeah," she answered.

"Aw'ight 'den. Learn how to keep usin' it."

The dream drove off through the airport traffic and disappeared as quickly as it came.

"Who was *that*?"

Tabitha turned and faced her foster sister Marisol, a hard-edged Mexicana who spoke only limited Spanish. Marisol represented the *opposite* of the dream of a fabulous life. Mari represented the bitter reality, wearing everyday blue jeans and a black sweater. She strayed from dreams and fantasy, while making it through the mundane headaches of yesterday, today, and tomorrow.

Tabitha spat, "Somebody *you* would probably never know."

Then she smiled as if the slight was harmless.

"Bitch, I'll kick your stuck-up ass right here in the middle of this airport. Do you hear me?" Marisol responded to her.

"I wish I didn't hear you," Tabitha told her.

"Well, why you pay my way to get here, if you feel all like that, *bitch*?"

"I ask myself the same question."

Marisol stood still with her bags in hand. "Are you gonna help me with this luggage or what?"

Tabitha answered, "You know what, I'm too damned *cute* to help you. So you pull your own luggage."

Marisol stood there and began to laugh.

She said, "It sounds like somebody got you *full* of yourself today. What, he just fucked you and told you it was good? The lyin' motherfucker," she spat.

Tabitha smiled back at her.

"At least he didn't kick my ass this morning."

Marisol dropped her bags. "Now wait just one motherfuckin' minute, *bitch*. You keep talkin' that shit out your *ass* up in here, and I *will* embarrass your motherfuckin' ass."

"You're already embarrassing me."

"Look, bitch, just shut up and find a cab."

After a few more profanities were shot back and forth between them, the shocked pink faces of passersby wondered if the two young women were insane.

"What the hell are y'all staring at? She's my damn *sister*, okay? We talk to each other however the hell we please."

When they made it inside of a cab, Tabitha sat up front with the driver.

"I don't wanna sit back there with her. She likes to fart too much," she commented.

"Aw, don't even try it, bitch," Marisol rebutted. "You're the one that be smellin' all foul after not washing your ass after all these men you creep with."

She said to the taxi driver, "Excuse me, we don't have any money on us, but she *will* fuck you for cab fare."

"I *got* money," Tabitha countered and pulled it out.

The taxi driver didn't know what to say. He sat there like a stiff and continued to drive to their destination.

"You are so embarrassing," Tabitha continued to tell her sister.

"Tabby, don't even try it. You do way more embarrassing shit than I do."

"That's not my name," Tabitha told the taxi driver.

"Oh, shut the fuck up, *Toni* or *Terrie* or whoever the hell you are," Marisol told her.

"Whatever," Tabitha muttered.

"Yeah, *what*ever," Marisol snapped back.

They settled down while they approached Tabitha's apartment complex.

Marisol noticed her sister counting the cab fare up front. She then looked around at the apartment buildings they were approaching.

"You mean to tell me that you gonna jump up out of a Lamborghini, and this is the best that you can do for yourself?"

Tabitha said, "Wait a minute, this is not a bad neighborhood."

"It don't look all that *good*."

"You mean that *expensive*," Tabitha countered. "Well, I don't spend money that way."

"What do you spend it on?"

Tabitha looked back and said, "You."

Marisol protested, "Don't even bullshit. I *hardly* ask you for that much."

"Is that a fact?" Tabitha questioned.

They climbed out of the taxi, collected their things, and were still going at it as they ascended the stairs to the second floor apartment.

"Could you keep your big-ass mouth down. I do have neighbors who like to *sleep* around here."

"Well, what are they doing asleep in the middle of the day?"

"I'm just telling you this for tonight," Tabitha explained.

Marisol looked over at her and said, "Girl, I'm not gon' be up bothering with you. I *sleep* during the night, which is more than *you* can say."

As soon as Tabitha opened the apartment door with her key and locked it back behind Mari, she took a deep breath. "So . . . how's everything going?" she asked her foster sister calmly.

Marisol sat her things down and took a deep breath of her own.

"Worse than you think," she answered. She paused and added, "I might be pregnant again."

Tabitha's eyes grew wide. She said, "I told you what you need to do. It's a simple procedure."

"Yeah, girl, simple for *you,* but I got scared. What if something goes wrong and I'm not able to have any kids?"

"Look, you keep talking about having kids, but every time you get pregnant you have another abortion."

"That's because I need a real *father* for my babies," Mari explained.

"Yeah, one who doesn't beat your ass and think you're cheating on him. Which I *don't* put past you," Tabitha snapped at her.

"Well, you're not loyal to one guy," her sister reminded her.

Tabitha said, "I *have* been loyal. I've had boyfriends. It just never seems to last long."

"So what you think I should do?" Mari asked her.

"Are you getting married?" It was the golden question.

Mari snapped, "Hell no! I mean . . . I don't know. Shit, girl, I don't know anything anymore. That's why I wanted to come out here with you. I have to figure things out."

Tabitha looked down at Marisol's bags and asked her, "How long you plan on staying?"

"Just long enough to get my head together."

Wrong answer.

Tabitha responded, "Shit, girl, you're not movin' in here."

"Tabby, you not even gon' be here half the time. You know how much you travel. You ain't even unpacked yet," Mari assessed from the stacked boxes that littered the apartment.

Tabitha looked away and mumbled, "I knew this was a bad idea."

"Well, where the hell else you expect me to go?" Mari snapped at her. "I would do it for *you.*"

Tabitha looked at her and frowned. "And when would you *need* to? I have never run to you like that."

"But if you ever *did* then I would be there for you."

"Yeah, at some oversexed man's house, so he can try and get me when you're not around."

Marisol stopped and chuckled at it.

"Girl, you still have an amazin' imagination."

"That happens all the time, Mari. You move a single woman into some-one else's house, and it's sure to cause trouble. You see that movie *Soul Food*?"

"Whatever. You're not in that situation no way. I'm over here at your house, and you don't have a man . . . you got plenty."

Tabitha grinned and kept her thoughts to herself.

The two foster sisters had gotten all of their zestful energies out by that evening. They rested on the living room couch in the dark and watched tele-vision.

"So . . . how's the old man and lady doing? Have you seen or spoken to them lately?" Tabitha asked Mari in reference to their foster parents, the Lit-tletons.

Marisol looked at her with little interest. "Have you?" she asked her back.

"Not recently. About a few months ago."

"Yeah, well . . . what do you want me to say to those people? I mean, how many times are we supposed to say thank you?"

Tabitha said, "It's not all about saying thank you, it's just about caring for them as they grow old as they cared for us."

Marisol said, "Look, Patrice has been doing enough of that for all of us. You know how much *she* loves them people."

"And what about Janet? How is she doing?" Tabitha asked of the fourth foster sister in their quartet. They hadn't all spoken enough about Janet. She had left the Littleton family earlier than the others on account of her health problems with leukemia. The state of Washington had stepped in and placed her in a foster family who could handle her health problems with more ur-gency.

Marisol answered, "I heard she's just making it. That shit sucks up a lot of money, you know. That's why they moved her away from us in the first place."

"Well, how much does it cost?"

Mari looked and frowned. "Are you asking *me*? The hell if *I* know. What, are you thinking about helping her?"

Tabitha paused, holding on to her thoughts. She then took a breath and changed the subject.

"Wouldn't it be great if we all had, like, a big old house away from every-thing, where we could all live in peace and have our own rooms and stuff."

"What, like grown-up orphan Annies in a fuckin' mansion? What the hell is wrong with you?" Mari snapped at her. "You've always been bringing that shit up. That's why you out here chasing these celebrities now. *Groupie*," she called her. "It's a wonder why you haven't married any of them, since you wanna live lavishly so much," she added.

Just as Marisol finished her rant, Tabitha's phone rang.

"There's one of them now," Mari said with a smirk.

Tabitha was apprehensive to answer the phone in front of her sister, but she was anxious to know who it was, and hesitant to let it ring.

"Go 'head. Answer the phone and see who it is," Mari instigated.

Tabitha answered it despite her apprehensions.

"Hello."

"Hey, girl, where you been at?"

It was Mr. Bennett, calling from his hotel room.

"Oh, I just got my family home from the airport," she told him.

Marisol sat there and grinned. Tabitha's life was better than the reruns on television. There was nothing that could compete with real-life sex, lies, and drama to keep a girl's blood pumping.

"You comin' back out t'night?" Mr. Bennett asked. "This my last night in town. You know I fly back out in the morning."

"Yeah, I know," Tabitha told him. "But I'm a little tired right now, sweetie. Maybe I'll come over there and surprise you in the morning. What time is your flight?"

"I'm gettin' out of here around nine in the mornin'. My plane leaves at eleven."

"Okay. I'll sneak over there and give you a wake-up around seven."

Marisol shook her head and struggled to keep herself from laughing. Tabitha stood up to take her conversation into the bedroom for more privacy.

"Don't leave," Mari whispered to her. "I wanna hear this."

Tabitha grinned and kept walking.

Mr. Bennett asked her, "Well, what am I supposed to do t'night?"

Tabitha stopped to think about all of the easy-to-order "escort girls" who worked the scene in Las Vegas.

She said, "Well, sweetie, I have to get a little bit of rest tonight so I can be fresh for my telemarketing job in the morning. You know, a girl has to pay her bills."

Mari overheard her in the short distance of the apartment and began to laugh out loud.

"That's a damn lie," she offered. "You ain't had no steady job in *years.*"

Tabitha covered the phone with her hand and moved quickly into her bedroom to shut the door.

Mr. Bennett said, "Look here, don't worry about your bills right now. If you come back out here and have a good time with me t'night, I'll take care of that. You hear me?"

She muttered, "Yeah, but I don't wanna be a burden on you like . . ."

He cut her off and said, "Look here, don't worry about that right now, I told you. You just get on back down here."

Tabitha chuckled openly at his urgency. She asked him, "Are you sure?"

"Hell yeah, I'm sure. And wear something real sexy like you always do, something to make these motherfuckers jealous down here at the craps tables."

"Oh, okay," she told him softly. "You made me do it."

Mr. Bennett laughed his ass off.

"Girl, I miss you already. How long will it take for you to get down here?"

"Thirty-five minutes," she estimated.

"I'll be waitin'," he told her.

After she hung up the phone, Tabitha walked back out to have a chat with her sister.

"So, I guess you're going out t'night, hunh, *Terrie?*"

Tabitha grinned at her.

"I don't even use that name."

"Whatever," Mari responded. "How do you do it?"

Tabitha played innocent. "Do what?"

"Girl, you know what the hell I'm talking about. How do you seduce all of these men?"

"I don't," Tabitha told her. "They do it to themselves."

A Life of Fantasy

Before meeting up with the private investigator the previous night, Tabitha had been able to maintain a feeling of peace while out in public with different men. She didn't care who watched her before, unless it was other men who watched her in envy. Otherwise, the more the better, and she was anonymous. However, anonymity was a treasure that she had *previously* enjoyed. Now that she was aware that others knew her game, it changed everything.

"What's wrong with you t'night, little momma? Roll 'dem damn dice," Mr. Bennett was telling her. He wore a dark suit and a derby hat.

Tabitha stood inside the casino at the craps tables with red dice in the palm of her right hand. She wore a dark blue blouse-and-skirt set of quality silk.

"Yeah, roll 'em!" the crowd of gamblers cheered her. She readied herself to roll the dice down the bold green table of lucky numbers covered by colorful chips.

"Seven!" the game teller called out after her lucky roll.

She rolled again.

"Eleven!"

Another winner. The crowd began to get excited with her hot hand.

"Yeah, girl! That's the way you bring that money back home to daddy!" Mr. Bennett hollered into her ear.

At the moment, Tabitha was not enjoying the extra attention she was receiving. As she began to worry more about who watched her, her winnings increased.

"Damn! I should have brought you over to these craps tables earlier," Mr. Bennett expressed to her. "You would have paid for my whole damn trip out here."

"I thought you said you didn't need to gamble to pay your way," she reminded him with a whisper and a smile.

"Yeah, well, every little bit helps. Now keep rollin' 'em."

Tabitha turned back toward the table to roll the dice again. She froze at the sight of Sylvia Green, the private investigator from the night before. Sylvia smiled at her from a distance before she disappeared into the busy crowd.

Tabitha remained frozen.

"Are you gonna roll the dice?" someone asked her.

"Look here, I'll tell her when to roll the damn dice. You don't tell her," Mr. Bennett snapped.

"Well, tell her then."

"Look, roll them dice, Teresa."

Tabitha didn't respond. Her eyes continued to focus on the woman somewhere across the room. It was a crazy predicament. The guilt of her lifestyle was intensifying.

"She's taking her time, that's all. Give her some breathing room," Mr. Bennett explained to the crowd.

Tabitha shook off her thoughts and rolled the dice again. A double one popped up. An automatic loser.

"Snake eyes!" the game teller called out.

"Shit!" Mr. Bennett snapped. "Look, you took too long on that one, Teresa. Now roll 'em quick. You were winning that way. It's a good thing I didn't bet everything on that one," he added.

At the rate at which he was betting, it would take them all night to win anything worthwhile. Mr. Bennett seemed too cautious a better.

Tabitha no longer wanted to roll the dice. Unfortunately, she was stuck in the middle of the game now. The eager crowd was taking over.

"Come on! Roll 'em!" they pressed her.

She was stuck in a whirlwind of confusion. Which way was up?

She rolled the dice again.

"Five!"

"Hey, roll 'em high! Roll 'em high!" someone yelled out.

"Just keep 'em comin'!"

Tabitha struggled to maintain her composure. She had had enough.

"Excuse me, I have to use the restroom," she told them all. She set the dice neatly on the table in front of her.

"You just can't quit like that," a dark-haired woman complained to her.

"Yeah, hold it in. You got money talking over here," someone else complained.

No longer could she hear her date's voice through the crowd. She quickly backed away without responding to them.

"You really have to go, right this minute?" Mr. Bennett's voice finally rang out. "You pick some real awkward times to pee, girl," he told her.

She said, "When nature calls, it calls."

An older blond stepped into Tabitha's place at the head of the craps table. "Hell, I'll roll 'em."

Tabitha slipped from the crowd on her way to the ladies' room. She knew that her old man, Mr. Bennett, and plenty of lustful men were watching her. However, she was more concerned about those inside the room who may be working with Sylvia.

"This is insane," she mumbled to herself. "I need to just ignore her. I haven't committed any crimes."

What kind of a private investigator propositions young women to become informants anyway? It seemed more like espionage, a spy game that Tabitha wanted no part of. Nevertheless, the role seemed to be chasing her down. And how much would it pay her?

She made it into the restroom, with no lines for a change, and realized that she did have to go. While inside the stall, a group of young ladies fluttered into the bathroom pumped with boisterous energy.

"Oh my God, he asked me to come up to his hotel room!" the first girl announced to the others.

"Oh, shit!" a second girl responded.

The third girl was more sensible.

"Isn't he, like, in his forties? Does he know how old you are?"

"Oh, who cares? What do we have fake IDs for, to tell people our real ages? Duuhhh!"

"Shut up, you slut!"

"Takes one to know one."

"What do you think you're gonna do up in his room?" the eager second girl asked.

Tabitha found the discussion interesting. She continued to listen in. What choice did she have?

The first girl responded, "I don't know. What do you think?"

There was a pregnant pause before they broke into laughter.

"Play a game of soccer and put the ball in the net."

"Or, maybe pool, and sock it in the left corner," they joked to one another.

"So, what are you guys gonna do?" the first girl asked.

"Wait a minute, you're actually gonna do it?" the sensible girl questioned.

"Well, yeah. Why not?"

There was silence. Was there a reason not to indulge in the passionate pleasures of men? Tabitha awaited an answer herself.

The sensible one said, "I would be flattered by the offer but . . . I mean, he doesn't know you. You don't really know him."

"He *is* sexy, though. He looks sexy in *all* of his movies," the second girl said. "He looks good out here in real life, too."

"So do guys we know who are *our* age. I mean, I just don't get it," the sensible one insisted.

Tabitha shook her head inside the stall.

"This is ridiculous," she whispered to herself.

Although she realized the three young white girls were probably not talking about African-American actor Isaac Abraham, the timing and the subject of their conversation was far too ironic. Had Sylvia sent them in there to do it?

The three friends quieted down when an older group of women entered the room.

"Oh, he is such a major *asshole,*" an older woman walked into the room venting. She was obviously full of steam.

"You just don't get his dark sense of humor," a second older woman countered.

"I get it all right. I just don't like it."

Tabitha finished her business and walked out of the stall to join the groups of old and young white women at the sinks and mirrors to wash her hands. The three high-school teens and two middle-aged women paid her no mind. They were engaged in their own worlds. Tabitha washed her hands and walked out.

Mr. Bennett was waiting for her outside the bathroom in his wool derby hat.

"Aren't you supposed to wear that thing *outside?*" she teased him with a grin.

"Yeah, but this is my lucky gambling hat," he told her.

She thought again of reminding him that he didn't *need* to gamble. Or so he had told her the night before at the MGM. All of a sudden, he seemed to be riding on his chips at the casino. He had a white bucket of chips in his big brown hands that he dared anyone to try and take from him. Tabitha noticed his tight possession of the chips and realized that it would not be a fun night for her. He was taking his chances too seriously, a sure way of ruining a girl's excitement for randomness.

"I see that you're pretty juiced tonight," she alluded. She needed to establish breathing room for her getaway. She yawned right after her comment to add to her hand of cards.

Mr. Bennett failed to acknowledge it.

"Yeah, I gotta find you some other games to play," he said. He seemed to be in a rush.

"What about you?" she asked him. "You're not gonna play at all?"

She definitely didn't want all of his chips riding on *her* luck.

He smiled deviously and said, "I just like watching."

"All right, well, let's play blackjack," she suggested. In her minimal experiences at the casinos, blackjack had been one of the easiest games to play.

"Let's do it then," Mr. Bennett piped.

She led him to the first available blackjack table while still watching for Sylvia through the crowd. She no longer planned to stay long at the casino that night, but she at least had to go through the motions.

She sat at the stool in front of the blackjack table. Mr. Bennett set his bucket of chips beside her and immediately reached his large boxing hands between her thighs from behind as she prepared herself to play.

Tabitha was no longer in the mood to play sex kitten. She planned to sock it to him where it seemed to hurt him the most: in his pockets.

"What are you betting?" the game teller asked her.

She answered him with the bucket of chips at her reach, "A hundred dollars."

"Whoa, horsy, start off with *twenty* dollars," Mr. Bennett told her. He quickly moved his hands to secure his bucket of chips from her.

She smiled and said, "I didn't know we were starting with a low budget."

"Shit, twenty dollars ain't low; it's sensible."

At that rate, they could be winning and losing all night.

"I always thought that if you're serious, you go for it. You don't nickel and dime all night," she instigated.

That put the old man on the spot, but she did it with a smile. Through her foster home experience, Tabitha had learned a long time ago that smiles made a world of difference in how people responded to her. Her positive results taught her to keep using her smooth cheeks, soft browns, and pearly whites to effect the change that she wanted.

"Ahhh," Mr. Bennett strained. He was having a hard time agreeing with her. "I already lost a lot today before you came and brought me good luck," he admitted to her.

"Well, let's quit while we're ahead then," she advised him. She faked another yawn. "I'm a little tired now anyway."

It was closing in on midnight.

Mr. Bennett said, "I'm *far* from being ahead out here t'night, baby."

Tabitha said, "I'm not, but let's do it your way." She had to let her man win. They *hated* to lose, even when they needed the lesson of humility. Manhood was about *winning*.

So they waged a measly twenty dollars a game and won and lost, won and lost, won and lost, just as she had expected. What was the damn point? After a while, the blackjack table became nothing more than background stimulus as Tabitha took in all of the glitz and noise from the casino. The bings, clings, clangs, spins, rolls, yells, screams, and shouts from the big-timers and the small-timers alike fell into a rhythm of delusion. How much of that money could have been used for more worthwhile purposes? How many of the suits, dresses, exotic perfumes, and colognes could have been worn to more important community or family functions? How much of the energy could have been focused on things that would really make a difference in the world?

Tabitha fell into her recurring daydream where she imagined herself and her foster sisters in a big house of love, where nothing could tarnish their happiness, and money was no longer an issue for them. She had spent many years wrapped up in that dream. It was one of the *few* dreams she had yet to pursue. How in the world would she be able to afford a big house of her own to begin with? She couldn't count on the wealthy men she dated for that. She understood their rules. Their rules were to *hint* and rarely demand, and do *neither* with great frequency. They had often cut her loose when she became too economically needy. That's what starstruck women were there for anyway, right? The money. With men of stature, women of every race, class, and creed were suspect. Because when all else failed, they could always take his ass to the bank.

On the other hand, a young woman served several advantageous purposes. They not only turned older men on in the sex department, but in the *need* department. Younger women often needed much less than a grown woman. Sure, a young woman's eyes were big with *want,* but wants could easily be facilitated or denied. However, the *needs* of a grown woman were more costly. They no longer responded in tantrums like the younger women often did, the needful older women responded in tactful execution for self-preservation.

It was Tabitha's tactful execution to remain a younger woman. The relationships came a lot easier that way. But she was grown now, and her expenses were increasing, as well as those of her loved ones. She needed more stability now. They *all* did. It was a fact of life that Tabitha had been avoiding. The illusion of the game was beginning to fade.

She responded again to the blackjack game in front of her. "I think we're up three hundred dollars now."

She sounded overly excited about it.

Mr. Bennett withheld his own response to read her facial expressions for sarcasm.

"Shit, three hundred dollars," he grumbled. He stopped short of telling her how many *thousands* of dollars he had blown that day.

"We're still ahead," she commented.

He got her point. If he wasn't planning on letting her go after major winnings, then the game was a waste of their time?

"Aw'ight. Let's fold this damn game up and get ourselves something to drink. We can buy plenty of *drinks* and *food* for three hundred dollars," he commented, "As long as we stay away from the wines."

Tabitha walked with him to the bar area and took another seat on a bar stool.

"Who you lookin' for in here, girl? I'm the only stallion you need," Mr. Bennett joked to her. He had noticed her rapid eye movement around the room.

She chuckled and placed an easy hand on his arm.

"Baby, I'm not watching for the competition. I just like watching people, *period*. Especially in these casinos. I think they're interesting to watch."

"What's so interesting about them?"

He caught her off guard with the question. Nevertheless, she had a ready answer for it.

"I always wonder what other people's lives are like. You know, what their dreams are, where they come from, what their struggles are; just stuff like that."

Mr. Bennett chuckled and ordered their first drinks, with a simple orange juice for the young lady.

He asked her, "What about you?"

"What about me?"

"You answer the questions you just asked."

"Oh, *my* dreams and stuff?"

"Yeah."

She smiled it off. "God, we'll be here all night."

Mr. Bennett held his just-arrived drink to his lips. "You got somewhere else you gots to be?" he asked her.

Tabitha was no longer anxious to leave. She relaxed at the bar with her orange juice and attempted to explain herself, or at least the parts that she wanted to reveal to Mr. Bennett.

She said, "I just figure that, if we're only gonna be here once, then why not do all the things you're allowed to do in life. And why not see everything? You know?"

He nodded to her. "Sounds like a winning idea to me."

"Then how come so many of us don't go for it?" she asked him. It was a serious question from her.

Marvin "Head Hunter" Bennett thought back to his own beginnings.

He held his drink in hand and said, "When I was comin' up in Newark, New Jersey, I started boxing because it was either that or goin' out and robbin' somebody."

She laughed at his brutal honesty.

He said, "I didn't have nobody to teach me or tell me what was out there to do. Shit, I figured you did what you could do in life, and that was it. So I started knockin' muthafuckas' heads off in the gym. The next thing I knew, I was in championship fights with thousands of crazy fans screamin' at me."

"Did you think about doing more things with your life once you got to that level?" she asked him. He had the open opportunity.

He said, "To be honest about it, I spent most of that time being a got'damned Santa Claus twelve months out the year. I had my first wife, Roberta, and she ain't never had no damn money before. I had three snot-nosed kids with the best of everything; brothers, cousins, nieces, nephews, every-got'damned-body. So before I knew it, seem like I was fightin' for everybody else. And it took me *years after* I had lost all my belts to realize that I needed to *keep* some of that money for myself."

Tabitha felt a pinch of guilt again. The majority of the celebrities she had been with were from similar situations. They were first generation wealthy, with hangers-on who took more than they gave, *if* they gave *anything* outside of familiarity and friendship. That was the trap for many celebrities. It wasn't as if they were *born* into it. They were all fresh fish out of water. As a foster child, Tabitha connected to them and understood their loneliness. She was a fish out of water herself. Fortunately, she had been able to get used to one tank of water rather than being shipped from one home to the next, like so many other foster children in the system.

"But we 'sposed to be talkin' about *you*, right?" Mr. Bennett backed up and asked his young date.

"Oh, yeah," she responded. "Where was I?"

"You were talkin' about goin' for your dreams."

"Yeah," she told him. She honestly had lost track of her thoughts on the subject. She had been all across the country with various athletes, singers, entertainers, and businessmen who had all faded away after short flings of lust with her. And what did she have to show for any of it? It was an equation of zero. She was always starting over from scratch.

"I don't know what I'm doing anymore," she blurted out. If anything, Tabitha had mastered conversation. She rarely spoke without being in step with whomever she was speaking to. It was her gift of connection to those she felt she could touch and change.

"You ever get that feelin' that you're swimmin' upstream in life?" Mr. Bennett asked her. "I mean, you know you're going somewhere because you're flappin' your arms and legs like hell. But while you're looking around, you see the same shit staring you right back in the face that you saw yesterday. And if you ever *stop* swimmin', everything moves right past ya' ass."

Tabitha laughed. She did have those feelings. She even felt that way as she sat there with him. She wished she had her own money to burn. She wished she had her own fancy hotel room at the casino. And she wished that for once someone was on *her* time instead of her always being on *theirs*.

"I know *exactly* what you mean," she told him.

He said, "Well, maybe that's why a lot of people don't go after those dreams you talk about. You figure, if you gots to swim that hard just to keep up with the Joneses, then how got'damned hard do you have to swim to keep up with the Rockefellers?"

She laughed again. He seemed a lot more philosophical that night. Losing money made thinkers out of everyone. There must have been ten tons of thought going on in Las Vegas. The distance between everything and nothing was a great conduit for deep thought.

She said, "I'm not talking about having Rockefeller money. I'm just talking about getting out there and just . . . living however."

He said, "You mean like a *hippie*? I know you ain't talkin' 'bout livin' like no hippie. Because that shit is just a *stage* of life as far as *I'm* concerned."

"Yeah, but a lot of those hippies became *millionaires,* too," she reasoned. "Because they just *believed* in living on the edge and taking chances."

Mr. Bennett ordered his second round of rum and Coke. He said, "Yeah, and all of those hippies are white boys, too. They're the only muthafuckas in this country who can fuck around for ten, fifteen years and then decide to get a haircut and become got'damned *executives* the next day. Only the white boys can do that shit. This muthafucka is *their* playground. And you betta' *believe it.* So you *know* how hard Don King had to hustle to get in *his* position.

"You *do* know who Don King is, don't you?" he asked her to make sure.

Tabitha nodded. "He's the boxing promoter with the tall gray hair."

Mr. Bennett said, "There ain't gon' be another Don King. You hear me? That's a once in a lifetime nigga."

After a few rounds of rum and Coke, Mr. Bennett was back to talking loud and crazy. Tabitha did more listening while she waited him out. He would be drunk again before the night was over. And she would make another entry in her diary. She had a lot of things on her mind to write about.

My Diary

Tabitha struggled to reach the elevator with Mr. Bennett leaning on her for support. He was loaded with alcohol again and barely able to stand.

"Good thing we ain't got far to go," he joked. "We almost there now."

With the strong fumes of his breath, she would rather he said nothing.

She made it up to his floor with him and helped him walk to the door.

"I guess I should pull out the ice bucket for when you throw up again tonight," she told him.

He was barely able to laugh. A laugh would have been too much pressure on his stomach, which was not at all stable. So he smiled instead, but even a smile was dangerous.

"Uhh," he gasped, mouth wide open. His stomach was already reacting to the overload of drinks.

Tabitha hurried to get the door open with the key card.

"Wait a minute! Wait a minute!" she told him.

Mr. Bennett continued to lean up against her at the door.

As soon as she got the door open, he got sick.

"Uuuggghhh!"

"*Shit!*" she snapped.

The contents of his drinks and the appetizers they had shared that night hit the right side of her blouse, her skirt, the back of her legs, and her shoes.

"Yuck. I feel sorry for you," a couple of girls commented from the hallway. They were headed to the suite a few doors down.

With no time to waste, Tabitha pulled Mr. Bennett into the bathroom and leaned him over the marble bathtub.

"*Uuuggghhh!*"

The sound of his hurling was amplified in the hollowness of the large bathroom, but Tabitha paid it no mind. She began to take off her things as quickly as possible. She wanted to wash them and have them dry-cleaned by the hotel staff, with the bill charged to the room.

"This is just . . . *beautiful*," she mumbled to herself.

Mr. Bennett was too busy feeling sick over the bathtub to respond to her. "*Uuuggghhh!*"

After the old man was sound asleep in bed and Tabitha had ordered her clothes to be dry-cleaned, she sat up in the lounge chair, wearing the white hotel bathrobe, while she wrote in her diary:

Sunday, February 17, 2002
Late Night
Casino Hotel
Teresa

I'm bored and frustrated right now. My sweet old man, Mr. Bennett, threw up on me tonight, but we had a good long conversation before that. We talked about going after your dreams and finding satisfaction in life.

I've already gone for a lot of my dreams, but I haven't found real satisfaction. I've been on boat rides, ski trips, fishing and hiking weekends, mountain climbs, and to all kinds of ball games, performance shows, and after parties. But then what?

What am I supposed to do with all of the things that I've done?

I'm having different thoughts about my life now. I need new direction. A clean start. I just don't know where to begin. I keep having thoughts of doing something crazy.

Maybe it wouldn't be as crazy as I think it is. Just an investigation. What do I have to lose?

Then again, what if I lose everything that I have? My privacy. That's about the most important thing that I have in life. Nobody really knows me but me. Or so I thought.

Maybe I don't even have my privacy anymore. And if that's the case, then what's the difference? I may as well do something crazy. At least I won't be bored with myself.

But not everyone knows me. Just a few people. And how much do they know anyway? How many of them know?

*I don't know. I just have a lot to think about right now. Maybe I'll just
ask a few questions first.*

In the morning, Marvin "Head Hunter" Bennett was all packed up and
ready for his return flight home.

"I apologize again for your clothes last night, Teresa. When will they
have 'em ready for you?"

"I guess any minute now," she answered. "I'll call back down and ask
them."

She was still wrapped up in the hotel bathrobe while finishing off their
room service order for breakfast.

"Maybe I'll fly you out to go shopping somewhere one of these days,"
Mr. Bennett offered.

"I won't hold you to that," she responded. "I know times are tight for
everybody right now."

She caught him off guard with her answer. It got him to thinking and
feeling guilty about his frugality with her the night before.

He broke down and said, "You know what? I might as well empty out
the rest of my pockets right now. You showed me a good damned time out
here. And all I did was throw up on you two nights in a row. You didn't even
complain much about it."

"It was nothing but a thing," she told him.

He dug into all of his pockets and pulled out a total of seven hundred
dollars and change.

She said, "I would never take all of your money. Just bless me with what
you can."

He looked at her and said, " '*Bless you*' with it, hunh?"

"Everything in life that you don't ask for is a blessing," she told him.

He nodded to her and gave her five hundred dollars.

"Well, there's your blessing."

"Thank you, Jesus," she responded and smiled.

He laughed. He said, "You know just what to say to an old-ass man."

When Tabitha arrived back at her apartment with her dry-cleaned clothes
that morning, she found her sister Marisol stretched out across her living
room sofa bed. She was watching the nineteen-inch color television set.

"Was it a good night, *Toni*?" Mari asked her in jest. "Or were you *Tamarra* last night?"

Tabitha ignored her and walked to her bedroom for more rest. She had been up long hours two nights in a row, and up bright and early the following mornings. Her body and spirit were exhausted. However, as she lay out on her bed, she began to wonder when she had told Marisol her aliases. She knew that her sisters knew *some* of the names, but . . .

She let it slide. She needed to rest with no more thoughts for the moment.

"So, you really lead an interesting life with all these guys." Marisol walked to the bedroom door and stated, "And they give you money where you don't have to work? Shit, I need to get in on that."

"Evidently I *need* to close my door," Tabitha snapped at her. "Isn't it obvious I'm a little tired right now?"

Marisol smiled. "Yeah, I guess you are." However, she stayed put at the door. She said, "A lot of the things you talk about make a whole lot of sense. I didn't know you thought that much about things. I always thought you were just a happy-ass."

Tabitha paused in alarm. She sat up straight in her bed and asked her sister, "What are you talking about?"

Mari continued to smile as if it were all a joke.

"You know what I'm talking about."

"No, I don't."

"I'm talking about the things you write."

"The things I write *where*?"

Tabitha wanted to get all of the facts straight before she'd lose it.

Her sister answered, "In all of those diary books you have."

Tabitha bounced up out of bed and hollered, "What are you doing going through my *shit*?!"

Mari was shocked by the outburst. She hadn't expected Tabby to be that defensive about it. She said, "I was just try'na help you un*pack* some of this mess."

"Well, I can't see what you *unpacked*. Show it to me!" she challenged her sister.

Mari was on the spot. She said, "Well, I got sidetracked."

"From reading my fuckin' shit!" Tabitha yelled at her.

"You are really *buggin'* over this," Marisol told her. She knew not to smile anymore. Her sister looked ready to engage in a physical confrontation over her diary.

She said, "I don't believe I just paid for you to fly down here with *my* money just so you can get in here and start going through my personal shit. I don't *believe* you!"

She brushed past her sister to retrieve the box that she had stored her diaries in.

Marisol said, "Well, at least I had something *good* to say about it. And I didn't *judge* you for anything."

"Whatever," Tabitha snapped to her. "I don't even wanna talk about it. You just never do that shit again. Now I gotta lock my things away somewhere."

Mari said, "You never talk to those *men* you date like that. You all fuckin' *soft* and *whiny* with them: If he could just *see* how much I *care* for him and open up his *heart* to something *special,*" she paraphrased from an entry in one of Tabby's old diaries.

"I mean, you really felt these high-post men were gonna be serious about you? I'm surprised you even got alone in a room with some of them. You got athletes, musicians, Hollywood folks, politicians. I'm impressed," Mari expressed to her. "You got with some real steals."

Tabitha froze and was overtaken by a flash of vengeance. Marisol was taking her feelings and personal life for granted.

Tabitha suddenly dropped her box of diaries and went after her sister with her right hand extended.

Marisol grabbed her hand in midair. "No you didn't."

Nevertheless, Tabitha's rush of action sent her sister reeling backward.

Tabitha followed up with a left-handed punch that caught Marisol square in the mouth.

"*Bitch!* You done started something now!" Mari yelled out. Tabitha had rarely been any good at fighting. However, Marisol had obviously underestimated her sister's rage. They were not kids or teenagers anymore. Tabitha had done a lot of growing up. And she didn't appreciate being taken lightly.

Mari tried to reverse positions where she could get the best of Tabby, but she couldn't seem to move her. Tabitha was far too effective in her attack.

"All I do is help you all the time, and you don't do nothin' but *fuck with me!*" she screamed, while throwing a fury of punches. It was as if the fighters from two nights before had taken over her body.

Marisol never had a chance. Before she knew it, she was flat on her ass and covering up from an ass-kicking.

"Stop! Stop, Tabby! I was wrong!" she yelled up to her sister.

Tabitha nailed her one last time before she let up.

"Shit!" Marisol shouted with a bruised face and ego. She covered her face on the floor and hollered, "You fuckin' buggin' out over some damn *diary*!"

"It's *mine*!" Tabby yelled down at her. "And you had no *right* to do that. And on top of *that* you're gonna sit up in here and rub it in my *face,* just because my old boyfriends happen to be more *important* than yours!"

"You trippin'," Marisol mumbled. "They don't care about you. You crazy."

"I may *be* crazy, but that's *my* business. And I'm not the one who needed to get away from . . ."

Tabitha stopped herself short and understood the hypocrisy of the situation. Mari had escaped an abusive boyfriend, just to take another beating from a vengeful sister.

Tabitha regained control of her cool head. She looked down at her cowering sister and apologized.

"I'm sorry for that. I didn't mean to—"

"Fuck you!" Mari spat into her hands, cutting her sister off.

Tabitha paused and shook her head.

"See, that's what I'm talking about. You have to learn to *respect* people."

After getting no response, Tabitha continued, "I can't even talk to you like a normal person. We gotta be all disrespectful to each other all the time. I'm just *tired* of that shit. I don't feel like jumpin' through hoops for you like that anymore. We're getting too *old* for that."

"Whatever," Marisol mumbled again.

Tabitha shook her head and walked away. She regathered her box of diaries and gave her sister one last warning.

"These are *mine,* Mari: *my* personal business. And that's all I have left to say about it."

She then walked into her bedroom and shut the door to think about where to hide her diaries . . . from everyone.

Marisol climbed to her feet and headed for the door. She needed to get out and smoke a cigarette while healing her damaged ego. She slammed the door hard behind her.

Bloom!

When It Rains . . .

T abitha paced her apartment for the next couple of hours, hoping that Marisol was not so upset that she wouldn't return.

"She has to learn to *respect* people," she insisted of her sister's behavior. She was nearly ready to leave and go looking for her to make certain Mari was still within sanity's reach, when the telephone rang.

Tabitha grabbed it anxiously after the first ring.

"Hello."

"Tabby, it's over with."

She took a second to recognize the voice.

"Patrice?"

"Yeah, it's me."

She didn't sound so great.

"Okay, what's going on?" Tabby questioned.

"It's over with," Patrice repeated.

"What's 'over with'? What are you talking about?"

Tabitha wasn't in the mood for guessing games. She was still concerned about Mari wandering around somewhere in Las Vegas.

"I caught Randy cheating last night," Patrice informed her.

Tabitha took a breath and fell silent. She just wanted to listen for a minute.

"You have nothing to say about it?" Patrice asked.

"Where did you catch him?"

"Coming out the bitch's house."

"This morning?"

"Last night."

"Did you say anything to him?"

"Yeah."

"What did he say?"

"Nothing. And he never came home last night."

Tabitha held back from being judgmental toward mistresses. She had knowingly been with *several* married men. She didn't want to *touch* the subject. Nevertheless, this was her sister's husband. She had been in their wedding.

"What did you say to him?" she asked.

"I cussed his ass out. I mean, how is he gonna leave me at home with three kids while he's out there fucking around?"

"How did you know where she lived?" Tabitha could just imagine someone tracking *her* down.

"I had a few people giving me tips on it. So while his ass was supposed to be out with his *friends* watching a basketball game, I had Cheryl watch the kids while I took her car and investigated the situation. Sure enough, there was our car parked outside this apartment complex over at Lake City. So I sat there and waited for him to come out."

"Did you see her?"

"Yeah, I saw her; some skinny-ass, dark-haired white girl. She kissed him at the door when he left. You believe that shit? He actually kissed the bitch at the door. How fucking romantic!"

Tabitha heard the breakdown in Patrice's voice as she began to cry over the phone.

"I can't believe this shit, Tabby. Do you still think everything's gonna work out between us now?"

Tabitha was silent, hurting inside. When it rains . . .

"Shit," she expressed aloud. She was thinking about everything that was going on in her own life, not just Patrice's situation. Her husband's cheating was only *part* of what was wrong with the world. Of course, it meant everything to Patrice.

She asked, "What am I supposed to do now? I haven't even been working. I can't afford day care like that, and Cheryl has her own life."

Tabitha was conflicted. She certainly had an answer, she just didn't feel safe about voicing it. But she *had* to. She *knew* the situation. Men had told her *their* side of the story.

"When he comes back home, you sit down with him and ask him what he's missing."

Patrice snapped, "What he's *missing*? I gave that man *everything*, Tabby. You *know* that! What could he *possibly* be missing with me? Unless he wants me to be a little-ass *white girl* now! I'm sorry, but I can't change who I am. I'm a big black woman from a foster ho-o-o-ome," she whined.

Tears fell out of Tabitha's eyes as she held the phone to her ear. She knew the feeling of unworthiness. Mari had just alluded to it. Who was a foster home girl to believe that she deserved a life with a man of stature? So Tabby felt vindication from the men she dated. She was *proving* that she belonged. Even a foster home girl could find her prince. But sometimes the princes felt unworthy themselves. They felt as if they were missing things. They were all as vulnerable to feelings of confusion and self-doubt as the women. Tabitha understood that about them.

She said, "I love you, Treece. You know how much I love you, but you have to trust me on this. Let him come back home and explain himself."

"Explain *what*? *Lies! Deception! Disrespect!* What the hell does he have to explain to me?"

Tabitha could hear the children in the background getting upset at their mother's tone of voice.

She said, "As much as you're hurting right now, you can't fight this thing and expect to win without staying in control."

"In control of *what*?"

"Of yourself," Tabitha stated to her. "No matter what, you *have* to stay in control. Look at your children right now," she told her. "*They* need you to stay in control. You have no control over him right now, but the more you have over *you*, the better off *all* of you are gonna be."

Patrice seemed to have gotten the point. She calmed herself down and then calmed her children. In her next breath, she said, "If you don't mind, Tabby, I think I'm gonna pack up our shit and drive out there to Las Vegas to stay with you for a couple of days. That way I'll show his ass who's in *control*, when he doesn't have a family to come home to."

That idea wasn't what Tabitha had in mind at all. But at the moment, she found it hard to deny her sister.

"You need to think this all through," she cautioned. However, she never said that she couldn't come. Nor did she inform Patrice that Marisol was already there.

Patrice told her, "I *have* thought everything through. And you're right. It's *all* about control. So I'm gonna show his ass who has it."

Tabitha hung up the phone with Patrice, the oldest of her foster sisters, and was stunned.

"This . . . my God," she uttered to herself. She could feel a headache coming on. She dug into her things in the bathroom and took two Tylenol with water.

Her fate was inevitable. She needed more money. *Fast!* She found the phone number in her purse to Sylvia Green and called her up for some questions and answers.

"Hello," Sylvia answered.

"This is Tabitha Knight. You kidnapped me from the casino the other night."

"I did what?" Sylvia quizzed her. She said, "You must have the wrong number," and hung up.

"Hello. Hello?"

Tabitha continued to hold the phone to her ear in disbelief.

"She hung up on me," she expressed to herself.

The Tylenol had no chance of working fast enough. Tabitha pressed both hands against her temples and closed her eyes to meditate.

She said slowly, "In two fucking nights, I am seriously about to lose my *mind*. Damn!"

The phone rang and broke her from her cynicism.

"Hello," she answered, expecting anything.

"Don't you ever do that again. Do you hear me? This is not a damn game." It was Sylvia Green, calling her back.

"I need to talk to you," Tabitha told her.

"About what?"

"You know what."

There was silence.

"Meet me at the same place tonight at ten. Alone," Sylvia told her.

"Of course."

The combined phone calls took less than a minute.

Tabitha grumbled, "This chick is dead serious."

In the next minute, Mari walked through the door and took a seat on the sofa bed in front of the television set.

"You want some Domino's pizza?" Tabitha asked her, with the phone still in hand.

Marisol took another minute before she answered.

"Yeah, why not?"

Tabitha immediately ordered pepperoni and pineapple with extra sauce; Mari's favorite.

Questions & Answers

Tabitha made it to the meeting place a half hour late and climbed into the dark, unmarked car with Sylvia Green, who was waiting behind the wheel of the driver's seat.

"You have a problem being on time?"

Tabitha answered, "I have a sister staying at the house who's a little high-maintenance right now."

Sylvia nodded. Then she smiled. "Sounds like you need some money."

Tabitha didn't like the candor of that, but it was true.

"How much is this job paying?" she asked. She planned to be as straightforward as Sylvia was.

"More than you deserve," Sylvia commented to her.

"And how much do you *think* I deserve?"

Sylvia paused. "No more than five hundred dollars."

Tabitha kept her cool. She said, "It would cost me more than that to even get close to him."

"Where there's a will, there's a way," the stern woman told her.

Tabitha reached for the door handle to climb out of the car.

"Well, I don't have no *will* for no chicken feed."

"That's why you're making a lot more on this job than what *I* would give you," Sylvia told her.

Tabitha held her position.

"How much more?"

Sylvia said, "Let's get something clear. This job is not about the money. It's about the *principle* of what you're doing."

"Bullshit, because if it's about the *principle,* then I'm not doing it at all. I told you that," Tabby reminded her.

Sylvia looked away from her and out the driver's side window.

"You'll be paid in increments as you get closer to him," she mumbled.

"How much?"

"Ah . . ." Sylvia remained hesitant.

"Look, do you want me to get involved in this thing or not?" Tabitha snapped in haste. It seemed as if the woman was trying to hold out on her purposefully.

Sylvia looked her in the eyes and said, "Ten-thousand-dollar increments with a total of a hundred thousand with his conviction."

Tabitha kept her cool.

"So I get ten payments?"

"That's the way it's *supposed* to work."

"When is the first one? Is it cash or check?"

"A bank account will be created for you. You can withdraw from that."

Tabitha looked at the private investigator and quizzed her. "And you don't think I should get that much money?"

"Of course not."

"Why not?"

She reasoned, "First of all, I don't agree with what you do."

"Do you agree with what *wives* do?"

Sylvia looked at her disgustedly.

"I *know* you're not trying to equate what *you* do to a *wife*."

Tabitha said, "The only difference is that they *keep* their wives and have *children* with them."

The private investigator stared at her. "You are *sick*. You really are."

"If I'm so sick, then where is *your* husband?"

She had Sylvia on the spot. She didn't have a husband. Men were pigs. Sylvia had worked with enough of them to know. You either accepted their ignorant sloth, ignored it in denial, or chose not to deal with it at all. Sylvia Green had chosen the latter. She even suspected that Tabitha was reading her now, and that she knew what she preferred.

"We're getting off the subject here," she commented.

"No, we're not. You want me to bring down this guy because he's an asshole. Well, a lot of them are assholes if you're gonna look at them in black and white," Tabitha reasoned. She was in a particularly cynical mood after all of the events of the day.

She said, "It's interesting to me how women choose which men are assholes and which men are not. I do the same thing. And you know who I choose? The men who I can predict a soft spot on to treat me right *some* of the time. But I haven't always been correct either."

She had the private investigator speechless. Sylvia was quickly learning why Tabitha Knight was so highly recommended for the job.

"So how do you plan to get close to him?" she asked the young woman curiously. She wanted to know for herself. How did she get these men to reveal themselves to her?

Tabitha said, "I read up on him a little bit tonight. He's typical of a powerful black man, or *any* powerful man for that matter. He likes to make his own rules. He wants to live outside the structure that the rest of us are locked in to. And he *does*. But he has a team that helps him to do that."

Sylvia nodded to her. Her homework was on point.

"He has a lot of protectors. That's why we've been unable to get to him," she admitted.

"That's how *I'll* get to him, through the people who surround him," Tabitha told her.

Sylvia shook her head. "That was attempted before. And the girl didn't get anywhere near him. She ended up being turned out by the help. So we want you to go right after the beast. We're not paying you this kind of money not to."

Tabitha disagreed. "I can't get to the beast without being walked in. If you did *your* homework, then you should *know* that. Isaac Abraham is not just a neighborhood *chief*, he's a crowned *king*."

Sylvia paused again. She said, "If you think this highly of him . . . do you think you can get the job done? Don't bullshit me if you can't," she added.

Tabitha leveled with her. "Like I said in the beginning, I don't agree with this whole thing. But I can get close enough to him to get enough information to break things down. And if I'm not able to get you all the information you need, then I don't get all of the money, right?"

"Right," the private investigator answered her.

"So . . . let me see how far I can get."

Sylvia thought it over and nodded. She had no other choice. Tabitha Knight was who they wanted.

"Okay," she responded softly. "I'll let them know."

Loose Ends

Over the next few days, the quiet before the storm, Patrice hit the road for Las Vegas with her three kids in tow and Tabitha got back in touch with her third foster sister, Janet, who now lived in San Francisco.

Janet sounded upbeat when she heard her sister on the phone.

"What made you decide to call me, stranger?" she asked.

"Girl, I've been meaning to call you for *ages*. You're always on my mind," Tabitha told her.

"Yeah, you've just been busy."

"You, too."

"How do you know?" Janet quizzed her. They hadn't spoken in more than a year. The last time was during the Christmas holiday season of 2000.

Tabitha answered, "I can hear it in your voice. You sound fulfilled."

"*Fulfilled?* I don't know about all of that. *Content,* maybe. But fulfilled is a little strong. I mean, is anyone fulfilled in life? Especially before thirty. I don't think so," Janet answered. Her voice was still slow and meticulous like an old, wise soul.

"You still doing computer work?" Tabitha asked her.

"Are websites still being created and designed to sell products and post information?"

Tabitha laughed. "You still got that smart mouth, I see."

"And you still have that spirit. I wish I had your smile. I could use it to light up my room at night."

"You still staying up late at work, hunh?"

"I like working. Working keeps my mind off everything I have no control over."

With that, Tabitha began to think about Janet's leukemia.

"So how are things going?" she asked her.

"Look, I'm living my life. And until this thing kills me, I got things to do. So I take my medicine and do what I gotta."

Tabitha smiled. "That's the spirit," she chirped.

"So how is everybody else doing?" Janet asked her.

"Tell her I said hi," Marisol mentioned, right on cue from the sofa. She was watching television again while twisting her straight dark hair in her fingers.

Tabitha nodded to her. She remained standing while pacing the room as she spoke into the phone.

"Marisol is right here, and Patrice is on the way," she informed Janet.

"What, in Seattle?"

"No, I live in Las Vegas now."

"And they moved there with you?"

Tabitha paused to think before she answered.

"We're having a sisters' reunion over here," she said. "All we need now is you. And Marisol says hi," she added.

Janet paused. "Is she still wild?"

Tabitha held back her laugh and smiled.

She turned to Marisol and lied, "Janet says what's up."

Marisol grinned. "Tell her I'm just trying to make it."

"She's just trying to make it," Tabitha relayed over the phone.

"I heard her," Janet said. "I see you're still trying to play peacekeeper. Somebody has to do it. We have enough war in this world. Now Mr. Bush wants to start World War III. So tell her I said me, too."

Tabitha relayed her response back to Marisol.

Marisol nodded. "That's good."

Janet said, "So they're all bum-rushing your place, hunh?"

Tabitha had to stop herself from laughing again. Janet was just being herself, an introspective straight shooter. Leukemia was rare in young people, so Janet had grown up fast and cut the chase of adolescent buffoonery. Her condition had forced her to speak nothing but the bare facts.

"I see you're still doing you," Tabitha told her.

Marisol looked up in alarm. "What did she say?" she asked. She knew how razor sharp Janet's tongue could be. They all knew it.

Tabitha lied to keep the peace.

"She asked me if I was still running the streets to try to find a father figure."

Marisol broke out laughing. She hollered, "Yes!" loud enough for Janet to hear.

"Are you?" Janet followed up.

"Of course I am," Tabitha answered.

Janet piped, "Yeah, Daddy Warbucks."

"Ain't nothing wrong with dreaming the big dream."

Janet said, "I had dreams, too."

Tabitha couldn't tell if her sister said it in jest or out of depression.

"We just gotta keep going for *whatever* in life," she responded.

Janet said, "You don't have to tell me. I don't need cheerleaders. I'm best without them. They don't know how far to go and when to stop sometimes."

"I know what you mean. Sometimes you just need somebody to be there."

"Exactly."

"So, would you ever want to be here with us again?" Tabitha finally asked her.

Marisol looked up in apprehension.

Janet chuckled over the line. "That's what this whole phone call was all about, wasn't it?"

"What would make you say that?"

"Tabby, are you still having those big house dreams of yours? What do you have, a grand plan now? A lucky lotto number?"

Tabitha smiled. "You never know," she answered.

"Well, I'm comfortable out here with my own space right now."

"Are you really? Because love is always around the corner."

"Or around the casino," Janet joked.

"It doesn't have to be," Tabitha responded.

"So you really do have a plan. What are you about to do? You hit the jackpot out there? Don't tell me you're about to get married to a croak."

Tabitha started laughing. "No, I'm not doing that, especially in the era of the prenuptial. That wouldn't make any sense."

"So what are you about to do then?" Janet pressed her. "I know you, and you don't start getting ahead of yourself unless you're getting close to making something happen."

"I'm always getting close to things."

"So, in other words, you're not gonna tell me."

Tabitha continued to grin.

"I did tell you."

Janet thought it over.

She said, "Somebody's gonna bankroll you for favors? You got it like that?"

"We'll see," Tabitha told her. Janet was the only one of her sisters whom she would trust to share so many details. Janet was mature enough to accept things at face value; but none of them got *all* of the details. Not even the diary.

"Mmpt, mmpt, mmpt," Janet grunted. "I'm scared of you. That smile has turned you into a life-size Barbie. And they're really falling for it, aren't they?"

"I can't say that," Tabitha answered. "If I could, I'd have a ring on my finger."

"True. True indeed."

≋

When Tabitha and Janet said their good-byes—for the meantime—and hung up the phone, Marisol was all over Tabby for information.

"So, what were you all talking about? Is she comin' here, too? Were you telling her things that you wouldn't tell me?"

Tabitha looked at her and said, "Gee, I wonder why. And no, Janet is not coming here."

Not yet, anyway, she thought to herself.

"You've always done that to me," Mari complained. "Is it a *black* thing? I thought I was your *sister,* too."

"You *are* my sister," Tabitha reassured her.

"So what was all that *ring* stuff about? You're gettin' serious with one of these *boyfriends*?" Mari quizzed.

Tabitha smiled and shook her head.

"Lesson number one: If you're going to eavesdrop, then make sure you hear all of the facts."

"Well, if you *told me,* I wouldn't have to *eavesdrop,* now would I?"

Tabitha ignored her and headed to her bedroom for privacy. She had some more writing to do.

Thursday, February 21, 2002
Nighttime
Home
Tabby

I talked to Janet today, and she's still the same old girl that she used to be. She says exactly what's on her mind. She sounds like she's doing okay in life. I still detect a bit of loneliness in her voice, though. I know she wouldn't mind being with us again, like old times. I can feel it in her.

Patrice is on her way to Las Vegas for a visit. I wasn't able to convince her to work things out with her husband from home. But just because she'll be here with the kids doesn't mean she's not going back. My guess is that she'll break down and get homesick after a couple of days anyway.

I don't know what I'm about to get myself in to, but it's better than doing nothing. Maybe if I had something to hold on to, I wouldn't have agreed to do this. Then again, I'm doing it to try and bring my sisters back together. At least that's what I tell myself. It's my dream, not theirs. But why is everything coming together like it is if it wasn't meant to be? I didn't ask for all of this right now in my life. I was pretty content. But I guess I'm not fulfilled. Maybe none of us is.

I would say I'm more fulfilled than my sisters are for one reason; I never let the foster home experience stop me from dreaming. Different people respond to things different ways. I guess I used the experience as a springboard to say, Why not? I mean, what have I got to lose?

Maybe I'm still crazy about the adventure of my life. One thing's for sure: This time I'm really outdoing myself. So I won't even mention his name until I'm successful at what I need to do. Or if I fail, maybe I'll mention his name then, too, just as a reminder of who I was after.

The Setup

Tabitha sat inside the unmarked car with Sylvia Green at their meeting place.

"Okay, here's the first step of the plan. Our guy has a premiere for his latest film, *All the Way,* at the Magic Johnson Theater in Harlem, New York."

Tabitha heard the words *New York* and froze.

"New York?" She wasn't too fond of the big city.

"Yes," Sylvia confirmed. "Harlem. He's doing this whole 'give back to the black community' campaign. So you'll have a lot of locals from Harlem mixed in with the Hollywood crowd."

Tabitha looked confused by it.

"In that case, they'll be on guard for anyone who tries to get anywhere close to him."

Sylvia told her, "This is just to get you familiar with who all of the players on his team are, because they'll all be there in New York. They'll stand out like sore thumbs. If the premiere were in L.A., it would be harder to tell who's really in and who's just faking it."

She said, "We felt New York would be perfect for you to blend in as an around the way girl. So make sure you wear a pair of tight blue jeans," she added with a grin. "They'll be having an after party at a club off One-hundred-twenty-fifth Street."

"So, how close do you want me to get to him in New York?" Tabitha asked her. "That's not really a place for intimacy. I mean, they're intimate there, but that's not the *easiest* place to get to know somebody."

Sylvia continued to smile. "If I didn't know any better, I would think that you're getting cold feet. What did you think, we were gonna wait around for him to come to Las Vegas so you can work your magic on *your* turf. Like you said, he's the biggest of the big. So we're flying you out to him."

"Will I have any contacts in New York? I don't know the city that well."

Sylvia pulled a black briefcase from the backseat. She opened it and began to finger through several snapshots.

"This is Wallace, and this is Angela. They were both contacted by a private investigator in New York. They'll be helping you out when you arrive."

Wallace was of medium build with a brown baby face that could fit in to any party. He had the boyish good looks of a star football player. Angela was a honey-brown model type with curled blond hair that fell past her shoulders.

"Looks like you're hooking me up with the star recruits," Tabitha commented.

Sylvia nodded. "Some real deep pockets are running the show."

Tabitha grinned. "I guess I don't get a chance to meet him."

Sylvia paused. She said, "You may already know him. He sure knows a lot about you."

Tabitha stopped smiling. "Who is he?"

Sylvia only laughed at her.

"That's not part of my job description. So let's get back to the script. Shall we?"

Tabitha asked her, "What exactly *is* your job description? Do you do jobs like this often?"

"Actually, I don't," Sylvia answered. "This is very new for me. But I'm finding it interesting. I'm sure it'll get a lot more interesting once it gets started."

She pulled out more pictures and began to go over the faces, one by one.

"This is Derrick, one of the bodyguards."

He was a wide-bodied man with a shaved head.

Sylvia said, "He's one of the few on the team who *won't* flirt with minors. But he allows it all to happen. So he's just as bad as the rest of them to me. Even worse, he serves as a lookout man. So if you want to get in with your safest mark, you choose him.

"This is Rafael," she said of the smooth-faced man in the next photo. "He's a wanna-be actor who couldn't make the cut. You've probably seen him in a few of Isaac's old pictures as an extra. He's now the traveling assistant. He makes all the personal errands. And he's particularly freaky. So I'd stay away from him. Unless you *want* to be freaked out," Sylvia added. "But if *he* gets you, then you're not getting to Isaac. Isaac doesn't take seconds."

Tabitha nodded and took it all in.

"This is Charles. He's the manager. He's the tight-ass of their crew. I'd stay away from him, too," Sylvia warned. "He'll prove to be the most skeptical. He'll call you out on everything. He's the main gatekeeper."

Charles looked like a strict image man. He wore tailored clothes from head to toe.

"He looks like a black man's *GQ*," Tabby joked.

"Yeah, that's what he thinks he is. But if he can afford it, and he *can,* then why not?"

She moved on to the next picture, a tall stately man with a deceptively warm smile.

"This is Teddy, one of the best publicists that money can buy. He gets good press by sleeping with any media woman who doesn't have her panties on lock. When he deals with male editors, he sends them willing lady friends."

Tabitha looked at her to make sure.

She asked, "Are you serious?"

"Believe it," Sylvia told her. "Big business is big business. Whatever it takes, he'll do."

"So he's like a media pimp?"

"And everybody's his ho."

"Damn."

"Interesting, ain't it?"

"Mmmph," Tabitha grunted. "Very."

"This one here is the lawyer, J.J. He's new. J.J. replaces the last lawyer, who got caught up in the hype and lost sight of his job after a very public affair with a B-rate actress."

"Yeah, I remember that," Tabitha told her. "That happened around the release of that movie *Alligator's Row.*"

Sylvia nodded. "Yeah. Then we have the agent, Michael Bent. He's the only one who goes by first and last name. He's eager to corner the market of young black actors and directors. Like Teddy, he'll do anything to get what his clients want. So disregard his choirboy looks. He's a snake."

Tabitha laughed aloud. The man did have a nerdish appearance in his tight, dark suit and wire-rimmed glasses.

Sylvia explained, "His looks make it easier for him to make deals with the white men who still run Hollywood. But his track record allows him to look that way and still pull more pussy than you would believe."

Tabitha stopped smiling. "So Isaac has a serious team. No women?"

"No. The only women in this camp are the wives, mistresses, girlfriends, and playthings."

"So, what would I be?" Tabitha asked rhetorically.

Sylvia frowned at her. She said, "The *wives* have known these men for years. The *mistresses* are like second wives. The *girlfriends* are future wives. And the playthings are everybody else. Now, what do you *think* you're gonna be? Not one of these guys is gonna be serious about a teenage groupie. So don't forget your role.

"Now that's the A-team, the real moneymakers. Isaac also has a B and a C team," Sylvia informed her. "They're mostly old friends and family members."

Tabitha stopped her and asked, "Do I really need to know all of these names and faces? You're gonna get me confused. I'd rather just get in there and do my thing."

"The more you know, the better," Sylvia told her. "I would advise you to memorize as much as possible. Because your *thing* may not work on this level."

Tabitha sat silently for a minute.

"This looks like a lot of work," she commented.

"What did you expect for a hundred thousand dollars? A cakewalk? This *is* work. So you best get ready for it."

She held the last picture up to Tabitha's face to nail it home. Isaac Abraham's smile was as magnetic and pure as it was on the big screen. And he was dressed all in white, of all things.

Sylvia said, "We have to stop protecting those who make a mockery of who we are as a people. He's not above the law. So he has it coming to him. I don't care *how* famous he is. He's gonna make a mistake and have to come to terms with his ways sooner than later. You just have to convince yourself that this *is* the right thing to do."

Second Thoughts

Friday, February 22, 2002
Late Night
In the Bathroom
Tabby

I'm already having second thoughts about this thing I'm supposed to do. I can't stand New York. I've only been there twice, and both times I felt so small. That place can really make you feel disconnected. I already spend a lot of time by myself, but that place made me feel like I was all alone—in a crowd, of course. There are plenty of people in New York. They just don't seem to care about you. Then again, who does? Maybe I'm overreacting.

I still can't decide if I want to be associated with bringing down a black male icon. White guys have their little personal lives, too, and no one seems to bother them. They do younger women all the time. That's the part about this that's messed up. How can it ever be fair?

Then again, how can I talk when I've been lying about my age for three years now. Men just seem to get more excited when you're young. Especially when you show a serious interest in them. I can see how their eyes stretch all wide with the possibilities as soon as I say I'm seventeen. I haven't been seventeen for almost ten years now.

A knock on the bathroom door stopped Tabitha from writing her entry.
"Who is it?"
"It's Patrice. What are you doing in there?"
"I'll be right out."

Tabitha stood from the stool and hid her diary deep into the sink cabinet. She changed her mind and tucked it under her arm to carry out with her.

"You know there's another bathroom in my bedroom," she mentioned on the way out.

Patrice said, "I don't have to go. I just wanted to see if you were up for a talk. The kids are finally asleep," she stated with a heavy breath. "I tell you, they are a complete handful."

She rubbed her hand over her weary brown face, letting it rest on her chin. She was already in her night clothes, an extra large, light blue one-piece.

"So, what's on your mind, Tabby? I can see you working something out up there. If we talk about *your* problems, I can stop thinking so much about *mine*."

Tabitha smiled. "Is that how it works?" She was still dressed in blue jeans and a white T-shirt.

"You know what they say, misery loves company," Patrice told her.

"How long have you been miserable?" Tabitha asked.

"What, you think I don't have a reason to be?"

"I'm not saying that. I'm just asking how long you've felt dissatisfied. I mean, this isn't all of a sudden. You've been expressing concerns to me about your life for a while now."

Patrice looked disoriented for a moment as they stood there in the living room.

"You know what? I can't ever remember being as happy as you are. Maybe misery is just my disposition."

"Well, what makes you happy?" Tabitha quizzed her.

Patrice looked confused again. She stopped in her thoughts and said, "Wait a minute. I'm supposed to be getting at what's going on in *your* head, not the other way around."

"My head is fine," Tabitha told her.

"Is it?" Patrice questioned. "Mari isn't here right now, so you can level with me, Tabby. How are you *really* doing? I mean, what is it about fast men that makes you want to keep chasing them?"

Tabitha paused. She said, "They're all fast, Patrice. Some are just faster than others."

Under the circumstances, Patrice had to agree with her.

"So, you just use their speed to cruise along and make yourself a comfortable living, hunh?"

"For the meantime. But it'll get old soon. Then I'll have to figure out what I wanna do."

"I see."

Tabitha changed the subject. "Well, you know I'm going out of town Sunday. I'll be back Wednesday night."

"Where are you off to?"

"New York."

"Whose treat?"

Tabitha smiled. "Somebody's."

Patrice shook her head. "I just can't understand how you do it."

"Me either. I just wing it."

Patrice studied her sister for a moment. She asked her, "Do you ever sleep with married men?"

Tabitha froze. What was the right thing to say? Of course she had slept with married men. Not to break up their families. Nevertheless, she wasn't sure how Patrice would react to her answer.

"What do you want me to say?" she asked cautiously.

"I imagine you have. You can't sleep with that many men without any of them being married."

"How would you feel if I did?"

Patrice thought about it. "Well, you know I don't like it."

"It takes two," Tabitha reasoned.

"Yeah, but you're going after these men. It's not like they're calling you out of the blue. You put yourself in the position to meet them."

She was right. Tabitha stood speechless.

"So what do you want me to say?" she repeated.

"I want you to stop *doing it*," Patrice admitted to her. "I want you to live a respectable life. Don't you want a normal home? We *all* want that."

"So why are you so miserable?" Tabitha asked her. "You have a respectable life and home."

"No, I *would have* had a respectable life and home if Mr. *Asshole* didn't fuck it up!"

Patrice began to rant and stirred the kids from their sleep.

"Shit!" she mumbled. One of her daughters cried out inside Tabby's bedroom. She had given up her queen-size bed for their visit.

Tabitha lowered her voice to a whisper. She said, "These men are just not satisfied. I've been with them. I know."

"And what do they tell you?"

"It's basically about enslavement. You're enslaved to your husband, and your husband's enslaved to you," she explained to her sister.

Patrice looked at her in awe.

"It's supposed to be about *love,*" she stated.

"Sure, it starts off that way, but where does the love go?"

"It doesn't go anywhere. You have to *work* at it. It's not a wham, bam, we in love thing. That's what's wrong with people now."

"So why are you here with me instead of back home with your husband? I told you to let him come home and explain himself. You were bent on getting away."

"Well, maybe I *needed* to get away. Why, you don't want me here? If you didn't want me here, then all you had to do was say it."

The increased volume in their voices stirred the kids again.

Tabitha whispered, "I didn't say that."

Patrice headed into the room to calm the children.

"You didn't have to," she responded as she left.

When Tabitha was alone again, she continued to think about her predicament. One hundred thousand dollars was a heck of a lot of money to turn down.

"I just need to stick to my decision on this," she told herself. "Either I can get the job done or I can't."

Patrice walked back out from the room and caught the tail end of her comment. She asked Tabitha what she was talking about.

Tabitha shook her head. "Nothing," she lied.

"I find that hard to believe, but I'll let you slide with that one," Patrice told her.

They both stopped and stared at each other.

Patrice exhaled and said, "Okay. I don't know how I can come down on you. It's not as if *my* life is all that great. I just feel like things are either falling apart, or on the *verge* of it. I guess I thought that if I came out here with you for a couple of days, when I drove back home, Randy would be sweating to have us back."

"He is already," Tabitha told her. "He's been calling here four times a day, worried about you and the kids."

"I know, but that doesn't mean anything. He can't change overnight."

"Nor can you."

"So what are you saying?" Patrice asked her. She was desperate for answers.

"I'm saying that life is a journey for all of us. It's really unfair of you to judge my journey without thinking about everybody else's," she answered. "I don't control what these men do."

"I already said that," Patrice reiterated.

"Well, now *I'm* saying it. Believe it or not, if people didn't have anyone to run to to understand them, there would be a lot more despair in this world than what we have already. Just like you ran to me."

With that, Patrice took a seat on the sofa in front of the television where Mari often sat. She didn't have a thing else to say.

"I just wish he could still talk to me," she grumbled a few minutes later.

Tabitha heard her words and understood the honesty in them. Nevertheless, she had learned that new conversations with new people were necessary for growth in life. How much were Patrice and Randy growing within their relationship? Were they growing together, or growing apart?

She responded, "He can," just to make Patrice feel better. There was always room for hope and reevaluation. They just had to figure out how to make that reevaluation work.

New York

New York, New York, was a giant urban terrain of twenty-four-hour hustle. New Yorkers hustled even while they slept. They dreamed about hustle. They woke up hustling. They hustled off to work in the morning. And they hustled back home and out to play after work.

Who in their right mind would want to leave the hot days and cool nights of Las Vegas, where everybody smiled and spent money without a care, for New York City's cold winter days and even colder nights of stiff-shouldered street peddlers? Visiting New York was the opposite of a vacation. It didn't put you at ease—it put you on guard.

Tabitha had a right to be apprehensive. She knew she was flying into some intense work. That was all that she could think about on the transfer flight to New York from Chicago: work and terrorism.

"Can I get you anything else to drink?" the Latina flight attendant asked her.

"Hunh? Oh, no. I'm okay," Tabitha responded with the jitters.

"Are you sure?"

"Oh, yeah, I'm sure. I'm okay."

The flight attendant smiled and went on about her business.

"This is your first flight to New York?" the middle-aged white man asked from the seat to the left. Tabitha was fortunate to have an aisle seat so she could leap for an exit if anything crazy happened.

"No, this is my third time," she answered.

"It's your first time since 'Ground Zero,' right?"

She stared at him blankly. "Who?"

"You know, the World Trade Center," he reminded her.

"Oh, yeah, that."

Tabitha nodded and planned to ignore him. She had a hunch that he was on a roll.

"So are you from Chicago?" he asked her next.

She undid her seat belt without a word and headed to the nearest lavatory. She squeezed inside and grumbled, "This is gonna be a long trip, but I got myself into it. No turnin' back now."

The plane went through turbulence, rocking sideways as soon as she sat on the toilet.

"Shit!" she cursed. "Is this a damn sign? I haven't even gotten there yet."

The rocky plane ride made it hard for her to finish her business in small quarters.

"I don't believe this," she continued to complain.

When it was all over, she walked out of the lavatory shaken by the experience.

"Pretty rough in there on ya', huh?" the man next to her asked.

Tabitha turned and stared at him right in the face until he got the point. She was not on that plane to be friendly. She had a high-priced job to do.

As the flight approached LaGuardia Airport, Tabitha became more antsy. Contrary to her fears, the landing went like clockwork. She found herself walking off the plane safe and sound.

"Have a nice stay," her friend from the seat to the left offered.

"Thank you," she told him.

Wallace, the stud who was sent to meet her at the airport, was waiting for her at the luggage pickup.

"You look just like your picture," he commented once he spotted her.

"So do you," she told him.

He wore a rust brown, three-quarter-length suede coat with a hood, black jeans, and black Timberland boots. Tabitha wore a full-length black sweater coat with blue jeans and light brown cowgirl boots.

"So, where do they have me staying?" she asked him.

"Times Square. Some of his team are having a get-together tonight at Bruno's Barbecue, on Forty-eighth Street."

"Am I going to that?"

"Not exactly. But we do want to be in the area when they arrive. So I made reservations for this Thai restaurant next door. We have a second floor window table so we can see who's coming and going at Bruno's."

"How do y'all know they're gonna be there?" she asked him curiously.

"How do you know the things that *you* know?" he responded with a smile.

She politely ignored it. "Here comes my stuff," she told him, watching the luggage belt.

"How many bags did you bring?"

She grinned before she answered, "Three."

He grabbed her first black bag from the luggage belt and grimaced. "Three bags for three days, hunh? What you need to do is shop when you hit the city. You need to blend in with the locals," he advised her.

She said, "I disagree. Blending in gets you ignored. You always want to look like you're from somewhere else. That gets you an extra look, and an easier conversation."

He stopped and stared at her. "I guess you would know."

She smiled. "I do. There's my other bags," she told him in a rush.

Wallace grabbed them all.

"So where's Angela?" she asked him.

They started toward the exit doors with the luggage. The cold New York wind blew into the airport from the sliding electric doors and shook Tabitha's bones before Wallace could answer her.

"Shit!" she responded to it.

"Not used to that, hunh?"

"Not exactly." She bumped into him when she spoke to buffer against the surprise of the sudden chill.

"Don't get it confused," he told her on beat. "I'm here to help you."

She appeared to be caught off guard by that.

"What?" she asked him.

He ignored it and answered her previous question.

"Angela will meet up with you tomorrow. She got some other things to do today."

"So that means I'm stuck with *you-u-u*."

The New York weather was kicking her ass as they walked right into it. It was the difference between the warm Pacific Ocean and the frigidness of the Atlantic. Tabitha had been prone to frequent the warmer areas of the West Coast and the South.

"Where's your car?" she asked him in haste. She wanted to get out of the cold as quickly as possible.

"We have to take the parking bus," he told her. He smiled at her and added, "Calm down. You're making it worse than it is. It's not that cold out here, that's just the airport. You'll be fine once we hit the city."

"I hope so," she told him.

Fortunately, they didn't have to wait long for a parking bus to arrive. Tabitha hopped on board and found a warm seat to begin rubbing her hands, arms, and legs.

Wallace climbed aboard with the luggage and joked with the other passengers, "Don't mind her, she's from Florida."

Tabitha smiled and held all of her thoughts to herself.

They arrived at the parking garage and walked over to a dark gray Ford Explorer.

"Have you ever been out of New York?" Tabitha asked him. She climbed in on the passenger side.

Wallace answered, "Of course. I've been all over. You name it."

He tossed her luggage in the back, with plenty of room to spare.

She said, "Hawaii."

Wallace climbed in on the driver's side. He said, "I flew over an active volcano in a helicopter. I surfed on the western beaches. I went to luaus. Horseback riding."

Tabitha looked over his chiseled brown face again.

"You model?" she asked him.

"Every job I can get."

That confused her. "So, what are you doing helping me on this?"

"I was told that I look good enough to help get where you need to go."

She nodded. It was a good enough answer for her.

He pulled out of the parking spot and headed for the city.

"What does Angela do? Is she a model or an actress, too?"

"All of us are trying to do something. What are you trying to do?" Wallace questioned.

"I'm just trying to live my life," Tabitha answered him.

"So why impose on other people's lives?"

He caught her off guard again. Was he just there to help, or did he have his own ulterior motives?

"Is that what you think I do? What have you been told about me?"

He said, "I don't know everything about you."

"But you know enough to *think* that you know me."

He smiled, looking forward and to the traffic on the road.

Tabitha stopped herself from more conversation with him. What he thought didn't matter. She had a job to do, and his sarcastic ass was there to help her. Or was he?

"So you think what we're doing is wrong?" she asked him anyway.

"To each his own. Or *her* own," he responded. "You gotta do what you gotta do anyway, just like everybody else, right?"

"Exactly," she told him.

They crossed from Queens over into Manhattan, where the dark sky-scrapers made the clouds and stars disappear.

Wallace piped, "Here we go, the big city. So I'll check you in to your hotel, and you do whatever you gotta do for two hours. Then you meet me down in the lobby at eight o'clock."

Tabitha was thinking that maybe she wanted to go by herself. That was how she had done her thing anyway. She imagined she would cut Wallace loose before the night was over, so she went along with the temporary plans.

"All right. I'll meet you in the lobby at eight."

Step 1

Sunday, February 24, 2002
Manhattan, New York
Millennium Hotel
Tabby

I start the big job in New York today. Or I guess I should say tonight. I was feeling nervous as hell about it on the plane ride from Chicago. But once I got here and hooked up with the asshole who's supposed to be helping me . . . I'm just ready to get this thing started and over with.

I don't have much else to say right now. I have to get my gear together for tonight. Some of these big-time players are supposed to be in touching range at a restaurant. I guess we'll see how untouchable they are. Then I'll have more to write about later on.

Tabitha closed her diary book and put it away. She unpacked her clothes to hang in the closet. Then she thumbed through her clothes for the appropriate outfit, starting with the colors of her shirts and blouses.

"Yellow is too feminine. Black is too opaque. White is too virginal. And green is too . . . *green*. Baby blue is too . . . *innocent*. That's perfect. Baby blue it is," she told herself and pulled the blouse out of the closet to iron.

She philosophized to herself as she pulled down the ironing board.

"Guys love innocent girls, but not necessarily *virgins*. They don't want to read through black all night. And they don't want to feel a need to *protect* a girl dressed in yellow if they're trying hard to get some.

"Of course, all of that is *bullshit* if they want some badly enough," she admitted. "They'll fuck a girl wearing red and white polka dots. As long as she got what they need when she's naked."

She decided to keep on her blue jeans from the plane ride, and wear a neutral brown leather jacket to cover up from the cold. The cowgirl boots fit as well.

She looked into the large dresser mirror at her final getup and was satisfied with it.

"Well, I don't look like I'm from New York. I don't know their look anyway. Seems like they wear a combination of a bunch of pieces. But that's probably from me looking in too many fashion magazines. Nobody really dresses like that."

While she talked to herself in the mirror, the phone rang.

"Hello."

"I've been waiting down here for twenty minutes. Was I supposed to call first?" Wallace asked her from the lobby phone.

"What time is it? I just got here."

Tabby hadn't even looked at the clock. It just *felt* like she hadn't been there long.

Wallace said, "It's eight twenty-five and counting. By the time you get down here, it'll be eight thirty-two. Then it'll take us fifteen minutes to drive and park, which makes us late for our reservation. We'll probably miss the grand entrance at Bruno's next door."

"Well, if they're already there, then let's cut to the chase and go to Bruno's with them," Tabitha suggested.

"That would blow your cover," Wallace told her. "We don't need you to do anything tonight. We just want you to see how they roll. Besides, you can't just walk up in Bruno's."

"Isn't that a barbecue place?"

"That's just the name. The place is still upscale."

"Well, you let me handle it when we get there," she told him.

"I think not. Just come down here and we'll talk about it on the way over."

"Whatever," she huffed and hung up the phone. "I wonder what this Angela chick is gonna be like. Because I'm not feeling playboy so far."

She made it down to the hotel lobby where Wallace waited for her. He wore a black leather jacket that was similar to her brown one.

"Aw, God, now we got the coordinated couple look," he complained.

"Trust me, I'm not thrilled by it either," she told him and kept walking. "Where did you park?"

≈≈≈

They made it to the restaurant on 48th Street in the Times Square area, where a full block of stretch limos emptied out important passengers.

"Looks like we may have missed their entrance already," Wallace commented.

Tabitha didn't respond to him. When they drove close enough to the restaurant through the jammed-up traffic, she peered through the dark glass to see if she noticed any of the men she had studied in the pictures that Sylvia had shown her in Las Vegas.

She said, "It's too dark to see anything in there."

"That's what I know already. That's why we needed a window-view table to see them roll up in the limo."

"But how long will that last? They're not gonna hang outside. They'll walk right in the restaurant."

"No, they like to showboat," Wallace told her. "They'll get out one at a time to be seen."

Tabitha frowned at him. "How else are they gonna get out of a limo? Three at a time?"

"Okay, you got jokes now," Wallace commented.

"The chauffeur has to open the door for them anyway."

"That would have given us time to watch them."

"Well, it's too late for that now. So what do you wanna do, wait for them to come out?"

It was close to nine o'clock. Wallace wasn't even sure if they could still get their preferred, window-view table.

"We'll see. Let me park first."

"All right, well, I'll go in while you park."

"Naw," he told her. "We have to look like a couple."

"Why?"

"So you don't look suspicious."

"Well, who's gonna want to talk to me if your ass is in the way?" she told him candidly.

Wallace said, "I told you. You're not here to meet them tonight. You're just supposed to *see* them."

Right as he spoke, Tabitha noticed Charles, the strictly business manager, step out of Bruno's front door while using his cell phone.

Instinctively, she hopped out of the Explorer to get a closer look.

"Fuck!" she heard Wallace scream at her back. It was too late to stop her.

She walked over toward Bruno's as if she were lost and looking for a friend.

Charles was talking loud with animation over his cell phone.

"That's not how it's supposed to go down. *You* were supposed to make sure that we could get our date. Now if we can't get the date that we asked for, then I don't know what to tell you about a next time."

It didn't sound like the kind of conversation that he would break away from to give her any attention. She made a left turn in rhythm and headed for the Thai restaurant without being noticed. As she headed on her way, Teddy, the publicist, walked out of Bruno's and caught her eye at a glance.

"Hey, Charles, let that go, man. I got some people in here who wanna meet you," he said, while still eyeing Tabitha.

His voice alone, after seeing his picture and hearing about him, was enough to give her chills.

"One minute," Charles told him with an index finger up. He even *sounded* like one in control. "Good. That's what needs to happen," he said over the phone. Just like that, he hung up and went back inside the restaurant.

Teddy went in after him. Tabitha was sure that he had taken notice of her. His stare was too strong not to. But she didn't know if that was a good thing or a bad thing.

She got the window table on the second level of the Thai restaurant and waited for Wallace.

Wallace walked in *steamed* at her.

"Look, you're gonna fuck up a whole lot of money for all of us," he said to her as he took his seat. "You gotta do things as planned."

"Do you even know why we're doing this?" Tabitha asked him.

"The man has overstepped his boundaries, and he needs to be put back in check," he answered.

"Yeah, but it sounds like we're all working for the money, not the principle of it. There are plenty of people we can go after with no payment, but what use would that be to us?"

She silenced Wallace. He lowered his eyes toward the menu deciding what to order.

"So what happened?" he asked Tabitha a second later.

"The timing wasn't right," she told him.

The waiter arrived at their table to take their orders. They made their orders and went right back to their conversation.

"That's what I told you. You have to work *with us* on this. So who did you see?"

"Charles and Teddy."

She stopped short of informing him that Teddy had eyed her. She didn't know what that meant yet anyway. What would Teddy do with the recollection?

"What do we do after this?" she asked Wallace.

"We get some rest."

"They aren't going to a club or something tonight?"

"I'm sure they are, but like I said—"

"I'm only supposed to see how they roll tonight. Well, if they go to a club, I can get a lot more details on who they are and what they like."

Wallace thought about that. "True, true. But I don't know if I want to chance that. They may notice you for when you try to zero in on Isaac."

She said, "You just have to let things flow a little. I mean, I can't work under all these restrictions. You have to understand that I have rules of my own that allow me to get close to men and maintain my self-respect."

Wallace looked at her incredulously.

"You keep your *what*? Self-respect?"

"Yes, I do."

He only chuckled at the notion.

"Anyway," she stated, "I think that trailing them to a club would be a good idea."

"*If* they're even going to a club tonight. They do have to prepare for their premiere showing."

"Well, let's just follow them and see."

Wallace shook his head. "You crazy," he told her.

"That's why I'm on the job."

Wallace thought about it.

"They'll be long gone by the time we eat and I get my car. All they have to do is walk outside and jump in a limo."

Just as Wallace finished his sentence, an entourage of Charles, Teddy, the lawyer named J.J., and the Hollywood agent, Michael Bent, walked out of Bruno's Barbecue with some other players Tabitha recognized from Isaac's B-team.

"Speak of the devil," Wallace responded, spotting them out the window. "So I guess you want me to fly down there and chase after them now like a superhero?"

Tabitha ignored his joke. "I have my plans," she told him.

"Plans to do what?"

"To find out where they're going. I know they're going somewhere. It's not even ten o'clock."

Wallace figured there was no way in hell they would chase them down after they had left. New York didn't have any dirt road shortcuts to make up lost ground.

Tabitha stood from her seat and said, "I'll be back."

Wallace looked up from drinking his glass of water and shook his head. He didn't even bother to ask her where she was going. She was wearing out his patience. He figured the less he had to say to her, the better.

Tabitha hustled down the restaurant stairs and made a quick dash out the door for Bruno's. She walked right into the restaurant. She began looking around as if she owned the place.

"Excuse me, may I help you?" a young male maître d' asked her. He was a young, college-age white male, wearing formal attire with a black vest but no jacket.

Tabitha faked bitter confusion. "Shit! I just missed them," she huffed.

"You just missed who?"

She answered, "There was a whole group of black men from Hollywood in here that I was supposed to meet with." She made sure to talk loudly enough to be overheard by other employees in the restaurant.

"May I ask what it was regarding?" the maître d' asked her.

"They wanted me to audition for them on the spot. Do you have any idea where they're off to?"

One of the waitresses overheard her and spoke up.

"I believe they're headed to a club called Good Times in the SoHo area."

"Good Times? Are you sure?" she asked the waitress.

"I believe so," she answered.

"Thank you." Tabitha hit the door to exit as swiftly as she had entered. She walked inside the Thai restaurant next door, back up to her window-view table with Wallace, and smiled at him.

"Have you ever heard of a club called Good Times in the SoHo area?"

Wallace stared at her with his hot plate of food in front of him. Tabitha's plate was on the table in front of her.

"What about it?" he asked.

"That's where they're headed," she told him.

"Who told you that?"

Tabitha just smiled.

Wallace stopped eating and shook his head one more time.

"I can see this is gonna be a long night."

≈

They arrived in Lower Manhattan, where things were still shaking and jumping.

"Now this is more like it," Tabby commented. She rocked to the music that flooded the cars and the various clubs that lined the tight streets.

"Okay, so we go in here and do what?" Wallace asked her.

"I shake things up and see what happens."

"*If* they're even in there."

She took a breath and told him, "Stop complaining so much and park the truck, Wally."

Wallace frowned at her before he parked the Explorer up the street from the club. They walked back to join a small line to get in.

"What's the cover?" they asked the salt and pepper bouncers at the door.

"Twenty dollars," the pepper bouncer answered.

"Damn, it ain't even packed tonight," Wallace mentioned.

"That's the way we like it," the salt bouncer added. "We keep it cozy and low-key."

Wallace paid their way to get in, while Tabitha used one of her several fake IDs; Tonya Kennedy from San Antonio, Texas.

"Mmph, nice," she commented about the club on entry. The blue, green, and yellow neon-lit club was not jam-packed, but it was packed enough to entice solid movement on the dance floor. The DJ was in strict control of the party, spinning Busta Rhymes's hit song, "Pass the Courvoisier," from his elevated platform in the middle of the room.

"Bingo," Tabitha told Wallace. "Charles, J.J., and Teddy are at the bar."

Wallace looked over and noticed the A-team members of Isaac Abraham's squad sitting at the bar to the left of the dance floor. They were relaxing with drinks in their hands and having light conversation.

"Okay, so now what?" he asked Tabitha.

"You get lost and let me do my thing," she told him.

She moved onto the dance floor in clear view of the team.

Teddy spotted her and recognized her immediately from the restaurant earlier.

"I guess it was meant to be," he mumbled to himself. He watched the young lady in form-fitting blue jeans, light blue blouse, and light brown boots before he mentioned the sight to anyone else at the bar.

"She got a wicked dance," J.J. commented. He was the most low-key of the team, in a basic black turtleneck with black slacks and shoes. Charles was tailored to the nines as always. Teddy, on the other hand, wore a loud, wide-collared beige shirt with cream zigzags to make sure he got noticed.

"Which one are you talking about?" Teddy asked J.J. for clarity.

"This girl over here in the light blue."

They all eyed the young lady as she danced in a slow twirl. She seemed to dance to a slower beat than the rest of the club, but she was somehow still on beat. Her movements were fluid and seductive.

Charles spoke up and said, "She makes everybody else look like they're dancing too fast."

"That's because most of these motherfuckers are showing off in here. They know who we are," Teddy commented with a grin.

"You think she knows?" J.J. asked.

"I'm about to find out," Teddy told him. He approached the young lady on the dance floor with his drink still in hand.

Charles, still at the bar, said to J.J., "She knows. Why else would she choose to dance right in front of us when she got all the room in the world out there?"

J.J. took a sip of his drink and agreed. "That's true."

Charles said, "Teddy knows it, too. He just likes making excuses to keep his thing wet."

J.J. smiled and said, "Like he needs an excuse."

Teddy approached the young lady and began to dance with her. He raised his drink up in the air in his right hand. The DJ was spinning P. Diddy's "I Need A Girl" remix, featuring Usher.

"I need one, too," Teddy ad-libbed to the song. "But some of y'all look too young in here for me. Who let *you* in here? Let me see that fake ID."

The young lady kept her poise and laughed. She said, "I'm *legal* now," sounding immature on purpose.

"Oh, you legal *now*. When? Yesterday?"

She only smiled at him. "I'm not answering that question."

"Gee, I wonder why?" he joked to her.

She smiled even wider.

"So what's your name, and why are you here? Because you're not a New Yorker," he correctly assumed. He had to lean into her ear to be heard over the bass thump of the music.

She leaned into him as well.

"My name is Tonya. But you'll never guess where I'm from, because I don't have the accent."

"That means you're from down South," Teddy assumed again. He was on his usual roll. As a top-notch publicist, he was well abreast of the various characteristics and flavors of people in the United States and abroad.

The young lady's mouth dropped open. She said, "You're good."

"I get paid to be," he told her.

"What do you do?" she asked.

"Basically, I do people favors, and then they write nice articles for me."

"Articles? What, you deal in public relations?"

He looked at her and dropped his mouth open. "You're good," he mocked her.

"Well, I *don't* get paid to be," she responded.

"What do you get paid to do?"

He put her on the spot.

"Oh, my God, I'm so embarrassed," she told him. "I really can't even tell you."

"What, you just got off the plane a week ago with your life savings, looking for a big break in New York?"

The young lady dropped her head, but her smile never left her face.

She said, "I guess you understand a lot of people if you deal in public relations, right? You know what makes them tick."

Teddy said, "Yeah, I guess you can say that. So what makes you tick? Why you think you got a chance in New York? What are you trying to be, an actress? A dancer? Don't tell me you're doing the video circuit."

"Not yet," she joked to him. She finally stopped smiling. She said, "But I don't know. Everybody gets a break *sometimes*, right? I mean . . . I don't know."

"You got a plan?" he asked her next.

She glanced to his feet on the dance floor again.

"You got me. I was just gonna come up here and wing it," she told him. She had genuine confliction in her face.

He read it and advised, "If you don't have a plan, I would tell you to go back home to Tennessee, or wherever, and find one. Unless *I* can help you in some way."

That was the pitch. Young hopefuls to the city of New York were always desperate to make it. They hated being told to go back home and start over. It had already taken a truckload of courage for the young woman to fly to New York in the first place. She fell hard for the pitch, as Teddy expected.

"How would you be able to help me? I mean, I can type and do office work, but . . . I never really did anything in public relations before," she told him.

Teddy began to shake his head. He said, "I wouldn't use you in that way. That would be a waste, having a pretty young girl like you in an office all day.

I don't even like that paperwork shit myself. So let's just agree to be friends for now."

He extended his right hand to her after switching his drink into his left hand.

"Teddy Liggins," he told her. "I don't have a business card on me, so I'm gonna need a full name and a number where I can reach you during office hours tomorrow."

She stopped and asked him with her youthful smile again, "That wouldn't just be your line to get my phone number, would it?"

He looked at her seriously and said, "Of course it is. Naw, if it was like that, we could find a Jacuzzi tonight," he answered. "I wouldn't even prolong the issue."

She maintained her smile and didn't respond to his forward flirt.

He said, "Now don't tell me you don't have a stable phone or a place to stay yet."

"As a matter of fact, I don't. I was gonna give you my cell phone number. I'm in a real complicated predicament right now."

"How complicated?"

"Well, I'm staying with a friend, who is *not* my boyfriend. But he wants to feel *privileged* in that way because I'm there."

"Has he *been* privileged?" Teddy probed her.

"No, he has not," she answered firmly. "But at the same time, until I can get my own place or whatever, I'm kind of, like, walking on eggshells."

Teddy started laughing. "He got your bags still packed up in the closet, hunh? He's just waiting for you to act up."

"Ain't that sad?"

He said, "It sounds like a young man to me. You don't get nothin' for nothin', and if ya' get somethin' from somewhere else, then ya' ain't gettin' nothin' from me."

"That is just *sad,*" she repeated.

"It sounds like you need room and board, too," he assessed. "So what would this *friend* say if you didn't come back to his place tonight?"

" 'Where were you?' "

"Out all night enjoying New York," Teddy answered for her.

"Is that something you would do, keep a girl pent up like that?" she asked him.

He said, "Hell no. I like my own space like a woman likes hers. I'd just give you your own place to live. And I'd make visits when you wanted me to."

"With no restrictions?"

"Restrictions as far as what?"

"When I come and go, or who I come and go with."

"Well, what kind of coming and going are we talking about here?" he flirted with her again.

She laughed out loud. "Aw, I set myself up for that one."

"Sure you did," he told her. "But you would be working for me in some capacity. I just have to figure it all out."

He left her speechless for a minute.

She asked him, "Are they your friends over there?"

Teddy answered without looking. "Yeah. Which one you like?"

He had her funny bone on a feather. She just continued to smile.

"I didn't say I liked any of them. I just noticed them staring at us."

"They're jealous. But I'll just tell them that you don't like me either. You know, we're talking about *business* opportunities."

She asked, "Are you always this convincing?"

He said, "Convincing of what? I haven't sold you on anything yet. You probably don't even believe I can put you in a Jacuzzi tonight. What color you want? Pink?"

She smiled and shook her head.

"You gon' make me ask you to prove it."

He got serious with her. He said, "This is what you do. You go home to your boy. You stay in your clothes. You tell him you got an errand to make and slip back out the door. I'll have a room with a Jacuzzi ready for you at the hotel. If I don't have a good excuse or a plan for you by the time you get there tonight, then I'll tell you to go on back home and cuss his ass out for not allowing you to have your privacy.

"Is that a deal?" he asked her.

She chuckled lightly and shook off the temptation.

"I mean, I don't know about all of that right now. I just got some things I need to work out without making more complications for myself. You know what I mean?"

He said, "I understand that. That's why I offered to be friends. I understand you're in a situation. I'll be happy to see you out of it and doing well. I just need time to figure out how I can help you."

She asked, "Is that a hard thing to do? Why would you bother to help me at all? I'm just a nobody up here."

Teddy looked at her and said, "We were *all* nobodies at one time. You need to understand that. So why *not* you? You just have to be brave enough to put yourself in positions to go after what you want."

She calmed herself and nodded to him. "You're right."

He said, "So if you still want to give me your cell phone number, then you do that. I'll call you, and we'll figure things out together."

The young woman paused and thought about it. She figured she had nothing to lose.

"Okay."

After receiving the young woman's phone number, Teddy walked back over to Charles, J.J., and the others at the bar.

"So how'd it go?" J.J. asked him.

Teddy ordered another drink. "And not so much ice this time," he told the bartender. He answered J.J. with a smile, "My game is strong as black coffee. This young girl *ripe* for pickin'. So I'ma take her home after a few more days out on the vine, warm her ass up real good, and toss her in the freezer for late-night munchies."

He laughed and said, "Boy, I love these young girls. They don't know if you Dracula or Santa Claus."

Charles sat there and smiled. He said, "And you don't know if they're angels or witches."

Teddy looked at him and frowned.

"Aw, nigga, you just mad 'cause you went ahead and got married too early. Ain't nobody tell you to buy that ring. You 'da fool."

Charles took a sip of his own drink and nodded pensively. "Yeah, we'll see." That's all he had to say about it.

Tabitha stepped out of the club with Wallace hot on her trail.

"So what went down in there?" he asked her.

She was walking briskly ahead of him toward the Explorer.

She said, "I just wanna thank you for letting me do my work. Everything is set up now."

"What does that mean?"

"It means I'm in."

"Just like that?"

"Just like that."

Wallace shook his head and didn't believe her.

He grumbled, "Whatever," and opened the door to his Explorer for her to climb in.

Girl Talk

Sunday, February 24, 2002
Late Night
Millennium Hotel
Tonya Kennedy

Interesting. Teddy Liggins is a real character. But if I wasn't on a job to get to know him, he wouldn't have a shot in hell at dealing with me. His intentions are all so obvious. If girls really go for his bullshit, then to each her own.

Teddy has made it easier for me to get in with the team, though. I just have to make sure I don't give him anything that he wants. I'll dodge him for a couple days if he calls me, and we'll meet up again at the premiere show on Tuesday night. I'll just act like it's a coincidence.

He didn't bring up the fact that he saw me earlier outside Bruno's Barbecue tonight. I'm sure he knows it. He doesn't strike me as a man who misses much. He also likes to flaunt his status in life. He likes playing a high roller.

If Teddy can't walk me in closer to where I need to go, then I'll try someone else on the team. Charles strikes me as a little uptight. Maybe he could use some unwinding. I can't really get a feel for him yet. I'll have to be patient to see what he's about.

Tomorrow I meet Angela, my second helper on this job. I'm glad, too, because Wallace has worn out his welcome with me. I've worn out my welcome with him, too, I'm sure.

Oh well. Some people just don't hit it off in this world.

No sooner had she closed her diary book, the telephone rang in her hotel room.

"Hello?" she answered skeptically. Who could be calling her there, after midnight?

"It's me," Wallace answered.

"Okay . . . and? Did we forget something?" she asked him. She was prepared to be extremely short with him.

"Naw. I just wanted to call to say I apologize. I guess you know what you're doing."

"Thank you," she told him.

Wallace added, "By the way, I really like the way you dance. I just wanted to tell you that. You dance with a lot of body control. It shows character."

She smiled at his recognition. "Thanks again. Now you know that I have some."

"Yeah," he mumbled.

"Okay, is that it?" she asked him. She realized by then that he was feeling her. He must have watched her dance in the club from a distance, and then held it to himself during the ride back to the hotel. After not being able to sleep that night without thinking about her, he called her up in desperation. Tabitha assessed his whole story before he could open his mouth to answer her question.

He said, "Well, I guess you're tired and all that."

"Yes, I am," she lied. She still had energy that night, just not for him. Her West Coast body clock was closer to ten than New York's one in the morning.

"Well, I guess I'll see you tomorrow or whatever."

"I thought Angela was supposed to be with me tomorrow," she quizzed him to make sure.

"Oh, yeah, but, you know, I'll still be around."

"Oh, okay," she told him with a pause. There was no sense in slamming his hopes against the concrete. "I'll see you tomorrow sometime then."

"Yeah," he uttered. He sounded as if he were trying to maintain his New York cool. But it was already too late for that.

Tabitha hung up the phone and smiled her ass off. She even laughed aloud.

"I don't *believe* this. After all of that, this boy is feeling me now. He was probably faking from the start. Mmmt, mmmt, *mmmph,*" she grunted.

The phone rang again a few minutes later. "Oh my God! Now he's gonna stalk me," she responded to the ring. She thought about not answering the second call. But she decided that she should, just in case it was someone else.

"Hello," she answered timidly.

"How did it go tonight?"

It was Sylvia.

Tabitha sat up in bed with the phone in hand and became more alert and professional.

"Oh, it went real well. I met Teddy Liggins at a party, and he came on to me real strong, but I turned him down *nicely*, of course. It's still an open kind of thing with him. He has my cell phone number, but I'm gonna use his connection to get to our main man. If I can't, Teddy already let me in on Charles and J.J. So I was thinking about trying Charles next. I have a real strong hunch about him."

"I see," Sylvia responded. "You sound excited. This must be fun for you."

Tabitha noticed the sarcasm in her tone and responded accordingly. "Whatever. Anyway, I had no help from—" She stopped herself mid-sentence. She changed her mind about reporting anything negative about Wallace. Since he had a change of heart with her, she decided to go easier on him.

"You had no help from who?" Sylvia questioned.

"Well, I'm the only one who really knows what I'm doing. Sometimes it's not even planned. It's just, like, a *groove* that I get into," Tabitha answered. "I mean, nobody can really help me in what I do."

"I agree. You are rather skilled at it," Sylvia responded slyly.

Tabitha held the phone away from her mouth and grumbled under her breath. "What is up with this chick? Anyway," she said back into the receiver, "I meet Angela tomorrow. So I get to powwow with what she thinks about everything."

"Yeah, that'll be an interesting meeting between you two," Sylvia told her.

Tabitha held her tongue. What was she saying with that comment? What exactly was Angela's connection?

"Okay, so I'll call you again around this time tomorrow for another update," Sylvia told her. "And I don't think I have to tell you, but I'll say it anyway. Always remember to keep your head out there. This is a game being played for keeps. The closer you get to your goal, the more costly the mistakes will be. So just remember that. Act very carefully."

Tabitha listened intently before she responded. "I hear you. But sometimes when you're *too* careful, you miss the point. Everybody makes mistakes. If not, then this is not even doable, because they would never let me slip in in the first place."

"So the answer is that you have to be more *perfect* than they are. Am I right?" Sylvia quizzed her.

Tabitha had to admit that she was. "Yeah, you're right."

"Good. That's all I'm saying."

When they hung up the phone, Tabitha felt a touch of nervousness again, like she felt while on the plane ride from Chicago.

"Shit!" she cursed. "They're cramping my style. I can't *work* like this."

She realized that too much pressure made her slow to react. A slow reaction resulted in a loss of natural flow. And the *flow* meant everything. So she forced herself to continue ignoring their advice.

"I'm just gonna have to fail or succeed on my own. If I listen too much to them . . . then I don't know *what* the hell might happen."

The phone rang again in the wee hours of the morning. Or at least it felt that way to Tabitha.

"Shit," she grumbled, moving to grab it.

"Hello."

"Did I wake you? This is Angela."

"Oh," Tabby responded to her. "Yeah. I guess I'm still on West Coast time. What time is it over here?" She didn't bother to look at the clock. She didn't even have her eyes open.

"It's after ten. But I can call you back later. I just figured we could start off the day by doing lunch or something."

"After twelve?" Tabitha asked her.

"Yeah. I can meet you in the hotel lobby around twelve thirty, and then we'll find something from there."

"Okay. Sounds good to me."

"So, should I call you back at, like, eleven thirty?" Angela asked.

"No, I don't need that much time. How about twelve?"

"Are you sure?"

"No, but I know I need some more sleep," she joked.

Angela laughed it off and agreed to it.

"All right, well, I won't hold you to any specific time. I'll just call at twelve and wait down in the lobby for you until you're ready."

"That's a deal," Tabitha told her. As soon as she hung up the phone from the comfortable bed, she grumbled, "She's pressed. I'm gonna have to side-step her, too."

However, after being woken, Tabby could not force herself into going back to sleep. She lay there and thought about things. Was Isaac Abraham really as magnificent as everyone had him cracked up to be? Maybe it was all a facade. Everyone was human. And if Isaac were *more* than human, how did they expect her, a mere mortal, to be able to crack his shell? Nevertheless, she was still excited by the challenge.

"Where there's a will, there's a way," she told herself.

She got back on the phone to see what was going on with her sisters at her apartment in Las Vegas.

Marisol answered the phone, sounding wide awake.

"Hey," Tabby piped to her, "you're up early. I expected Patrice to answer the phone."

"She's thinking about driving back already," Mari informed her.

"She talked to Randy last night?" Tabitha asked of her sister's estranged husband.

"Wore your phone bill out with him," Mari told her.

"Well, at least they talked it all out."

"If you wanna call it that."

"What, they mostly argued?"

"And I had to keep the kids while they were at it," Mari answered. "So I can just imagine how they're gonna be when she gets back to Seattle."

"That's another full day of driving."

"I know. But you know how she gets when she makes up her mind. She drove all the way out here, didn't she?"

"Let me talk to her."

"Hold on."

Marisol went to get Patrice while Tabby shook her head against the phone in New York.

"Is this what marriage is about? Treece is going insane," she told herself.

Patrice came on the line.

"Yeah," she huffed. She still sounded irritated.

Tabitha cut straight to the chase with her. "Are you planning on driving back to Seattle before I get back to Vegas?"

"Yes, I am."

Tabitha paused for a minute. Marisol was right. Patrice had already made up her mind.

"Okay. Well, call Marisol at the apartment when you and the girls get back," Tabitha told her. There was no sense in arguing a losing battle.

Patrice said, "I talked to his ass good and long last night, and we got down to the bottom of a lot of things."

"Like what?" Tabitha asked her.

"Well, he kept talking about how he felt swallowed up in the house. Like, how the hell am *I* supposed to feel? At least he gets to *leave* the damn house every day. I don't even get to do that."

"Well, maybe you should get a part-time job doing something you like, and pay for a baby-sitter or day care with it," Tabitha suggested.

"And what purpose would that serve if all of the money is gonna go right back to day care? I can hear Randy's mouth now, 'You just spending time away from the kids for nothing.' "

"Well, you tell him that this is for *you,* to make sure you feel like you have more to offer the world than just being a mom," Tabitha advised her. She said, "You used to have all kinds of ideas and motivation before you got married, Treece. I used to ask *you* for advice. Now it seems like you only complain about things.

"I hate to see you like this," Tabby leveled with her. "I mean, to be honest with you, you're not making marriage seem like it's worth it."

"Well, maybe it's not. And maybe you're right. But I'm in it now, and I don't have men wanting to fly *me* around the country for late-night rendezvous. So I have to live with the cards that I've been dealt," Patrice huffed at her.

Tabitha kept her poise and let the diss slide.

"Okay. Have a safe trip back home," she offered weakly.

"I plan to."

When they hung up, Tabitha found herself numb. There she was in New York, trying to make enough money to buy a big dream house for all of them to live in in peace, while the reality seemed that there would never be peace. Peace was indeed the journey of life. However, peace on earth seemed to be more of an illusion. There was always too much to be dealt with between men, bills, and unfulfilled desires. It made a sane person want to throw up their hands and say "To hell with even trying." Nevertheless, Tabitha's life had always been about forward movement and exploration. That's what she planned to do; continue moving forward.

Tabitha was ready to meet Angela before she even called up to her room at noon.

"I'm on my way down," she told her as soon as she received the phone call from the hotel lobby.

"Wow! You weren't playing," Angela commented. She was surprised by it. She said, "I just bought a magazine to read."

"Well, you can flip through the pictures, like a man, before I get down there," Tabitha joked to her.

Tabitha had no idea what to expect from Angela. All she knew was that the girl looked like a new-style model with curly golden locks, and she was pressed to be on time. Tabitha didn't know what Angela expected from *her*, either. So she made sure to wear white to project virginal imagery.

She made it down to the hotel lobby and met up with the young woman at the lounge chairs near the hotel's restaurant.

"Hi," Tabitha piped to her.

Angela stood up and immediately towered over her.

"How tall are you?" Tabby asked on instinct.

Angela laughed. "I'm five-eight, but I guess my posture makes me appear taller. People always ask me that." Angela seemed to laugh at everything, too easily pleased.

"Yeah, because I'm five-seven with heels on, and you still tower over me," Tabitha commented.

"Well, I do have two-inches on."

Angela motioned to the heels of her burgundy leather boots. They matched her burgundy leather jacket and the purse she carried.

"Well, aren't you all coordinated," Tabitha told her.

"I try. Anyway, what do you have a taste for?"

"Well, since it's New York, I know they have a lot of Italian food, right? So let's get some fattening pasta."

"Okay. Italian it is."

As soon as the two young women walked into the streets of New York, the eyes and loose lips of men let them know they were noticed.

"All right now! Work it all out!" a parking garage attendant let out as they strolled by.

"I bet you get that all the time here," Tabitha commented to her new helper.

"You learn to ignore it."

"So, when *don't* you ignore it?"

"When you know who it's coming from, of course."

"Of course," Tabitha agreed with a chuckle.

They made it to a restaurant called Remi nearby the hotel.

"I heard you met the team yesterday," Angela commented.

"Some of them," Tabitha answered.

"Teddy is always out front. He's like the gatekeeper," Angela said.

"I thought Charles was the gatekeeper," Tabitha questioned.

"Well, for business, he is. But for pleasure, Teddy is the gatekeeper."

Tabitha smiled. "Oh, okay. So, how well do you know them all?"

Angela answered, "Too well."

They ordered their food and made small talk until it arrived. As soon as they began to eat, Angela revealed her history with Isaac Abraham and his team.

She said, "I made it all the way to the top, three years ago. But I wasn't out to . . . I mean, I just admired who he was and what he stood for."

"Isaac, you mean?" Tabitha asked her, for clarity's sake.

"Yes, Isaac. But the rest of them were all so interesting in their own little ways."

"So you got caught up in the rest of them?"

"Basically, I was just happy to be anywhere near him. And when I finally got a chance to sit down and talk to him, it was all that I expected and then some."

"Is he egotistical?" Tabitha asked her.

Angela thought about it and grinned before she answered.

"In a very sly way. I mean, he's not outright with it. But of course, being a man in his position, he is very confident."

"Does he look as good in real life as he does in his movies?"

Angela was obviously still infatuated with the man. Her loud smile said everything.

"With no makeup needed," she answered.

"Really?"

"Really."

"Does he smell good?"

Angela broke out laughing and had to be careful with her mouthful of food.

"Of course he does. I mean, you can't make as much money as he does and not smell good."

Tabitha rolled her eyes. "You'd be surprised."

"Well, there's only good surprises with Isaac."

Tabitha had to pause and reflect for a minute. She believed in the men she had been with. She supported their careers, visions, and crafts, but she rarely talked about them openly. She logged her feelings in her diary instead. Maybe Angela needed a diary to express herself and move on, because she obviously had not. She seemed to be caught up in a dream of what *was,* or what could have *been*.

"How often do you think about him now?" Tabitha asked her.

"Actually, I try not to. But every time he has a new movie out, or he's in the news for something . . . What can I say? It's like yesterday all over again."

"Does that bother you?"

"Does it bother *you?*" Angela asked her back.

Tabitha reflected on it and thought about her sister Patrice. Tabby refused to be bitter about her life's expectations.

She answered, "When you think too much about it, it just gets you upset that you can't have things the way you want them in life. So, I try to take it all as a learning curve."

Angela nodded. She said, "I know what you mean. But . . . I don't know. I mean, he was married, three kids; I was only a sophomore in college. What did I know?"

Tabitha raised her brow with her drink in hand and her straw to her mouth.

"How old are you now?" she asked.

"Twenty-three."

"I thought you were—"

Tabitha stopped herself mid-sentence. No woman liked being insulted about her age.

She said, "Well, I don't know what I thought, really."

"A lot of people think I'm older than I am," Angela told her.

"How does that make you feel?"

She shrugged her shoulders.

"It doesn't really bother me either way. I know how old I am."

Tabitha began to wonder how old *she* looked to Angela.

"How old do I look to you?" she asked.

Angela studied her face for a minute.

"You look like you can pass for college age."

"Is that *too old* for him?"

"No. Why would you say that?"

"I heard he likes to deal with teenagers," Tabitha stated.

Angela looked puzzled for a minute.

She said, "He does deal with a lot of young women, but I wouldn't necessarily say *teenagers*. But if that's true, then I guess that's why he didn't get too intimate with me. *I* was too old," she added with another laugh.

"If you don't mind me asking, how intimate did you get?" Tabitha asked her.

"Not very."

"What does that mean?"

"Well, I gave him a blow job, but he didn't want much else."

Tabitha had to stop herself from laughing. The girl seemed so embarrassed by it. She was sorry she had even asked her.

"You're not from New York, right?" Tabby guessed.

"Unt, unh, not *hardly*. I'm from Nashville," Angela answered. "And yes, we *do* have black people there."

Tabitha smiled. With her being black and from Seattle, she knew the feeling.

She asked, "So what happened after that? He just told you to leave?"

"No. We basically just lay in bed naked and talked."

"About what?"

Tabitha was really enjoying the conversation, or the interview as the case may be. She didn't know how Angela was supposed to help her, but she surely planned to suck her dry of information.

Angela said, "You know, he just has a lot of ideas about life and stuff."

"Did you learn a lot from him?"

"Oh, of course. He taught me a lot of things."

"You talked to him a lot then?"

Angela paused to get her facts straight.

"No, not really. I just took in everything he said when I was with him."

"It was a onetime thing?"

"If you wanna call it that. But I relive it all the time. It's never been a one-night stand for me."

"But you *have* only been with him *once*?"

"I guess, officially."

Tabitha began to smile at her across their small table.

Angela attempted to explain herself.

"I know it sounds crazy, but you only get one chance to meet someone like him. So I've learned to treasure that moment."

Tabitha decided to move on with her line of questioning.

"What about the rest of the team? What do you think about them?"

"I don't. Or I try not to."

It sounded like she was in denial. Tabitha pressed her about it.

"Have you been involved with any of them?"

Angela took a deep breath. She said, "I figured this question would come up. But since I agreed to help you . . ." She decided to tell all. "I had an ongoing thing with Teddy and Walt Nesbitt before he got into trouble with his wife and this other woman that led to him being fired and exposed by the media."

"And what happened to Teddy? Nothing?"

"Well, as you'll find out, Teddy can be . . . how should I say, *elusive* about what he's doing. Walt wasn't. And he really got caught up in everything."

"He didn't threaten to tell everybody what was going on?"

Angela looked at Tabitha squarely across the table. She said, "Are you kidding me? He would *never* do that to Isaac. All the bad media attention that he got after they fired him was just a warning."

She said, "You don't fuck with Isaac Abraham. He's connected to too many people who make good money."

That made Tabitha stop and think for a minute.

"Do you know what I'm supposed to do?" she asked.

Angela answered, "Yeah."

"And you're still helping me?"

"I wanna see if you can actually do it."

"And what happens to you?"

"What do you mean?"

"How do you feel about it? I mean, you still admire him, right?"

"Yeah, I do."

"Well, this seems like a conflict of interest to me. How can I trust you?"

"How can you trust anyone?" Angela asked her.

She had Tabby on the spot.

"Good point," she answered. What else could she say?

"So evidently, you really don't believe that I can do this?" she asked candidly.

"Anything is possible. You have nothing to lose."

"Oh yes we do." Tabitha told her. "We lose the privacy of our relationships."

"Well, you'll lose that if you succeed, too," Angela leveled with her. She was right. It was a no-win situation as far as privacy was concerned. Once a scandal hit the news, people wanted to know who it involved. The media would sacrifice human souls for the public's interests, and for the public's dollars.

"But just look at it this way; with the way that America loves true stories now, we may just become celebrities in our own right," Angela suggested with a grin.

"Yeah, celebrity hoochies," Tabitha joked.

"Well . . ." Angela responded.

Tabitha shook her head. "That's not how I'm trying to go down."

"What do you think, you'll just ride away in the sunset?" Angela asked her.

They were finished with their barely eaten food. They were both far too interested in their conversation.

Tabitha answered, "You're not helping me to be that optimistic about things." She looked away and added, "Everybody has their issues."

Angela nodded and understood what she meant.

She said, "Believe it or not, I haven't met too many people who I can talk to about it. Half of them don't believe a word you say, and the other half condemn you for doing it. So I just learned to keep it to myself."

"That's the only thing that you *can* do," Tabitha agreed.

"So, how did you get started?" Angela asked her. "Was it one special person or just people in general?"

Tabitha thought about it. Her first one was not really a celebrity, but he was brutally honest. He explained to her that sex and love for men and women were worlds apart. He also knew what he was doing in bed, as if he were training her to know what works the best for her own satisfaction. He told her to be her own person, and to live how she wanted to. He also told her not to be a fool for so-called love. Take life as it is and enjoy the ride. However, she still cried when he left. She cried because she learned how complicated love could be. From that point on, she wanted to understand more than feel. And she wanted to feel through her understanding.

She answered, "We all have a first one, but after that, it becomes people in general."

"And what about *'the one'*?" Angela asked her next.

Tabitha said, "Unless you're talking about God almighty, *'the one'* is a fallacy. I've just been around too many miserable people to believe that. Then you have those who *supposedly* are in perfect marriages, who fly out of town on business, get them a little piece, and then fly back home like nothing happened."

"I thought that was a married man's privilege," Angela responded.

Tabitha looked at her to see if she was serious.

Angela took in her look and smiled at her. She said, "That's *always* been the case. Is it because there're more women in the population than men?"

"What, with a quarter of the men in jail, a tenth of them gay, another quarter not worth your time, and the rest married, engaged, or lying about it?"

Angela laughed so hard she began to clap her hands at the table.

"Sounds like you did your homework."

"Of course," Tabitha told her. She said, "So what's up with this guy, Wallace? Are you familiar with him?"

Angela stopped her laughing and turned serious again.

"Now see, Wallace is the opposite of the guys you're about to deal with," she stated. "He looks just as good as they do, but where they're confident, he's not. Where they make things happen, Wallace has to *wait* for them to happen. Where they dictate what's going on, Wallace has to ask and be told. And it's like, once I got involved with men of a higher caliber . . ." She shook her head and concluded, "There just was no going back to guys like Wallace. I mean . . . for what?"

Tabitha nodded her head and agreed. "Amen."

Step 2

Monday, February 25, 2002
Nighttime
Millennium Hotel
Tabby

I wasn't so sure of Angela when I first met her. She seemed kind of naive. She had me wondering how I seemed to people. But I use naiveness to my advantage. Who knows, maybe she was doing the same to me. After a while, her true colors began to show, and I could see that she had a strong head on her shoulders.

I guess I've been able to let go of things a lot easier than other people. Then again, I never let go of my family and my dream of keeping us together. I still think about my blood family like everyone else. But we all have met our blood families, and they were such disappointments to us that we all decided to continue with our love for one another instead of dealing with them.

I think people really take companionship at any level for granted. They don't realize how special it is. I mean, just open up and converse with someone. You have everything to gain from it. So many people are so afraid of real confrontation with themselves, their beliefs, and their shortcomings, that they'd rather not talk to anyone.

I know my life has been enhanced by being able to talk to people. I'm not afraid at all. Maybe, one day, I'll even use my real name and age with people. I wonder how the conversation would change then. Would I learn less? Or more? Hypocrite!

Anyway, tomorrow is the big day. I didn't get a phone call from Teddy tonight, nor did I see Wallace. I'll see both of them tomorrow. I'll also see the big man himself. But I still won't mention his name until I get where

*I need to be with him. From what I was told by Angela, he should be well
worth the wait. We'll see.*

It took a while for Sylvia to call New York for an update. In the meantime,
Tabitha called home to see how Marisol was doing and to see if Patrice had
hit the road and called back to check in yet.

"Girl, your phone has been ringing off the *hook* today," Marisol told her.

"Did you take any messages?" Tabitha would rather Mari let the phone
ring so the messages could be recorded.

"I didn't know you wanted me to," her sister answered. "Hold on," she
said inadvertently.

Tabitha froze after hearing noise in the background.

"Who are you talking to?"

"I'm talking to you," Mari answered.

Tabitha paused. "Do you have somebody in the house?"

Marisol thought before she answered.

"I have a friend over," she admitted.

"A *friend*. Well, he doesn't have his *own* place?"

"Aw, don't even start that, Tabby. It's not even like that. We grown folks
anyway."

"Well, 'grown folks' still have to respect each other's house."

"I know that. But if I had my own *room* in the big house, then what? You
gon' tell me the same thing?"

She had a good point. What kind of rules would they have if they decided to all live together again like Tabitha continued to dream about?

She said, "Well, let's wait 'til we have a big house first."

"Aw, girl, you're crazy. What if you didn't know? Would you be upset
with me then?"

"What, you had him over there last night, too?" Tabby asked.

"I'm not saying," Mari told her.

"Well, that's just as good as confessing."

"Whatever."

Tabby decided to move on.

"Anyway, has Patrice left and called back yet?"

"Yeah, she left. But she didn't call nobody yet. You know how she is. She
won't call until she gets there. Unless her car breaks down or something."

Tabitha shook her head against the phone while looking outside the
hotel. New York was a crowded city of everyday work people.

"What time did they leave?" she asked her sister.

"They didn't even leave until after twelve."

"So, she has to stop and rest at a roadside motel or something."

"Yeah, I guess."

"Shit! She is so hardheaded."

"So are the rest of us," Marisol responded.

For once, she was right.

Tabitha said, "All right, well, call me when she calls. Because she won't even answer her cell phone while she's driving."

"Yeah, and what good is that if someone's trying to get in touch with you?" Marisol stated.

She was two for two.

"Well, like I said, I would feel more comfortable if you took your friend back to *his* place," Tabitha reiterated.

"Aw'ight. I'll think about it."

Tabby took a deep breath and did not respond.

Marisol told her, "I was just *joking,* okay? So put away your damn *boxing* gloves."

Tabitha cracked a grin.

"I'll talk to you later."

"How's New York?" Mari asked before they hung up.

"It's very interesting," Tabby told her.

Marisol chuckled and responded, "Yeah, I bet."

Tabitha waited up for Sylvia to call but she was interrupted again by Wallace instead.

"I'm sorry I missed you two kittens today. I had some other things I had to do. Did y'all miss me, though?"

"Oh, terribly. I don't know how we made it through the day without you," Tabitha bullshitted him.

He said, "Easy. All you had to do is go shopping."

"In New York? I heard the prices are robbery."

"Yeah, they are. Anyway, tomorrow is the big day. But you know Isaac is in town tonight."

"Yeah, I know."

"You're not anxious to do things your own way again and try to see him tonight?" Wallace quizzed her. "He's staying right over at the St. Regis.

That's walking distance from you. Or you just wanna warm things up with me tonight instead?" he added.

"What?" Tabitha asked him. She didn't say it in a nasty way. She was just trying to make sure she heard him right.

He laughed it off and said, "Don't mind me. I had a few tonight at the bar. Sometimes that good liquor goes right to the wrong head."

"And you didn't take home a girl? What, your game is slippin'?" she teased him.

"Naw, I don't talk to them girls. It be the same ones there week after week. Then when a new one steps up, she got issues, too."

"Why are you after me then? You think I don't have issues? You think I'm easier than them? Why, because I'm doing the things I do? I still have to choose. I'm not a hooker," she told him.

"Oh, I know that. I'm just sayin' . . ."

The reality was, he didn't know what he was trying to say. All he knew was that the girl turned him on. It was her sexual liberation that he found hard to ignore. It was like knowing a girl is into threesomes. It makes a guy want to experiment for the hell of it.

Before they could explore the conversation any further, the second line of her hotel phone buzzed.

"I have to take this call," she told him.

"Aw'ight, do what you gotta do."

"I'll talk to you tomorrow."

Wallace hesitated as if he had something else to say.

"Oh, aw'ight. So, you try'na go out t'night or you staying in?"

Obviously the alcohol had stirred him. He wasn't taking a hint.

"Call me back in a half hour," she told him.

"Aw'ight. I'll do that."

Satisfied with that, Tabitha hung up with him and clicked onto her second line.

"Hello."

"How was your meeting with Angela?" Sylvia asked her.

"Damn, no hi or nothin', hunh? You're just straight business."

"Okay, how was your day today?" Sylvia backed up and asked.

"Oh, it was a nice day. I got a lot of things accomplished," Tabitha answered civilly.

"Did you find Angela to be helpful?"

"Oh, very. She knows the ins and outs."

"And you know *more*?"

Tabitha was confused by the question.

"What do you mean by that? I know more about what?"

Sylvia explained, "Getting around the rich and famous men, and keeping your head about it. Because Angela obviously didn't."

"Well, I haven't dealt with men on this level," Tabitha responded. "There are a lot of different levels of men."

"I don't think you were paying attention to the levels that you were dealing with," Sylvia rebutted.

"What makes you say that?"

Sylvia spoke as if she knew more about the men Tabitha had dealt with than she previously let on. Tabby had not yet explored all that the woman knew about her.

"So, how much do you know about my life?" she asked on cue.

"Enough to have faith in you. Same with my employer."

"But you said I wasn't worth the price," Tabitha reminded her.

"Not worth *that* price, but definitely more than what *I* would offer. But what can I say? The rich can do what they want with their money."

"How rich is this employer who's running the show?" Tabby asked. There were still a lot of details that went unexplained. She still considered herself in the dark about a lot of things.

"I don't know the extent of his pockets myself."

"But he's paying you well?" Tabitha asked.

"You, too. Your first deposit has been made today."

"That's good to hear," Tabitha piped. "So if I finished the job tomorrow, I would have the rest deposited the next day?"

"That's highly unlikely. We predict that this job will take you at least two to three months."

"What, to sleep with him?"

"To build up enough information for a case against him," Sylvia clarified. "The truth is, you wouldn't be able to take him to court anyway, because you are of age. But if you can get close enough to get around the other young girls who are not of age, that's where our case will be built."

"So, why not use a girl who's really that young to do the job?"

It was the point Tabitha had made earlier in their proposition to her.

Sylvia said, "As you should have found out from Angela, young women are like putty in this man's hands. We're hoping that you *won't* be. So we couldn't chance a younger girl who may get things confused. It would have been against our best interests to put a minor in that situation to begin with, not to mention illegal."

Tabitha nodded her head with the phone in hand. She said, "Okay, let me just stop asking questions and do what I need to do before I get confused myself. I just feel like a damn guinea pig."

"Well, you need to ask questions for clarity. This case is complicated to begin with. But it's not something that you can't handle. You seem to thrive in complicated situations."

"Okay, so let me get this straight. You want me to get close enough to connect to an inside girl who we can build a case around?"

"In a nutshell, yes."

"Okay, that's all I need to know. So let me go ahead and take care of business."

She hung up with Sylvia and was ready for bed when Wallace called back again.

"So what's up?" he asked her.

"Sleep, Wallace. I'm tired," she told him. "I'll see you tomorrow."

And she hung up on his late-night ideas.

Magic Johnson Theater was jam-packed on 125th Street in Harlem before showtime that Tuesday evening. Tabitha stood in line disguised as her alias, Tonya Kennedy. She was dressed as a local in her black form-fitting jeans, with baby-girl looks. She had her hair twisted in long curls past the shoulders, wearing black eyeliner to make her youthful eyes pop even stronger.

BET cable network reporters and local camera crews were there to record the crowd's response before and after viewing the film.

"What do you expect from this movie?" a hip, black woman asked with a microphone in hand. A cameraman was right behind her. They were interviewing a group of teen girls just a few feet in front of Tabitha. Wallace and Angela were not allowed to be seen with her at the premiere. She was out on her own.

"I don't know. I mean, he's gonna be sexy as always. He's gonna save the day. And he's gonna make me dream about him some more," one of the young women answered.

Her friends laughed and made fun of her response.

"You're pressed. That's all she talks about is his sex appeal. He's too old for you anyway. She doesn't even care what the movie's about."

"And you do, obviously," the BET reporter asked the friend.

"Yeah, I do care what the story's about. Isaac is always giving his all in his performances to make it believable. That's why *I* like him."

They moved the cameras and microphone along to interview an older woman, just two steps in front of Tabby.

"I've been following Isaac Abraham's films for years, and he always seems to have a social message behind them for the community. Even having the premiere here in Harlem is a part of his outreach to the fans who support him. And I just honor what he stands for."

Tonya Kennedy didn't have anything supportive to say to the reporter about the man she was there to bring down. She shook her head and waved the cameras away when they approached her. The more she heard about the man, the harder it made her job.

A minute later, the energy picked up in the theater as security began to make room for the arrival of the stars.

"That's Frances Watkins!" someone yelled.

The camera crews hurried into position to interview the stars now.

"How does it feel to work with Isaac Abraham? Isn't this your third film working with him as a costar?"

"Yes, it is. And Isaac, of course, is just a professional and a total gentleman to work with. He really is. He helps everyone along with their roles to make sure that we get the total performance from everyone. He is just a grand professional in the art of filmmaking."

"How well do you think this film is going to do at the box office?"

"Well, you really can't predict anything like that. We know the people are going to like it, but we don't know how *much* they'll like it. Nor can we predict the other factors involved, like reviews and the good word of mouth, that really make a film go. All you can do is promote, promote, promote, and then just *hope* for the best."

The overwhelming support was making Tabitha feel nauseous. But what did she expect at a premiere film showing for the man's latest work? Maybe she should have been flown out to his regular hangouts in Los Angeles instead. However, Isaac's MO was that his dates with young women generally took place *away* from home.

The energy picked up another notch when Isaac's full entourage arrived; absent were his wife and three kids. Tabitha spotted Derrick, the lead bodyguard out in front of the pack, while security continued to clear a path through the crowd.

"Here he comes! Here he comes!" several fanatics yelled.

Tabitha took a deep breath and prepared herself for her first up-close sighting of the man. The reporters and cameramen were just as anxious. They continued to jockey for front and center position for their interviews.

Derrick, the bodyguard, was followed by Rafael the personal assistant, Teddy the publicist, Charles the manager, and Isaac, the star himself.

A rapid fire of questions shot off from the eager reporters as soon as he was in range.

"Isaac, what's your take on this film?"

"Why a premiere in Harlem?"

"Any hopes for an Academy Award on this one?"

"One question at a time. I don't have six pairs of ears," he joked to them.

The camera crews and reporters laughed as they continued to badger him for responses to their questions. With all of the hype involved in the night's affair, Isaac Abraham showed up in regular blue jeans and a Bill Cosby–like sweater. He seemed at total peace with all of the fanfare.

"Why a premiere in Harlem?" he addressed. "Magic Johnson happens to be a dear friend of mine, and so are the citizens of Harlem. I grew up in a Harlem myself, called Detroit. So it's always good to remember where you come from and give back the love that the community gives you."

"I heard you'll be working with Spike Lee again in the near future? Is that true?"

"Who in Black Hollywood *hasn't* worked with Spike Lee?" he answered. "Spike has had us on *his* A List long before Hollywood figured out they can bank an opening night on black faces."

"Is it true that you and your celebrity friends are gonna start your own Hollywood film company similar to the Dreamworks team?"

"That's a little premature at this point, but it's definitely a long time coming for black folks to be able to greenlight our own film projects. Don't you think? We surely have enough professionals and enough money for it. We just have to have the willpower and organization to do it.

"But I thought we were supposed to be talking about *All the Way* tonight?" he asked the reporters as his entourage moved toward the theater doors.

"Are we going all the way to blockbuster status? I guess *Harlem* will have something to say about that. Am I right, Harlem?" he asked, playing up to the crowd.

"Yeah! Number one!" they yelled back to him.

"That's what we're talking about, *support*," Isaac told the reporters. He seemed to be turning their questions into his own campaign for the people.

Tabitha moved closer into the crowd and spotted Teddy Liggins eye to eye again.

She smiled at him politely, but didn't budge a muscle to speak. She realized that he would have to make the first move; otherwise she would be blown out of the inner circle before she even got there. She had to be *invited* in. It was a game of self-control and patience.

Once Teddy saw that she was not making any moves toward him, like clockwork, he slipped through the crowd toward her.

"Small world we live in, ain't it? I just keep bumping into you. That must mean something."

"Not if you don't want it to be," she told him.

"Oh, I want it to be. But as you can see, I had a big piece of prime rib on my plate," he said, in reference to publicity for the premiere.

"So, you just happen to do publicity for my *favorite* actor," she told him.

"Who, *that* guy's your favorite actor? *Isaac*?" he teased her. "I thought you'd like the younger guys; Mekhi Phifer or Omar Epps or something."

"I like them, too. But they're not on Isaac's level yet as far as *real* establishment is concerned."

"Oh, yeah, no doubt," Teddy agreed. "You talking about two different types of careers. It'll take those guys another ten years of consistency to touch Isaac."

She asked, "Would I ever be able to meet him? I mean, if you're all gonna start your own film company, you're gonna need fresh new talent, right? Or a typist for the screenplays or whatever?"

Teddy nodded to her and smiled. "I'll see what I can do," he told her. "Let me get back over there."

As soon as he left, she cursed herself. "Shit! That was too strong."

She realized that she came off like any other fan and had distanced her connection to Teddy far too fast for him to carry their relationship further. He didn't really know her to do her any favors, especially if it no longer involved him as the power figure. There was no way he could introduce her to Isaac without having her under wraps for himself first, which was not the case. So for all practical purposes, the bridge through Teddy had just been burned to the ground.

However, Tabitha caught Charles's eye just long enough to know that he had been watching her. Was that a good thing, or a bad thing? She still couldn't tell with him.

They were ushered into the theater and watched the film with Isaac, the co-stars, the director, producers, and everyone's entourage. The film was a good one. *All the Way* involved a retired track star who returned to the sport to compete in the Olympic Games after being disqualified from performance for illegal drug use twelve years before. It was a film about unbreakable determination.

The film made Tabitha more determined in her own right to at least meet Isaac on private terms. She just wanted to talk to the man about his lifestyle. However, she got nowhere near him or his team on the way out. Security rushed them out the exit doors at the back of the theater and to their awaiting limos in a hurry. The general crowd was not allowed to follow out the back exit at all.

Tabitha met back up with Wallace and Angela away from the theater. She was pretty sour about the events of the premiere as they talked inside the Explorer.

"So how'd everything go?" Angela asked.

"The *movie* was good," Tabitha told her. She sidestepped what Angela really wanted to know.

"You didn't get anywhere near Isaac, hunh?" Wallace asked her on cue.

"Nope," she answered. "They had everything down like clockwork. I couldn't even sniff his cologne."

Angela said, "I expected that. It won't be as chaotic at the after party. Only guest-list people can get in. We already have connections for that. We have you down on the list as Teresa Kelly."

Tabitha said, "But I already told Teddy my name was Tonya. I bumped into him and screwed things up at the premiere. I ran my mouth too fast to him about meeting Isaac. So if I show up at this party trying to get near him, Teddy's gonna spot me immediately. Charles and J.J. know my face now, too," she added.

Wallace shook his head and grinned. "I told you creeping up on them Sunday night wasn't a good idea. Now they can *all* make you out."

"Isaac can't," Angela commented. "He hasn't met her yet. So I'll need to show up to get Teddy away from this after party before you come. I wouldn't worry about Charles and J.J. They don't get into the personal affairs as much as Teddy does. So you'll have to get in there and do your thing now with Derrick and Rafael and get to Isaac.

"He'll be meeting plenty of privileged people tonight," she told her. "That's what these after parties are for. But he may only be there for an hour or so. So be prepared to work fast."

Wallace said, "Aw'ight, so you go to the party early, then call us when you're on your way out with Teddy, and we'll show up after that."

Tabitha could imagine that Wallace was loving his new teamwork assignment. They would be joined at the hip until they received word from Angela.

"Okay, well, that's the plan," Angela confirmed.

"What if Teddy doesn't want to leave with you?" Tabitha asked her.

Angela smiled. "You just leave that up to me. But if push comes to shove, I may just have to distract Teddy while you get to Isaac. Or . . . you'll just have to introduce yourself to him at another time."

Wallace nodded his head and agreed with the last idea.

"That sounds like the best-case scenario to me. You need to meet him in L.A. or somewhere else, away from Teddy. Because New York is Teddy's turf. That's where most of the black press is. We don't get that much press in Hollywood. Not even Isaac."

Tabitha smiled and said aloud to Wallace in front of Angela, "You just want me to yourself, don't you?"

Angela started to laugh.

Wallace went to save his ego. "Don't get it confused. I'm just here to help you."

Tabitha continued to grin. She said, "I know. You wanna help me real badly."

Angela walked into The Revue restaurant and nightclub on Malcolm X Boulevard off of 125th Street and searched the large room for old friends. On the outside she was calm waters, but inside she was a nervous shipwreck. She didn't let on to it earlier, but Tabitha was right: What if Teddy was uninterested in any proposition from her? She hadn't spoken to the man in more than two years, after their fiasco had ended. There was no reason at all for him to want to go back. He wasn't that desperate for trim. There were always new women around to entice, who didn't have an embarrassing history with him. She didn't know how she'd act so close to Isaac again, either. What if he actually wanted to speak to her that night?

Fortunately, the team had not shown up at the party yet. Angela walked over to the bar through the crowd and had herself one strong drink to take the edge off.

"Been a long day?" the bartender asked her.

"Not yet," she responded to him.

"You're expecting a long night?"

"Sure am."

"Man problems?"

Angela looked at the bushy bearded man and grinned.

"That's about the only problems we have, hunh?"

"Well, women seem to find ways to get money," he answered. "And what else is there to be concerned about?"

Angela answered, "Family."

The bartender smiled. "Ain't nothing we can do about our blood ties but learn to ignore them."

They shared a smile before he moved on to serve the next customer.

Angela watched the front door until she spotted the bald-headed body-guard Derrick, clearing the way for the entrance of the A-team, featuring the ringleader himself, Isaac Abraham.

Angela took a deep breath and wasted no time marching toward Teddy. He filed into the club from the back of a fifteen-member group. She couldn't concern herself with Isaac and the others at the moment. Tabitha would have to express the details on Isaac and the rest if she was able to play *her* part that night.

"Hey stranger. I figured I'd see you here t'night," Angela commented to Teddy away from the group. Teddy had always been one to stray into his own mission.

He looked at her and was pleasantly surprised.

He said, "I haven't been a stranger. I'm doing the same thing in the same city. You're the one who disappeared. So how you been?" He looked over her fit body and added, "I see you're still healthy."

That was a good thing. He was flirting with her early. She didn't know the extent of it, but it was still a good start.

She said, "I don't know how. I haven't been using my health much."

"So what have you been doing?"

"Lately, I've been reminiscing."

"On what?"

"Everything that used to mean something to me."

"And what does that mean now? Are you trying to reclaim a position of old? And who with?"

He was basically asking her what she wanted, and if she wanted it from him or from Isaac. Teddy always understood the pecking order with Isaac. He knew to stay out of the boss's way, especially when it came to the pick of the litter with women.

Angela answered, "Well, I came here looking for you, if just to remember what we had at one time." She knew he didn't want to hear anything about permanency. So she made a clear attempt to let him know it would only be a temporary encounter between them.

"Not to say that I'm not flattered, but what makes me so special?" he quizzed her. Candy didn't come *that* easy. Teddy needed to understand her full logic.

However, if Angela knew anything about Teddy Liggins, it was that his curiosity was his worst enemy. But if you told him everything he wanted to know, he tended to close his book on your mystery. So she planned to say no more about it.

"Some things I can't explain myself," she told him.

Teddy looked over at the elevated VIP table where the rest of the group was seated and ordering drinks. He wondered how long they would need or want his company. There were surely some other fish to fry in his batter that night, but none who were jumping into his net without wanting anything in return like Angela was offering. He had to think real hard on her proposition.

Finally, he nodded his head and said, "Let me buy us a drink for old times' sake."

≈≈

Wallace received Angela's call on his cell phone and was a little disappointed to hear that she had succeeded in her task.

"Aw'ight, we're on our way there in a half hour," he told her from a late-night soul food spot around the corner.

"He bit on it?" Tabitha asked Wallace of Teddy. She was having a plate of boneless fish with hot sauce, candied yams, greens, and corn bread. Wallace was having fried chicken, rice with gravy, and macaroni and cheese.

He answered, "Yeah, I guess so. So we gotta wolf down this food now or what?"

"Can't they make us a carry-out bag?"

"Yeah, but . . ."

Wallace wasn't trying to give up that hot plate so fast.

Tabitha said, "Well, we're only around the corner. Let's just keep eating and see how much we get finished before it's time to go."

Wallace nodded to her. "That's cool with me. 'Cause I'm hungry."

She smiled. "I understand."

He jammed a load of food into his mouth and mumbled, "So what's your plan?"

Tabitha shook her head and grinned. He couldn't have asked her that before or after he packed his mouth full of food?

She answered, "I don't have a plan. I'm just gonna try and wing it, and see what happens."

Wallace paused. He warned, "That's what got you in trouble the last time."

"Well, you can't really make plans with things like this. My thing has always been to hook up with available and interested parties that I choose and who choose me. I haven't really been chasing after specific people. So I've been able to field people out. But in this case, he's able to field *me* out."

She stopped and said, "Why am I even telling you all of this?"

"Because I'm here to help you."

"Here you go with that sorry line again," she told him. "You're here for the paycheck like everyone else. Or maybe Angela's not here for that."

Wallace said, "Those bills have to be paid by all of us."

"So how much are they paying you to help me?"

He answered nonchalantly, "A couple thousand dollars."

Tabitha wondered if he was lying. She figured her asking him a monetary question would catch him off guard. When he answered so openly, it made it hard for her to take his answer at face value.

"Will you be proud of yourself if we succeed?" she mumbled to him through her own mouthful.

"Proud of myself? For what?"

"For a job well done."

He frowned at her and said, "Naw. I'll just move on. Same as you."

She nodded and said no more about it.

When they approached The Revue nightclub for Isaac Abraham's after party, Tabitha took a breath and got nervous again. Wallace stepped up and gave their names to the hostess at the front door who held the guest list.

"Here we go again," he said as they walked in.

The Revue was jumping five times stronger than Good Times had been on Sunday night. They had invited some really energized people for a Tuesday evening.

"Damn, does this seem like a Tuesday to you?" Tabitha asked Wallace.

"Naw, but that's the kind of pull he has."

"I see. So I'll see you again when it's over," she told him.

"Aw'ight. Be safe."

Tabitha nodded to him before they separated.

She looked in the direction of Isaac's elevated VIP table at the back of the room and wondered how in the world she would be able to slip through everyone to reach him. His well-guarded table looked a mile away.

"This is ridiculous," she muttered to herself. She had rarely felt that distant from men. She could usually just walk past them and get some form of reaction. This was a whole new ball game for her.

"It looks like somebody keeps showing up in awkward places," a commanding voice said to her from behind.

Tabitha turned and spotted Charles. He was zeroing in on her with a drink in his hand. His eyes were like dark stars with steady focus. His brown skin was flawless. She was close enough to smell his understated cologne, sweet enough to make her wonder and strong enough to convince her.

She smiled at him. "Hi?" she uttered. "You're not tired of seeing me, are you?"

She still could not read the man.

He said, "I'm just wondering what your goals and intentions are."

His nature was more of a wasp, flying in strong for the kill, where Teddy's had been more of a bumblebee, hovering in circles while still deciding whether or not he should sting.

Peculiarly, Tabitha found herself at ease with Charles. She realized that there was much less game to figure out with him. He was a straight shooter. He just needed a reason and a desire to speak to you.

She said, "I guess we're just choosing the same places."

She was forcing herself to keep things simple with him.

"How'd you get on the guest list?" he asked her.

Maybe his sting was too much for her after all.

She backed up on her heels and answered, "I wasn't on the guest list." She wouldn't chance putting it on Teddy. She didn't know if he was a guest list kind of guy or not. It would have been an easy setup for her to lose another bridge.

Charles looked her over and nodded. "You charmed your way in?" They made necessary room for such. But only for the pretty young women. Security had been informed.

"You have to do what you have to do," she answered.

He said, "I didn't get your name the other night. Teddy got it."

"It's Tonya Kennedy," she told him, just in case he checked the guest list and found Teresa Kelly on it.

He extended his hand. "Charles Grandison."

She took his hand in hers and said, "Pleased to meet you."

"Are you?" he asked her.

"What do you mean?"

"Who are you here to meet?"

The answer was obvious. It was Isaac's party, and she had already made her acquaintance to Teddy. So either of them was an easy guess.

"Actually, I just wanted to be here," she answered. "But since you asked, I would love to meet the man of the hour like everyone else."

She smiled as widely as she could to lessen the forwardness of her advance.

What golden luck she would have if he actually agreed to it. But if he didn't, she could see enough interest in his eyes to think of an alternate route through him, as she had expected earlier.

He asked her, "What do you want to know about him?"

"I already know enough about him. I just want to meet him for myself," she answered.

"How much do you know?"

He caught her off guard with his third-degree line of questioning.

She tossed her hands skyward and answered, "He's Isaac Abraham. A superstar. I mean, how many articles have been written about him?"

"You've read them all?" Charles asked her with no smile.

"Are you kidding me? Nobody can read them all."

Finally, the man cracked a smile, with a noticeable dimple in his right cheek.

He said, "You'd be surprised. Come on, I'll take you to meet him."

Tabitha kept her cool. They walked through the place hand in hand, with eyes glancing at them in envy. She knew the game. No one wanted to look at them directly, but they all knew that she had been chosen to meet the man. She was alone, she had the right young look, and Charles, an A-team captain, was leading her across the room toward their treasured VIP section.

Before they arrived, Tabitha spotted another young woman who seemed alone in the room. She wasn't far from the VIP section, but she wasn't close enough to be connected to it either. She was in easy sight range, a perfect island-tanned brown with thick dark hair that seemed wet under the party lights. Her jeans fit her curves just right, and her top was sexy but still taste-ful. When their eyes met momentarily, Tabitha knew from instinct that the girl was an insider. She seemed far too calm within the room of adults, as if she knew where her place was: above theirs. Tabby made note of the girl for later.

Before she knew it, Charles was helping her up the VIP steps and past Derrick to introduce her to Isaac.

"This is Tonya Kennedy."

Isaac stopped and gave her a quizzical look.

"Uh, oh, you're not related to the famous ones, are you? A black sheep of the family? Another Jefferson clan?" he joked. Everyone laughed around him, including a few older women. They served as great props of adult content. However, everyone knew where Isaac's fetish lay.

Tabitha laughed as well. She answered, "No, I would have to ask my daddy." She wanted to keep all of her words short and explosive to give Isaac more to respond to and less to ignore.

"Where you from?" he asked her.

"San Antonio, Texas."

"With no accent," he commented.

She shook her head. "No accent."

"You wanna be an actress?"

She smiled. "Doesn't everybody?"

He looked straight through her and answered, "No."

He waited for the laughter around him before he added, "But you do have a good voice and good presence about you. Where you go to school?" He assumed that she was still young, in her late teens or early twenties.

"I packed up and came here. I'm not in school anymore," she answered.

"Oh, so you need a job now."

They laughed all around him again. Isaac was excellent at being a ham. Nevertheless, Tabitha was reading right through it. The man was still acting. He was terribly lonely within his crowd. His life, or at least his public life, had become a show. He seemed bored with it.

"Are you hiring?" she asked him. It was a loaded question.

"For what?" he answered. It was a loaded answer.

"For whatever's available," she responded.

He looked around at his entourage as if he needed them to understand the girl's eagerness.

Rafael, his personal assistant, spoke up about the job, "Can you travel?"

"Of course."

Isaac looked at Rafael and asked, "What, are you ready to hire her? We don't know that she's talented in yet."

"You already said she has a good voice and presence. I'm sure we can find someplace for her to work."

Isaac threw up his hands and said, "You see that? We come to Harlem for a screening and give away a hundred jobs. Make sure you get all of her information, Charley."

Charles nodded to him.

"Nice meeting you," Isaac said with his hand extended to the young woman.

She took his hand and read his eyes. "Thank you."

"You're welcome," he told her. And that was it, an anticlimax.

As soon as they walked away, she decided to tease her host.

"He calls you Charley?" she asked Charles with a grin. He damn sure didn't seem like a *Charley*.

He said, "It's a personal thing. He likes to show closeness with it."

"How does that make you feel?" she asked.

He shook his head. "It's no big deal. I got used to it."

"That doesn't mean that you *like it,* though," she noted.

"Let's move on from that," he told her.

All the while, Tabitha kept her eyes on the young woman she had spotted earlier. She was dancing now, but not allowing her dance partner to get close to her. The DJ had dug deep into his crates and pulled out Michael Jackson's "Billie Jean."

"Okay, so you met him," Charles commented of Isaac. "Now what?"

They had moved back out into the general crowd.

Tabitha asked, "Is he always that jokey?"

Charles countered, "Have you seen his films and read his interviews?"

His point was well taken. Isaac was a man of expansive range.

"So, I guess he puts on a show for them, hunh?" she asked, revealing her intellect on the matter.

Charles smiled slyly. He said, "All of public life is a show. Even yours. What you choose to wear every day is part of it. And it never stops."

She smiled back and agreed with him. "I guess that's true."

With no time to waste before their entourage would leave, Tabitha wanted to find out more about the girl she had spotted.

"I'll be right back," she told Charles. "I have to use the restroom."

"Do your thing," he told her. But as soon as she moved, he moved.

"Where are you going?" she asked him. She felt they had bonded well enough to continue in each other's company. Or so she had *hoped*.

"I have some other people to meet here," he told her. "But I am flattered," he added with a smile.

She decided to go bold with him. The business type honored boldness.

"All right, well, I *will* find you when I come out," she told him.

He chuckled. "Take your time. Life is all about those sixty minutes."

She nodded. "I'll remember that."

When she turned to find the restrooms, she searched for Wallace. She spotted him on the dance floor getting his grind on with a big-butt girl. She motioned for him to follow her.

Wallace didn't look as if he wanted to. Tabitha waited him out until he did.

"Damn, you pick a fine time to need me," he complained near the restrooms.

"Cut it out," she told him. "This is important. There's a girl in here I want you to try and talk to."

"For what?"

"Because we need to know who she is."

"Why?"

"Look, just trust me on this."

"Aw'ight, what girl?" he asked her in haste.

"Okay, I'm gonna go to the bathroom, and when I come out, I'm gonna walk right past her and turn back to you. So you need to pay attention."

"Yeah, whatever," he told her.

She frowned at his lack of professionalism and went to use the restroom.

"I don't know who she thinks I am," Wallace mumbled to himself in her absence. "I'm not no little brother type. I'm the big-ass brother."

Tabitha walked out a few minutes later and spotted her mark again. "Okay, she's still there."

"Just point her out to me then," Wallace suggested.

"No. My way is more tactful. So just follow me with your eyes," she told him.

"Aw'ight, aw'ight. Go ahead and do it."

She weaved through the crowded dance floor with her back to him until she reached her mark. She then turned and faced him before she continued on to the bar area.

Wallace spotted the girl and was stunned.

"Shit," he mumbled under his breath. "Somebody has good *taste*. Mommy look *good* in here."

He made his way to the dance floor right as the music changed. The girl stopped dancing and dismissed the advances from the tall partner who danced with her.

"Uh, oh," Wallace mumbled. "She shootin' people down in here."

Nevertheless, he was making *money* to be there. So he approached her with gusto.

"Hey, how you doin'? I don't wanna dance, I just want to know who you are."

She looked into his face with calm serenity and asked him, "Why?"

For a moment, Wallace felt paralyzed by her undivided attention.

Damn, she fine! He panicked to himself.

He stammered and said, "Ah . . . I don't know."

His answer caught her off guard. She found herself tickled by his honest confusion.

"Well, if you don't know, then why should I tell you?"

It was a good question.

He got his bearings together. He said, "I need a little more time to think about that. But anyway, my name is Wallace."

"I know," she told him.

"You *know*?"

She caught him off guard as well.

"Aren't you a model?" she asked him.

"Oh, yeah, sometimes."

"I saw you in that Hawaii swimsuit spread in *Honey* magazine a few years ago."

"And you still remember that?" he asked her. He was impressed by it.

"I don't forget a face," she told him. "That was one of their first summer issues."

"Yeah, but you remembered my *name*, too," he reminded her.

She smiled and leveled with him. "Not really. I just knew your face."

The Insider

Wallace was damn near in love, and he didn't even know the girl's name yet.

"So, who are you here with?" he asked her. "You look a little young to be in here. And you read *Honey* magazine," he teased.

"And? You were *in Honey* magazine," she responded. She didn't seem offended by it. She was only expressing the facts.

He told her, "A paycheck is a paycheck."

"That's all it meant to you?"

"Well, naw, you know, if it was consistent. But since it's not, what else can it mean?"

"Sounds like you need a better agent or a manager," she told him frankly.

"What do you know about all of that?"

Before she could answer him, she read a look from Derrick, the bodyguard, that signaled their entourage was ready to leave.

Tabitha read the same from across the room, where she continued to eye them all.

"Well, I gotta go, Wallace. Nice meeting you."

The girl headed in the opposite direction, to the restrooms.

"Wait a minute, wait a minute," he called after her.

She ignored him and disappeared into the crowd.

"Hold on, what's your name?" he yelled. He wasn't able to make his way through the crowd as swiftly as she had. He bumped into several dancers and caused static.

"Watch yourself," someone warned him.

By the time Wallace made it to the restroom, there was no sign of the girl. He figured she had gone inside, so he waited there patiently. And in vain.

≈

"I guess you all are ready to head out of here now," Tabitha commented to Charles. He was making his final rounds through the club before leaving. "Thank you for the introduction," she told him.

He nodded, with new drink in hand that was nearly finished.

"So, what are you doing once the smoke clears?" he asked her.

She shrugged her shoulders. "Going to bed, I guess."

"Where do you stay?"

She smiled. "Your friend Teddy asked me the same question. I told him it's a complicated situation. I'm basically staying with a male friend until I can find my own place."

"Can you afford to move out?"

"Not yet."

"How long have you been there?"

"Only two weeks."

"How long do you figure it'll take?"

She shook her head and looked hopeless. "I don't know. I'm hoping sooner than later."

He nodded to her. "I see. Did Teddy offer to help you?"

"I don't know if he was sincere about it. He hasn't called me yet."

"Did you expect him to?"

"He said he would, but guys say a lot of stuff."

Charles began to smile. Over his left shoulder, Tabitha could see the rest of Isaac's team making their way for the door. However, Charles was still giving her his full attention.

He said, "Some men like words, other men like the follow-through."

"So what are you saying?" she asked him. He definitely had the room temperature heating.

"I think you know what I'm saying already. But you take it how you want."

"You're saying that you would get me a place?"

"Not yet," he leveled with her. "We barely know each other. Maybe you don't even need the help. And I don't know if you want the attention."

His style was drastically different from Teddy's. Charles had Tabitha nervous again. She was supposed to be on the job, but she was beginning to have a conflict of interest.

"What kind of attention are you talking about?" she couldn't help but ask him.

He sucked down the rest of his drink. "You're a big girl. Do your homework."

She said, "I need time," and felt her knees shaking.

"That's fair," he told her. He put his drink down on a nearby table and began to head for the door.

"Where are you going?" she asked him again.

"I'm sure I'll see you around somewhere. Just keep following the people with the money," he told her.

His comment left her frozen and speechless. He spoke as if he knew her lifestyle in and out.

"Tabitha . . . Tabitha?" someone called.

"Hunh?"

She broke from her daydream and turned to face Wallace.

"That girl disappeared on me."

"She's going with them," Tabby told him.

"With who, Isaac and them? Naw."

Wallace didn't want to believe it.

"That's why I told you to find out who she was," Tabitha explained. "Did you get her name?"

"Nope. I was about to, but that's when she broke camp."

"How old do you think she is?"

"Man, about . . . seventeen, eighteen. She probably, like, a senior in high school. But I can't see none of them high school guys dealing with her. She probably cut them loose after her *sophomore* year."

Tabitha began to smile at him.

"It sounds like somebody got their nose pulled open."

Wallace said, "Shit, I wasn't prepared for that. She even knew who I was."

Tabitha froze. "Wait a minute. She knew who you *were*?"

"Yeah, she saw me in the swimsuit issue in *Honey* a few years ago. It was that same shoot in Hawaii that I told you about. Ain't that ironic?"

Tabitha nodded. "How did she talk to you?"

"Oh, she was real cool until it was time for her to go. Then she just broke out on me."

Tabitha smiled, knowing the game. A girl had to do what she had to do to catch her boat.

"Did she seem mature?" she asked him.

Wallace thought about it. He said, "I couldn't really tell. We just got to talking and . . . I mean, I wasn't really paying no attention to that."

"Of course not," Tabitha told him.

"She *looks* young. I *did* tell her that."

"But you didn't get any valuable information from her."

"Naw." He grinned, and was embarrassed about it.

Tabitha asked him, "Would you deal with her?"

"Yeah," Wallace answered eagerly. Then he backed up and tried to explain himself. "I mean, you know, if she was old enough."

Tabitha pressed him. "You mean you wouldn't take her right now if she's only seventeen?"

"Man, I'm sayin'—"

"Yeah, you would," she cut him off and stated.

Wallace only smiled at her.

When Tabitha arrived back at the hotel, she went straight for her diary to write another entry. It was her last night's stay in New York.

Tuesday, February 26, 2002
Millennium Hotel
Premiere After Party
Tonya Kennedy

I'm really confused right now. I met the man I was supposed to meet tonight, but it was all so fast and impersonal that it felt meaningless. All that buildup for two minutes. Now I'm attracted to his manager in a real way. But how much of this is real anyway? They want to pay me all that money for this? I don't get it.

I did see an interesting girl at the after party tonight. I'm quite sure she's an insider. It just made sense when I spotted her. And she left when they left. But that's all I know. I don't know her name, her age, where she's from, or anything. All I know is what she looks like.

It seems like I need more time here in New York. I've been here for three days now. So why does it feel like I just got off the plane? I'm supposed to fly back tomorrow, but I feel confused about it. It's like I'm beginning to like the place and the new friends that I've made. If I can call them friends. Maybe they wouldn't even talk to me if we weren't all working together. And maybe I wouldn't talk to them.

The phone rang before she could finish all of her entry.

"Hello?"

"How did it go tonight? Did you get a chance to meet him?" It was Angela.

Tabitha answered, "Yeah, I met him, but it didn't feel like I did anything special. He was putting on a show for his entourage."

"Yeah, you can't meet him out in public and expect much from him. He gives the people what they want," Angela explained.

"So, I'll have to meet him again anyway," Tabitha concluded.

"Yeah, of course. What did you expect? At least he knows your face now. You just bring up the meeting to him again and go from there. 'Hey, nice meeting you again.' "

Tabitha said, "I saw a young woman there tonight who looked around eighteen or so. She was a touch browner than me, and a little shorter, with a nice body, and that wet-look hair. Do you know her?"

"No, but I can find out."

"Well, I won't even be here when you find out," Tabitha stated sourly.

"Yeah, time just flew by, didn't it?"

"Too fast. I was actually starting to like it here."

"What, you didn't like New York?" Angela sounded surprised by it.

"Girl, the last couple of times I was here, I couldn't *wait* to leave," Tabitha told her.

"That's because you hadn't met me."

Tabitha smiled at Angela's open gesture of friendship.

She said, "You have to come out to Las Vegas and visit me now."

"I will."

"And you'll bring Wallace with you? I'm sure he'll love the women out on The Strip."

Angela laughed. "I bet he will."

The second line buzzed.

"Uh, oh, I might have to call you back," Tabitha told her new pal.

"Take your time. And call me back at the Marriott on Broadway. I'm in room twenty-one ten."

Tabitha paused and got nosy.

"Was it good?" she asked of Angela's rendezvous with Teddy.

"I wish," she responded. "But I'm damn sure gonna enjoy this twenty-four hour room service and the movie selections."

Tabitha laughed hard at that. She knew the feeling. Every man didn't get the job done.

She clicked over to the second line and found Sylvia.

"You need another day or two?" Sylvia immediately asked her.

√

"You're reading my mind." Tabitha perked.

"I hear you got a lot accomplished tonight," Sylvia mentioned.

"Yeah, I met him, but it was so brief that I felt cheated. But I think I may have found a young woman to talk to."

"I heard Charles introduced you tonight."

"Yeah, and then he made a play for me. So I'm two for two now."

"How was Isaac?"

"Guarded. He had a bunch of people around him. He gave me the co-median role."

"I see. He'll be different when you meet him again. We'll fly you to his next event outside of New York. His guard won't be as high then."

"Yeah, but I *do* want to find out who this girl is. She could be the one who *really* gets us inside. That's why I'd like to stay a couple more days."

"Not a problem. Wallace is on the case already."

"Yeah, she put the whammy on him," Tabitha joked. "His nose was wide open."

"What did you expect? Isaac doesn't pick any ugly ones."

"I see."

"Is Friday morning good enough?" Sylvia asked her.

"Yeah, that's good. I still have a house to get in order."

"By the way," Sylvia added, "stay away from Charles. He's not as forgiv-ing as Teddy."

Tabitha nodded and heeded her words. "I hear you."

As soon as she hung up with Sylvia, Tabitha called Angela back at the Marriott.

"Guess what?"

"Isaac's coming to your room tonight?" Angela answered in jest.

"I wish," Tabitha responded. "No, I just found out I'm staying until Fri-day. Now we can find out more about this girl together."

"Really? Cool."

"Yeah, you're not rid of me yet," Tabitha joked.

Angela responded, "Damn! I guess I have to share the spotlight for two more days."

Step 3

Your phone was ringing off the hook again," Marisol told Tabitha from Las Vegas. They hadn't spoken since that morning. However, Tabby was only concerned about one thing.

"Did Treece make it home with the kids yet?"

"Yeah, they got there. She called about an hour ago."

"Good. I'll give her time to settle in, and I'll call her later. I won't be home until Friday now."

"Yeah, well, I'm getting a little homesick," Mari told her. "I've been out here in Vegas for about two weeks now. And you're not even here."

"You knew I wasn't gonna be around anyway. I'm never in one place that long," Tabby reminded her sister.

"Yeah, but I didn't know you were gonna be out of town."

"I didn't either. Definitely not for this long."

"Anyway, your guy Terrence Madison said to call him on his cell phone. He said don't worry about the time. I wasn't trying to take his message, but he sounded really pressed to talk to you."

"You mean Terrence *Matthews*?"

"Yeah, whatever. That's what he said."

"Okay, thanks."

Tabitha hung up the phone and thought about it.

"Hmm. I guess I will call him. See how he's doing out in Memphis. Tomorrow sometime."

Tabitha met up with Angela and Wallace for lunch at T.G.I. Friday's in the middle of Times Square to go over their plans for the day.

Wallace looked dead tired and was slumped over their table. He had been up late gathering information.

"Aw'ight, I got her name, age, address, and high school. She lives in Queens with her aunt, but she's from Long Island. I heard her mom kicked her out the house," he added with a grin. "They say the girl likes to do things her own way."

"And you got all that in one night?" Tabitha asked him. "I'm impressed."

He smiled sheepishly. "Actually, it was easy. She was at the St. Regis last night. So I sat up there and kicked it with a few of the doormen. I let 'em know I had money on me, and after a while, one of them pulled me aside on the down low. He knew everything."

Angela looked at Tabitha while drinking a cup of coffee.

"Mmm," she grunted, "the things that people know for the right price."

Wallace said, "Them doormen on their grind like everybody else."

Tabitha asked, "So, what's the plan? We catch her at her school, or near her house?"

Angela and Wallace looked at her in confusion.

"What, you're going after her? What are we, detectives now?" Wallace joked.

"Why not? I want to talk to her."

"But won't that blow your cover?" Wallace asked.

"How? You think she travels with him?"

"I doubt that," Angela commented. "He doesn't need them to travel. He has them set up in every city already."

Wallace shook his head with an envious grin. "Damn!"

"Wish you had it like that, hunh?" Tabitha teased him.

"I'm just sayin', I mean . . . what are you gonna say to her?" he questioned. He was still confused by it.

Tabitha said, "Well, what's the use in getting all of this information if we're not gonna use it? I know how to talk to her. It's best that I do it, because I'm not gonna be here."

Angela nodded. "She has a point."

"Okay, so we drive out there to Queens, and then what? You just jump out the car and go talk to her?"

"We'll figure it out. Maybe we'll just follow her from school. If she catches a train or a bus, or doesn't go straight home, then I'll have her," Tabitha answered.

Wallace shook his head. "You crazy. I see why they hired you."

Tabitha smiled. "I just go for it. Life is a big party. I'm having a good time with this. And we're getting *paid* to do it," she added.

"Amen to that," Angela told her.

They arrived at a high school in Queens in Wallace's gray Explorer, right before dismissal. Angela sat up front with Wallace, while Tabitha sat in the back.

"Damn, we just made it," Wallace commented. A few faculty members and security were walking out before the bell.

Wallace stopped directly across the street from the main entrance.

"Drive down the street and act normal, Wallace," Angela told him. "We don't want to *look* like we're waiting for somebody out here."

Wallace drove to the middle of the block and found a parking spot as the final dismissal bell rang.

Nnnrrrrrnnnnkk!

"Wow, I haven't been back to a high school since I graduated," Angela commented. She watched all of the wild energy and colorful, eye-blinding outfits as the teenagers began to pour out of the exit doors.

"When was that, last year?" Wallace joked to her.

"Yeah, a day before you."

As Wallace and Angela continued to joke, Tabitha spotted a shiny dark blue Lexus IS, parked not far ahead of them. She began to wonder.

"Aw, man, they got, like, six different doors letting out," Wallace complained. "We got no idea which one she's coming out of."

"If we already know where she lives, we can just ask someone which buses go that way and catch her at the bus stop," Angela suggested.

Tabitha was still concentrating on the exit doors to their left, while she went over her line of questions in her head. She was still trying to figure it all out for herself.

"Oh my God, here she come, too!" Wallace said excitedly. He was looking back to the main entrance down the street.

"See that," Angela told him.

Tabitha turned and looked for herself. The girl looked fabulous in a light brown, three-quarter-length, hooded fur coat. She wore faded Iceberg Jeans and light brown Timberland boots. Her hair still looked wet, and her baby-doll brown face was flawless in the daylight.

"Oh my God, she got the fox fur on! She's ghetto fabulous out here!" Wallace stated.

Angela looked at him and huffed, "Would you stop sweating her?"

"Aw, you just a little jealous in here. Calm down."

"You're the one who needs to *calm down*; all yelling and screaming over some high school girl."

Wallace looked back to Tabitha. "Don't she sound jealous to you? She in here hatin' 'cause she ain't fab."

"I never wanted to be *'ghetto'* fabulous," she told him.

"Yes you do. On the low, *all* girls want that shit. So don't even *front*."

Tabitha was laughing from the backseat while trying to concentrate.

"Wait, she's walking our way. Nobody look at her," she told them.

They all turned in their seats to look normal.

The girl crossed the street and headed straight past them.

Tabitha said out loud, "If she gets into that Lexus . . ."

Wallace lost his cool again. "Oh my God, she got a *I S* in *high school*! I *know* she ain't fuckin' with these kids. How do the *teachers* even let her do that? They *know* something gotta be up. They *know it*!"

Tabitha laughed and said, "She has a rich uncle."

"Yeah, named Isaac Abraham," Wallace responded.

Angela was speechless.

Sure enough, the girl popped open the blue Lexus with a keyless remote and climbed in behind the wheel.

"She don't even have no *friends* riding with her," Wallace stated. "She out here *solo*."

"That's how you do it," Angela mumbled. "Friends get in your way."

Tabitha nodded in agreement from the backseat.

Wallace said, "Yeah, I guess y'all *both* know. I got two *vets* in here."

Angela shook her head and didn't comment.

Tabitha said, "All right, once she makes it to the corner, we start to follow her."

Wallace was on the case. "I got'chu." He pulled out of his parking spot slowly. Once the Lexus made a right turn at the corner, he sped down the street after it.

By the time they made it to the corner, the Lexus was at the next corner.

"Damn, she *whippin'* that ride," Wallace stated.

"Well, don't rush after her like a damn *fool*. We can still see her from back here," Angela warned him.

"I got'chu," Wallace repeated.

Tabitha continued to smile. The New York action sure beat flying back to Las Vegas for Marisol's drama.

The Lexus sped down another street and made a left.

"Aw'ight, she's not going back home, 'cause she lives the other way," Wallace commented as he continued to follow her.

The Lexus then hit Queens Boulevard.

Wallace said, "I bet you a hundred dollars she's going to the mall. Her sugar daddy just gave her some money last night, and she's going straight to the mall with it."

Angela said, "Please, spare us your small-minded commentary."

However, when the Lexus made another left turn toward the Queens Center Mall parking garage, Wallace became more animated.

"I told you! *I told you!*" he hollered. "And then women wonder why we call y'all *chickens!*"

"Excuse me," Angela huffed. "You are really starting to get under my *skin.*"

Tabitha couldn't stop laughing. She didn't care. She lived her life, and everyone else lived theirs.

She said, "Okay, now she's made it easy for me. I'll just walk up to her in the mall and say, 'Oh, didn't I see you at the premiere party last night?' "

"And where are we supposed to be?" Wallace asked her.

"You can hang out in the mall somewhere, I guess. As long as you don't walk in with me."

"We can't park behind her, either. That would be suspect," Angela advised.

"Right, so just drop me off, and I'll go in there and see where the entrance from the garage is. I wanna catch her on the way in. That way I won't have to look all over the mall for her."

They dropped Tabitha off next to the Queens Center Mall on Queens Boulevard. She hurried around to the garage area to catch the girl coming in. As soon as she arrived, she spotted the girl on the second level parking bridge walking across to the mall.

"Shit. A second later and I would have missed her."

Tabitha slipped into the mall to catch the girl on the other side. Once inside, she looked to find an escalator without losing sight of her target. She jumped on the escalator going up and arrived on the second level just in time to catch the girl walking into a small jewelry store.

Tabitha then slowed down her role.

"Okay. Raven Johns," she reminded herself. There wasn't much sense in catching a young girl in a jewelry store unless she was actually buying jewelry. Jewelry store owners were usually too aggressive to allow idle conversation between strangers. Tabitha realized she needed more space and privacy. So she waited three stores down for the girl to walk out.

When she finally made her exit, she walked in the opposite direction, away from Tabitha. She wasn't walking slowly either.

"Shit. I'm gonna have to chase her down."

Tabitha walked behind her at a quick pace and looked down at her watch as if she had an appointment to keep.

The girl led her right into a Macy's department store at the far end of the mall.

"Perfect," Tabitha told herself. She would be able to approach the girl in a natural rhythm at the perfume counters. The girl was testing a bottle of Burberry.

"Hi, didn't I see you last night in Harlem at the after party for Isaac Abraham's movie premiere?" Tabitha asked her.

She appeared to have caught the girl off guard. She hit her with too much information at one time.

She looked at Tabitha, confused. "No. I'm not from Harlem," she answered.

"Well, I'm not from Queens, but I'm over here," Tabby countered.

"Well, I'm sorry, but you got the wrong person," the girl told her. She maintained her poise with no attitude when she said it.

"Are you sure? Because I think I heard someone say your name was Ramone Johnson, or something like that."

The girl shook her head. "No, that's not my name."

Tabitha snapped her fingers and said, "*Raven*. Raven *Jones* or something, right? I'm sorry, but I'm just *terrible* when it comes to names."

The girl repeated, "Like I said, you have the wrong person," and began to back away from her.

Tabitha said, "Okay, if you wanna play it that way, then be my guest. But we both *know* who we know. I just wanted to give you some information. F–Y–I."

Tabitha stood there and waited for her response.

The girl looked around for privacy. She finally asked, "Who are you?"

"Toni. Toni Karson."

She reached out her hand to the girl.

Raven stared into her face and didn't budge.

"And what do you want from me?" she asked.

"You wanna talk?" Tabitha, disguised as Toni, asked her. Although Raven *had* spotted her brief meeting with Isaac at the after party in Harlem, she had thought nothing of her.

"I don't know you," she responded. She was still trying to figure out how to play it. The girl seemed persistent. Why? What did she really want?

The stranger lowered her tone. "Don't be like that, Raven. This is inside talk. Okay? I'm just here as a friend."

"A friend to do what?"

"Do you want to talk or not?"

"I am talking."

"Okay, well, here's the deal then. How old are you?"

"Why?"

"Look, I'm nineteen myself now. I've been knowing him for five years. We always play like we don't know each other while out in public. That's our game."

Raven shook her head. She said, "I don't know what you're talking about. And I don't have time for this."

"I think you should *make* time," Tabitha warned her. "Especially if he's giving you things."

She had Raven frozen in her fur-coat-wearing, jewelry-buying, Lexus-driving tracks.

She asked, "What are you trying to say?"

"Let's talk."

Raven looked around and said, "Where?"

"In the kids' section. They won't bother us there. They'll be too embarrassed. Unless they think we're trying to steal something for our babies," Toni joked.

Raven cracked a smile. "All right. I'll go first."

Tabitha followed her to the kids' section while still gathering her game plan. She had to make up something believable and convincing.

Raven stopped at the little girl dresses. "Okay, so what are you talking about?"

"I-A is in trouble back home in Detroit. They had a couple of underage girls say that they had sexual contact with him. Now they have investigators looking to find more girls wherever he goes. I don't know if you're still underage, but I just wanted to tell you to watch out. Unless you wanna go to court."

Raven looked on without words. She didn't know what to say.

Tabitha added, "I don't know if it was necessarily *wrong* for me to sleep with him all these years like I did, but I know it wasn't *right,* either. You know what I mean?"

Raven was still speechless. Her mind couldn't seem to figure out an answer to the equation being given. She slowly nodded her head.

"All right," she mumbled in response.

"So what are you thinking?" Tabitha asked her.

Raven was still slow to answer.

"I mean . . . I don't know."

"Well, they haven't contacted me yet. I don't know what I'll say if they do," Tabitha told her. "I had a friend who told me he has girls in every city. I'm still trying to deal with that. I mean, that could be dangerous. We used to go unprotected sometimes. *A lot* of times."

She was pouring it on the poor girl. Raven stood as stiff as a nail.

"I'm sorry I had to tell you that. But once I saw you in the mall, it was just too much of a coincidence. I felt it was my *duty* to tell you."

A thousand thoughts ran through Raven's mind at that moment.

Tabitha read her face and decided to stop right there. It was obvious she had said enough already.

"Are you okay?" she asked the girl.

Raven shook her head. "Not right now," she answered. "But I'ma *be* okay," she added with determination.

Tabitha nodded to her. "Good. That's how you *have* to be. I had to learn to be that way myself. It's all about survival. I'm not giving up *my life* for nobody. Especially for somebody who wouldn't give up his life for *me*. And I *know* he wouldn't. I'm just *one of* like everybody else. He's *married*."

Raven looked away and was ready to move on. She didn't want to hear another word of it. She just wanted to be alone with her thoughts.

"Sorry," Tabitha apologized again.

"Whatever," Raven huffed as she began to walk away. "Thanks a fuckin' lot," she grumbled.

For a minute, Tabitha found herself in shock. She had no idea her plan would work so well.

"Oh my God," she mumbled to herself. "That was too much."

She tried to follow Raven, but the girl was making a fast exit to get away from her.

After that, Tabitha wanted to get away herself. She didn't even want to be in New York anymore. As far as she was concerned, her job was done. She felt absolutely *miserable* about what she had done.

"That was *wrong,*" she murmured as she walked back out into the mall area.

With Raven already out of sight, Tabby pulled out her cell phone and called Angela for her pick up.

"I'm ready to go."

"Did you catch up to her?" Angela asked. "We're in the food court on the bottom level."

"Yeah, I'll tell you about it," Tabitha answered hastily. She wanted to get the hell out of there. She didn't feel safe anymore. It felt like a dark cloud was hanging over her head inside the mall.

She made it down to the food court area and searched all around her for signs of Raven, as if the girl would pop up out of nowhere and curse her for her terrible lies.

"So what happened?" Wallace asked her. They were eating burgers and fries.

"Can y'all eat that on the go? Where did y'all park?" Tabitha asked them in a rush.

Wallace answered, "Down the street. We just got here. We had to walk two blocks."

Tabitha didn't want to hear it.

"I want to get back to Manhattan."

"What's the rush? Sit down and tell us what happened," Angela told her. They were not budging from their seats.

Tabitha took a breath and sat down with them.

She said, "I caught up to her, and I said way too much."

"You blew it?" Wallace muttered through his mouthful of food. He was smiling at her.

"No, I didn't blow it," she answered, "I blew it *up.*"

"What does that mean?" Angela asked her.

"Let's just say that . . . I said enough."

"Well, what did you say?" Wallace wanted to know.

Tabitha shook her head. She answered, "I can't even remember all of it. I'm already trying to erase it from my mind."

"Was it that bad?" Angela asked her.

"Yes."

Wallace began to laugh.

"Is somebody after you now?"

"Why?" she quizzed him.

"You look like it. What she say to you? She was gonna have somebody kick your ass in here?"

Tabitha didn't respond.

"Well, what did you *say*?" Angela pressed her.

"Let's just, um . . . let's just move on."

Wallace noticed the cold shoulder she was giving them. He shook his head and said, "Damn, you must have said some fucked-up shit to her, hunh?"

Tabitha still didn't respond. She was in a daze. She wanted to be alone with her thoughts now, too.

She didn't speak much on their way back to the hotel.

"Are you okay?" Angela finally asked her before she climbed out.

"I don't know," Tabitha answered. It was just after six o'clock, and the sun had gone down.

Wallace said, "You not gon' hang out wit' us tonight?"

"It's still early," she told them. "I'll think about it."

"All right, girl. I hope you feel better," Angela told her.

Tabitha climbed out of the Explorer on her way into the hotel.

She looked back at them and said, "I hope I feel better, too."

Guilty
Conscience

Wednesday, February 27, 2002
Evening
New York
Tabitha Knight

Party over. I feel terrible right now. I did the job, even though I didn't really believe in it, and now I'm feeling the pressure from it.

I really said some mean things today. I don't even believe in getting in people's business, but here I am in New York, stirring up all kinds of trouble just to see if I could.

Who gave me that right? I feel like the biggest hypocrite in the world right now. I don't even want the money anymore. I just wanna be able to take back the things that I said today. But it's too late for that.

It's not too late for me to quit, though. I'm done. This isn't fun anymore. I wanna go back home and get back to my own life. If I can. Funny how one event and one day can change so much in our lives.

I don't even feel like writing anymore. I just want to go to sleep and wake up from this bad dream.

Tabitha closed her diary and slipped into her pajamas by eight o'clock. She then flipped on the movie selections to see if there was anything worth watching.

"I could use a *Sleepless in Seattle* right now," she joked to try and lift her spirits. However, only the more recent movies were part of the selection.

"I may as well try something different," she told herself. She selected Bruce Willis and Samuel L. Jackson starring in *Unbreakable*.

By the middle of the slow-moving film, she was already falling asleep. The only thing that saved her was a call on her cell phone.

"Hello," she answered groggily.

"Hope you don't mind. I got your number from Teddy."

Tabitha immediately sat up from her slumped position in bed. In a flash, she was back on alert. It sounded like Charles Grandison.

"No . . . I don't mind," she responded.

"Your roommate breathing down your throat?" he asked her.

"No. He's not even here right now."

"So, why are you there? He has someplace to go, and you don't?"

"Sometimes I just like peace and quiet," she answered.

"I can understand that. Silence is golden. Only then can you hear your own heart beat."

Tabitha began to daydream that the man's sultry voice had turned in to the full body and had crawled under the sheets with her. He then slipped off her pajamas and massaged her naked body from head to toe. Before she realized how far they were going, he began to pound into her for being such a bad girl that day.

I'm sor-ree. I'm sor-ree, she pleaded in her daydream.

"What's on your mind?" Charles was asking her.

"Oh, shit, I'm sitting here daydreaming. What were you asking me again?"

He paused. "I'm not one for repeating myself."

"But what if I didn't hear you?"

"Then it wasn't important to you."

She thought about it and said, "You're right. I was thinking about something else."

He asked, "I called at a bad time? Or do I even have time?"

His words were as loaded as the verses in the Bible. And it was killing her, in the right way.

She said, "I was thinking about you, actually."

"In what way?" he asked her.

"Sexually," she admitted.

"Why?"

"I just wondered what it would be like."

"Any conclusions?"

"I was thinking it would be very deliberate. And that's what I actually need right now," she leveled with him.

"Hmmph. You said a mouthful with that," he told her.

She asked him, "Are you smiling?"

"Yeah."

"I can feel it."

"I'm sure you can. It's deliberate," he told her.

She smiled herself. "So what are we waiting for?"

"A place, a time, and a reason."

She paused. His words seemed to dive into her for the deepest effects.

She said, "I thought you told me you don't like words. You could have *fooled* me."

He said, "Maybe I don't. But we still have to use them, right? So why not use them to move things forward, like business."

"But this isn't *business,*" she reminded him. "This is *personal.*"

For a moment there was silence between them.

"Where do you want to meet?" he asked her.

"Downtown Brooklyn," she answered. "Let's just be different. You name the hotel, and I'll meet you there. In one hour. And the reason . . . is because I want you. And you want me."

"And the truth . . ." Charles started.

" . . . shall set you free," Tabitha ended.

And they laughed like old friends.

Tabitha hung up the phone, took a deep breath, and launched herself from the bed so she could freshen up, redress, and take a taxi ride over the Brooklyn Bridge.

It was an unexpected invitation for companionship, and after the events of the day, she needed closeness. Charles wasn't a bad choice for the job.

"Sylvia said to leave him alone," she told herself as she ran the shower water. "To hell with her. I'm off this job now anyway. I'll do what I want."

After her quick shower, she re-dressed in a fresh pair of blue jeans with no panties and slipped on a new eggshell-colored turtleneck with no bra.

She gave her body a good once-over with Bijou perfume and made sure her face and hair were in order. She then grabbed her brown leather jacket, bag, and cell phone, and walked out the door.

She rode the elevator down to the lobby and headed briskly for the hotel's front entrance.

"Taxi, please," she told the doorman.

"No problem."

"Taxi!"

Taxis were plentiful in the Times Square area. Three pulled up immediately. Tabitha jumped in to the first one in the line.

"Where to?" the Middle Eastern driver asked her.

"The Flatbush Hotel in downtown Brooklyn."

"You have an address?" he asked her.

"We can ask once we get over there," she told him. She had no time to waste.

"O-kay," the driver agreed.

He took off into the busy New York traffic.

During the ride, Tabby began to assess her thoughts on the day. What was so wrong with loving who you love? Did age really make a difference? Most women wanted to look up to their men anyway. If they didn't, then they had the right to choose otherwise. But was the playing field lopsided with ultra successful men?

Of course it was. Such was life. There was no real equality in partnership. There were married women with college degrees who had given up everything for *average* men. So what chance did a girl in high school have with a multimillionaire? It was easy pickings. A battle between a gnat and an elephant.

Tabitha didn't know how to call it. She had dealt with older men for the majority of her life. Then she had moved on to successful men. They had more to love. They were more complicated. They were more organized. They were more skillful. They knew more. They experienced more. That's why they were successful. And they were on the winning side of the game called life, with the opportunities to call the shots. Why wouldn't a girl be attracted to that?

Tabitha's cell phone rang right as she hit the Brooklyn Bridge in her taxi. She looked and read the number on the Caller ID. It was Angela.

Tabby shook her head and ignored the call. She had her own mission for the night. She planned to turn off her cell phone and ignore the world as soon as she met up with Charles at the hotel.

"I see it," the taxi driver told her of the Flatbush Hotel. It was located on the south side of the bridge, with a perfect view of the bay.

"Nice view," the driver added.

"That's what it looks like," Tabitha perked. She was pleasantly surprised, and glad that she had mentioned Brooklyn. She just didn't want Charles anywhere near the St. Regis in Manhattan, where Isaac stayed. But what if they had already spoken, and Raven had pointed her out from the premiere party? Could she be walking right into her own trap?

She doubted it. She hadn't even thought about it earlier. Charles was already attracted to her, and he had his own life to live. Nevertheless, Tabitha climbed out of her taxi at the hotel and paid her driver with a last-minute feeling of anxiety.

"Shit. Why am I thinking about this now?" she mumbled to herself as she walked in to the low-key hotel. It was a dark, quiet, elegant place for insiders only.

"May I help you?" a hotel receptionist asked her. He was a twenty-something white man with a tactful presence, wearing a white dress shirt and black tie.

"No, I'm okay," Tabitha told him. She wanted to blend in to the hotel setting until Charles arrived, but the receptionist was not allowing her that opportunity.

"Are you here to meet someone?" he asked her.

She was just about to ask him why when he asked, "Is your name Tonya?"

She looked at him calmly and answered, "Is there something you need to tell me?"

He said, "I have a key for you, compliments of your stay with us."

He slid the small key cover into her hand with the room number attached.

"Enjoy," he told her. Then he went on about his business.

Tabitha responded to the gesture with a nod. "I see."

Charles was taking care of business.

She read the room number on the seventeenth floor before turning to find the elevators.

"I bet he has a great view of the bridge and Manhattan, too," she told herself on the way up.

Sure enough, her window had the east side view of The Big Apple.

A minute later, the hotel phone rang. Tabitha was hesitant to answer it.

But who could it be but Charles? No one else knew she was there. Or did they? She answered it anyway.

"Hello."

"Do you like the view?" Charles asked her.

She smiled, at ease with the sound of his voice.

"It's like heaven on earth."

"Not yet. I'll be there in another five to ten minutes."

Tabitha chuckled. "I love a confident man."

"Who doesn't?"

"People who can't take it."

"Or people who can't take themselves," he responded. "Everyone's confident. They're just not confident when it counts."

"And you are?"

"I am what I am."

"And what exactly is that?"

"We'll talk about it when I get there."

Just like that, New York was exciting again. But only for that night. Charles would be back to his normal life in the morning, a life that didn't include her. That was the problem in dealing with the men Tabitha dated. They were never hers. They belonged to everyone *but* her. She was only stealing the time in between. If that's what you called it. But whose time would it have been if Charles had decided to fall asleep for the night instead of meeting with her for a rendezvous? Wouldn't that have been *his* time? Things were far too complicated to think about.

Just let it be what it's gonna be, Tabitha reminded herself.

She could already imagine his hands all over her body. She even flirted with waiting for him naked under the sheets. But that would cheat her out of the thrill of having him strip her and find that she wore no underwear. Or maybe that would turn him off. Maybe Charles was an extra tactful man.

"Just let it happen," she reminded herself aloud.

The wait was killing her. She usually just *flowed* into her alliances with men. She didn't have to *wait* for it. Sex happened readily. Naturally.

By the time Charles arrived at the room, Tabitha was staring out of the window, hypnotized by the view. It beat thinking about a million other things that would never change. Sex would always happen with men and women. If it did not, there wouldn't be any more men or women.

"What are you thinking over there?"

Charles had already undone his tie. He wore a beige wool suit, a yellow dress shirt, and dark brown alligator shoes.

"I see you had big business today," she mentioned to him. She had not budged from her window view. She figured correctly that he would join her there instead.

Charles took off his jacket to toss across the high, king-size bed. He walked over into her range and said, "Every day is big business. That doesn't mean you close out every deal, but you're working on it."

He opened his arms and gently pulled her into them.

She placed her head against his shoulder. "You smell good," she told him.

"I was supposed to tell *you* that."

"Do I?"

"Of course you do."

He fingered through her hair. She relaxed into his arms and brought her chin up to face him.

"Is this the part where I kiss you?" he asked her.

She smiled, subtly. "I hope it is."

He kissed her, with his hands sliding around to her back.

"Soft skin is the biggest aphrodisiac in the world to me," he told her.

She said, "I have plenty of it."

"I see."

She pulled away just enough to undo his dress shirt.

He moved his hands to her breast and carefully massaged her nipples.

"So young. So ripe," he told her.

"Is that how you like it?"

"What's there not to like?"

She undid his dress shirt and pulled up his tank top to kiss his chest and softly bite *his* nipples.

"Mmmph," he hummed to her. "You have the perfect touch on that."

"Not too hard . . . not too soft," she told him.

Before Charles knew it, she had slid her hands inside his pants to find that he was not wearing any underwear himself.

"Have you been like this all day?" she asked him with a grin.

"Not hardly," he told her. "But once you know you're not gonna need them for much longer, you find a bathroom and do a Superman."

Tabitha laughed harder than she expected. Charles had a real personality that he appeared to hide under too much male armor. She understood him perfectly now. He was a cub in a lion's mane, with a lot of play still left in him that he wasn't able to utilize much.

She undid his slacks and allowed them to fall to the floor. His boy woke up and said hello to her while she massaged him in her hand.

Charles did the same with her jeans, finding her girl moist and eager for company.

He pulled her turtleneck over her head and allowed her twins their freedom, the freedom to be milked by soft lips and probed by a cool tongue.

"Mmmph," Tabitha responded to him. She cradled his head into her bosom and whispered, "Thank you. It's been a long day."

She kissed the smooth hair on his head and rubbed it like a mother would a newborn.

He stood again to face her. "Do you want this?" he asked.

She looked at him with dreamy eyes and uttered, "Yes."

He took her hand in his and led her to the bed.

"Under the sheets," he told her.

While she climbed into bed and slipped under the sheets, Charles fumbled inside his suit jacket for his protection. Finding them, he slid one on and climbed under the sheets with her.

"Tell me if it hurts," he told her.

"Okay," she responded softly.

Charles aimed, but did not enter. He played at the door instead. Tabitha was far too satisfied with things to complain. She realized that they were just getting started. And if things failed to be as strong as she desired, she would take matters into her own hands.

However, just when she began to tire of his tease, he pushed his way in unexpectedly.

"Unnhh," she responded to him.

"Tell me if it hurts," he repeated. It was his game of reverse psychology, hinting at pain where there was really pleasure.

"O-kay," she whispered in response.

Deliberate he was, deliberate in driving her crazy. He established a rhythm and drove her into a frenzy of excitement.

"Ohhh . . . mmm," she moaned.

"Does it hurt yet?"

"No-o-o," she moaned to him.

"Are you sure?"

"Yes-s-s."

"I don't wanna hurt you."

"You're not, you're not."

With every question, he poured on the heat.

"You still want it?"

"I do, I du-u-u-u," she pleaded.

She felt her first episode of the shakes, as Charles continued to dig into her. And it wasn't her last. She experienced several levels of joy, while the man gave her everything she imagined it to be. And when they were finished, she felt she knew him.

"Wow," Tabitha stated to the ceiling.

"You're surprised?" Charles asked her.

After their first energies had been depleted, they lay there in bed, naked under the sheets side by side.

She answered, "Well . . . you said you like the follow-through. Now I guess I know."

"What do you want from a man?" he asked her out of the blue.

She thought about it and answered, "Honesty. But not honesty with his words; I want honesty with his actions. If we have a relationship, and that's what it is, then that's what we have. Be real about it."

"So, what's supposed to happen with it?"

"Whatever we decide on."

"But sometimes things change."

"I know," she admitted. She looked over at his ring, an open symbol of his marriage. "Did things change with her?"

"What do you think?" he quizzed her. "How much do you know about the institution called marriage?"

She said, "I know a lot of people are still trying to figure it out."

He nodded. "What do you think about that? Are you interested in it?"

She drew a blank. "Actually . . . I don't know right now."

"That's an honest answer," he told her. "But let me tell you something I want you to always remember."

Tabitha gave him her undivided attention in the silence of the room.

"Okay. I'm listening."

He said, "Marriage, for a woman, is about a legacy. Her legacy is established through the name that she acquires and the children she bears. And as long as that man is building the family castle, her legacy grows. But if she steps out of her position for divorce or whatever the reason, chances are, she doesn't get that legacy back."

"Unless you're Jackie Kennedy Onassis," Tabitha responded, implanting her alias as Tonya Kennedy.

Charles nodded to her. "Right. But how often does that happen for a black woman?"

Tabitha smiled at him. "So, you're saying that, no matter what, your wife should never leave her legacy?"

Charles didn't even flinch. He said, "Emotions are temporary. The flesh gets old and wrinkles up. New friends come and new friends go. But family legacy is blood on the grave."

"So why go outside of the family and chance ruining it then?" she asked him. It was an honest question. "And why do it with young women at that? I mean, give them a chance to grow into their *own* legacy as wives, instead of them being ruined at young ages."

Tabitha was off the job and asking questions for herself now. Charles was that interesting to her, more interesting than Isaac.

He said, "Some eggs are always gonna fall out of the nest. That was the case before us, and that'll *be* the case after us."

"But why do *you* have to be the one to take them?" she asked.

"In most cases, I'm not. But after being around long enough, I noticed that those eggs are still falling. And the question becomes, 'Who's gonna catch them?' You understand me? Is it gonna be good hands, or bad hands?"

He had her speechless. She couldn't deny it. He actually made sense. If a girl was ready to be turned out, then it was only a matter of time before she met with her fate. Maybe if Tabitha hadn't been a foster child, she would have had stronger visions of a daddy who would always be there to protect her. But the reality was, she had never met her daddy, and she had fallen into the kind hands of another man who raised her. How many other young girls shared her story?

"Do you feel that you're ruined?" Charles asked, breaking her from the thoughts of her upbringing.

"I don't know," she answered.

"Can you still marry?"

"Yeah, I can. There's nothing stopping me."

"Exactly," he told her. "But you know why you *won't*?"

She read the seriousness in his eyes and asked him, "Why?"

"Because you feel guilty," he told her. "Now you know how much *bull-shit* is out here, and you're afraid to be a part of it. You don't *believe* you can be a part of it. So you tell yourself not to be, and you try to keep living outside the box."

He said, "But just like you told me you want honesty in actions, you have to *accept* that same honesty in a relationship with a husband and say, 'This is what it is.' And you design your own needs and wants inside and outside of that marriage. Because the perfection that you believed in before you found out the truth was a lie to begin with.

"Am I right, or am I wrong?" he asked her.

"You're right."

He said, "So don't ever feel guilty about what you know in this world. You use it to your advantage and learn to grow with it."

Tabitha nodded to him in silence. She understood everything.

Charles said, "Now, if I get excited again and roll over on you, are you gonna feel guilty and push me away?"

She smiled. "No."

"What are you gonna do?" he asked her.

"Spread my legs, and invite you back in."

"But that'll make you ruined," he teased.

She said, "I'm already ruined . . . and I like it."

Charles chuckled, and smiled his ass off. What else could he say?

What's Going On?

Thursday, February 28, 2002
Early Morning
Brooklyn, New York
Flatbush Hotel
Tabby

What a wonderful time I had last night. I can't say it was a good day, but it sure ended with a bang. Pun intended.

I had the most delicious forbidden fruit. And as always, I learned a few new things. There's no need to be confused about my lifestyle. Just keep doing me. I can't continue to feel guilty about it either. Everybody has their own issues.

It's almost time for me to head back home now. I feel like I'll miss New York. I have to admit that. But I don't know what that girl Raven is about to do after I dropped that bomb on her yesterday. Shit could really hit the fly when or if she acts up.

I also need to call my contact this morning and give her an update on what's going on. I know she's wondering where the hell I am. It'll be interesting to hear what she has to say when I tell her I quit. Of course, I don't plan on telling her that until after I get back home. I wouldn't want her trying to cancel the flight on me.

Well, I have one last day in New York. Let's see if I can make the best of it without anything crazy happening.

Tabitha closed her book and gathered her things to take a taxi back to the Millennium Hotel in Manhattan. Charles had left her there in Brooklyn in the wee hours of the night, but at least he stayed *that* long. Tabby had gotten used to busy men who often needed to leave her before the sheets had even cooled down.

Right as she opened the door to walk out, the hotel phone rang. She smiled, believing it was Charles calling her again.

"Hello."

"Miss Kennedy, your car is waiting for you at the front of the hotel whenever you're ready," the front desk informed her.

Tabitha paused. "Okay."

She hung up the phone and said, "Charles must have sent me limo service. But I can't go back to the hotel with that."

She was confused about what to do. Had she left a minute earlier, she wouldn't have known that a car had been sent for her.

"Shit. I'll just tell the driver I'm going to Manhattan for something. But for what?"

She walked back over to the bed and took a seat to think things through. It was not even nine o'clock in the morning yet.

She snapped her fingers and said, "Job interview. I'll tell him I have an interview with MTV."

Fortunately, Angela had pointed the MTV offices out to her in Times Square the day before.

Tabitha took a breath and headed down to her limo with her story right. She returned the key card at the front desk.

"Did you enjoy your stay?" they asked her.

"It was wonderful."

She headed out the door and arrived at the black Lincoln Town Car parked out front. An older man in a dark suit rushed to open the back door for her to climb in.

"Hi, I need to go to Manhattan for an interview," she told him.

"Oh, okay. Where to?"

"The MTV offices in Times Square."

"Oh, that's a popular building. You're trying out to be a VJ?"

"We'll see," she told him. "They have to interview me first."

The driver closed the door behind her. He strolled around to the driver's side and hopped in behind the wheel to take her to her destination.

"What time do you have to be there?"

"Eleven o'clock," she answered. "I wanted to go shopping first to buy some more exciting clothes. I think I may be dressed a little too conservatively right now," she added with a smile.

He looked up into his rearview mirror to peruse her outfit.

He said, "I like conservative. Everyone doesn't have to show everything. But when you're dealing with that MTV crowd, I guess you know what you're talking about."

He said, "I only get to watch it with my grandkids, just to see what they're in to, you know. You can never be too old for change."

"That's the truth," Tabby responded. "But it's not so much about your personal tastes anymore, unless your personal tastes are in line with what the *young* people like."

" '*Young people*,' " he mocked her. "You're still young yourself."

When the driver arrived in the 42nd Street area of Manhattan's Times Square, Tabitha climbed out of the car at the corner and said, "Thank you."

"You'll be all right here?"

"I'm a big girl," she told him.

"All right then. Good luck."

Tabitha walked in the opposite direction of the Millennium Hotel toward the shops to at least *appear* to be interested in shopping. Many of the stores wouldn't open before ten, but she could window-shop.

However, once her driver fled off in his car, she doubled back toward the hotel and turned her cell phone on. She had missed seven calls. Two of the calls were from Sylvia. She also had phone calls from Angela, Wallace, Marisol, and Patrice. Since it was still a new cell phone number, she hadn't set up the voicemail service as of yet.

"I'll call them all once I get back to the room."

There was no sense in using her cell phone. The hotel's phone bill was included in the expenses of the job.

Tabitha arrived back at the Millennium. She took the elevator up to her floor, walked past the cleaning ladies in the hallway, and calmly entered the room with her key. When she looked into the room, she froze.

"What the fuck?" she cursed.

Someone had recklessly thrown her clothes all around the room and had dug into all of her luggage. They had no intention of being discreet. They obviously *wanted* her to know that they had been there.

Tabitha walked back out into the hallway with the cleaning ladies.

"Did you see anyone come out of this room?" she asked one of them, who was still in the hallway.

The immigrant woman looked at her in confusion.

"No," she answered.

"Did any of you go in this room yet?"

The woman shook her head. She then walked to the room to take a peek inside.

"Ohhh," she hummed. "Who did that?"

"That's what I'm trying to find out," Tabitha told her. "I don't know who did it."

They stood there in dismay before Tabitha announced, "Okay, let me try and figure this thing out."

She shut the door to be alone. She didn't want the woman to continue staring at all of her personal things spread around the room.

"What the hell is going on?" she asked herself as she began to organize the mess.

The hotel phone was blinking with messages left there as well.

Tabitha sat down at the desk phone and retrieved them.

The first message was from Angela. She sounded hysterical:

"I don't know what you said to that girl today, but some guys just grabbed me and forced me to tell them everything I know about you. I've been trying to get you on your cell phone to warn you, but you weren't answering.

"They were two black guys, dressed in dark suits, like detectives or something. They were asking me all kinds of questions about what we were doing.

"So be *careful*, Teresa. That's the name I gave them for you. But I don't know what's going on right now. I'll just keep trying to call you."

The second message was from Wallace:

"Yo, what the fuck you say to that girl in the *mall* today? Some stiff, suit-wearing muthafuckas just *bum-rushed* me about that shit!

"What you get us into, girl? They're after *you* now, so watch your ass! That's all I got to say.

"This shit is *crazy!*"

Tabitha's heart began to race as she listened to the third message, from Sylvia:

"I don't know where you are. *Hopefully* you're on the *job* right now and not on *pleasure*, if you know what I mean. But you need to *call me* when you get a chance. You know who it is."

Tabitha took a breath and continued to listen to the phone messages as if her life depended on it. The fourth message was left from the unknown voice of a man:

"We know who you are. We know who you're working for. We know what you're after. And it's not gonna happen.

"Now all you have to do is give us the diaries. Keep your mouth shut. Go back home to where you live. And we'll disappear and leave you alone."

Tabitha was frantic. They knew everything—even about her diaries.

"*Shit*!" she expressed as she listened to the last urgent message from Sylvia:

"Okay, I *need* you to call me! There's *a lot* going on, and if you're *okay* over there, then call me *immediately*!"

Right as Tabby listened to the end of the message, her cell phone rang from her carry bag and startled her.

"*Ahhh*!" she overreacted to it. Her nerves were at pressure cooker level.

She struggled to get her cell phone out of her bag with shaky hands. She looked at the screen and read the number. Sylvia was calling her again.

Tabitha answered the phone nervously. "Hello."

"Thank *God*!" Sylvia told her. She sounded relieved. She said, "I was just about to catch a flight out there. You need to get to New Jersey's Newark Liberty International Airport, *right now*! I have to get you out of there. They're on to you. So do *not* go to LaGuardia!"

"I know," Tabitha agreed with her. "I just got the messages. But you know what? We can settle all of this right now by just giving them the diaries. I'm not sweating that.

"I mean, I'm just not *feeling* this anymore," she punked out. "I was gonna tell you that last night. This isn't worth it. So I'll just give them the diary and go on back to my regular life.

"I'm *sorry*," she concluded.

Tabitha was quite determined about her decision. The money wasn't worth her loss of sanity, nor was it worth running for her life.

Sylvia said, "*Diaries?* Who asked you about diaries?" She sounded confused by it.

"They left me a message on the hotel phone right before *your* last message."

"And they asked you about *diaries*?" It didn't add up for Sylvia. "Have you been telling people about that? How would they know about that?"

Tabitha stopped and thought about it. She *hadn't* told anyone about her diaries. Angela and Wallace didn't know about them either.

Tabitha panicked anew with ill thoughts about her rendezvous with Charles Grandison, and how Sylvia had warned her to stay away from him. He was the most skeptical of the team. How convenient was it for them to ransack her hotel room right after she left to be with him.

"Did he . . ." she quizzed herself and stopped. She wondered if Charles had snuck into her bag and found her diary while she slept. But if so, why didn't he take it?

"Did he *what*?" Sylvia asked her. "Who did you tell about these diaries? Wallace?"

Tabitha snapped, "Please. I wouldn't tell that boy about anything like that. I *never* talk about my diaries. It's *personal*."

"You must have told *somebody* about it," Sylvia pressed her.

"No I *didn't*," Tabby shot back. Her sisters and foster parents were the *only* ones who knew she kept diaries. She had always written them in private and kept them to herself. Unless her family members had told people about them. But how would they connect to her job in New York?

Tabitha immediately thought of calling Marisol for questions and answers.

She told Sylvia, "You're right. How *did* they know about my diaries?" She kept her rendezvous with Charles Grandison to herself.

"I didn't know about these diaries either," Sylvia admitted. "So evidently, they know more than *I* know. And I don't particularly *like* that."

"Well, who sent *you* after me?" Tabitha questioned.

Sylvia continued to withhold that information.

"We'll talk about that once I get you out of there."

"*No,* we need to talk about that *now*!" Tabitha snapped at her.

"*You* need to get the hell out of *New York,*" Sylvia snapped back.

Tabitha could see that it was a wasted argument. She would just have to find out who employed her later.

"Okay, so what do I do with the diary? I just leave it in the room for them? I give up already."

Sylvia didn't have an answer for the diary question. She was still trying to figure that part out.

"I wouldn't leave that if I were you. If they still *want it,* then they still have to *get it* from you. So you use that as your safety net to get out of there."

"But what if I bump into them on the way to the airport?"

She was already nervous about stepping outside her hotel room.

Sylvia said, "You have to think of a way for them to allow you to get on the plane. If not, then you just tell security that they're trying to kidnap you or something. I don't know. Give me a minute to think about that."

Tabitha panicked and said, "Wait a minute, you don't *know* what to do? You're the *police* officer."

"Private investigator."

"Whatever," Tabitha huffed at her. "You got me in this mess, and all I want to do is give them the diary so I can go back to my life. They told me they would disappear and leave me alone if I gave it to them."

Sylvia was baffled. She took a breath and said, "Well, they're not out to kill anyone. They just had some rough talk with your new friends to find out who you were and where you were staying."

"Yeah, and then they came here and tore up my room, looking for the diary," Tabitha informed her.

"They were in your *room*?"

"*Yes!*" she stated.

"Well, where were you? We were all trying to call you last night."

Tabitha heard a jingle at the door. She shouted in panic, *"Who is it?!"*

"Cleaning," a meek, accented voice answered.

Tabitha yelled, "Not right now!" She got up to make sure the latch was on the door. It was. She returned to the phone.

She told Sylvia, "Look, unless you can get me a police escort out of here, if I run into these guys on the way out, I'm just gonna give them what they want and tell them I don't remember a *thing*."

Sylvia said, "Stay in the room and I'll see what I can do."

"All right," Tabitha agreed in haste. She had managed to dodge the question about her whereabouts the night before.

As soon as she hung up the phone with Sylvia, she called Marisol at her apartment, bent on letting her sister have it about the diaries and information on her trip to New York. She was wondering if Marisol had run her mouth over the phone to a stranger the last couple of days. She said there had been a volume of calls there.

Marisol answered the phone in a panic herself. "Hello."

"It's me," Tabitha barked at her.

Mari beat her to the punch.

"Tabby, somebody broke into your place last night and went through all of your things."

Tabitha stopped with her plans and said, "What?"

Marisol explained, "I went over to my friend's place last night, like you told me to do, and when I got back to the apartment this morning . . . I mean, everything was just all *over* the place. But it doesn't look like they *took* anything. So I don't know what they wanted."

She said, "It looks like a wild *animal* was in here."

Tabitha was *really* confused after Marisol's information.

She had hidden her old diaries at her apartment to keep them away from Mari, but what did the *old* diaries have to do with the New York situation?

"Something real *weird* is going on right now," she commented to her sister.

"Why, what's happening in New York?" Marisol asked her.

"Somebody broke into my place *here,* too," Tabitha answered. "And they were looking for my *diaries,*" she emphasized. "Now, have you *told* anybody about that, Mari?"

Mari answered emphatically, "*No!* Why would I do that? Especially after you just kicked my *ass* over it. I've never said anything about your diaries to anybody outside our family. And the only reason *we* know is because we all *started* them together. You were just the only one who kept going with it."

"Well, somebody obviously wants them now," Tabitha told her.

Mari said, "It's probably one of those—"

She stopped herself from saying it, but it was the only idea that made any sense.

"From one of these rich *guys* I've been dealing with, right?" Tabitha finished.

"Well . . ." Marisol hinted. She said, "I'm sure a lot of them wouldn't want you keeping a *record* of the things you did, especially if they're *married* and whatnot."

Tabitha thought it over. *Who* had known about her diaries? Why were they searching for them *now*? And *how* was it all connected to her mission in New York?

Nothing added up. Tabitha drew a blank and became frustrated.

"This is . . . What the *hell*?" she expressed out loud.

"You have no idea, do you?" Mari questioned her. "Mmm, hmm, I bet you'll think *twice* about that diary now, *and* about how you live."

Tabitha was speechless. Would Marisol be vengeful enough to put her in a bad situation and then lie to her about it? Tabitha doubted it.

She paced the hotel room, thinking of any of the men she had been with who may have had a reason to fear something she had written about them. Of course, the Isaac Abraham situation came to mind. However, she had never had any connection to him outside their recent two-minute meeting. Why would he have people looking for diaries at her house?

"Somebody knows more than they're fucking telling me," Tabitha snapped to her sister.

"Well, I *told* you everything that *I know*," Marisol insisted. "I haven't told anybody about your *diaries* either," she repeated.

"Okay, well, with these phone calls that I'm getting, has anyone asked you a bunch of questions?"

"Questions like what?"

"I don't know, about where I'm at or whatever."

"Yeah, they all wanted to know that."

"And did you tell them I was in New York?"

"No, I did not," Marisol told her. She finally said, "Look, do you think I'm a fool or what? Now, I may have read your diaries the other day, and I admitted that I was *wrong*, but I don't give out your personal information like that."

"You *joke* about it," Tabitha reminded her.

"Yeah, but anybody can joke about shit, Tabby. That don't make it *true*."

"Yeah, but still. You can give people *ideas* with that."

"*Whatever*. If you're trying to *accuse* me of something I didn't *do*, then I'm gonna defend myself. I'm not gonna let you just *pin* anything you want on me. So forget about that shit."

Tabitha scratched the Marisol hunch and started thinking again about who had hired her for the New York job. Only Sylvia had that information.

"I'll call you back when I figure out what's going on," she told her sister.

"Yeah, you do that."

Tabitha called Sylvia back.

"Hello," Sylvia answered.

Tabby informed her, "Somebody trashed my apartment in Las Vegas looking for my diaries, too. Now are you ready to tell me who hired me for this job? Because things are not making sense, and I don't know what it all has to do with Isaac Abraham.

"I barely spoke to the man, and everything I have on him is in the diary that I have in my bag. In fact, I haven't even written his name in the book. So why would he have people trash my apartment at home? How would he even know where I *live*?" she added.

Sylvia responded, "First of all, you don't know *what* he's capable of. They're obviously sending you a message that you're out of your *league* here, and I'm obviously out of *mine*. Now I'm trying to get you some protection for your flight home as we speak. So if you'll just hold tight, we'll get to the bottom of this *together*."

"Yeah, that's easy for *you* to say, nobody's after *your* shit," Tabitha snapped at her.

Sylvia took a breath and said, "Let me work this out for you. You're not doing yourself any good by not allowing me to do my job."

"And what is your *job,* to get fuckin' *paid* by sending me on a crazy-ass *mission*?!"

Tabitha had finally lost all of her cool.

"You need to calm down," Sylvia told her.

"No, *you* need to tell me who the hell *hired* me!" she shouted instead.

Sylvia paused a minute, while the girl calmed down and waited.

She said, "I was told by *my* contact that he represents a wealthy banker, and the whole story about the banker's daughter and Isaac Abraham. They then gave me all of the information on *you,* set up the scenario, and asked if you would be willing to do it."

"A wealthy *banker*?" Tabitha repeated. She started to think about who she had dated who was a banker.

"Yes," Sylvia told her. "We'll sit down and talk it all through once I get you out of there. But now I have to redial the call that I was on to get you some protection."

"And why was that information such a big secret?" Tabitha asked her.

"Just like you want *your* privacy . . . they wanted *theirs,*" Sylvia answered.

Tabitha said, "Yeah, and Isaac Abraham wants *his* privacy, too. So this is *all* hypocritical, just like I thought in the beginning. It was my dumb fault for doing it, though," she admitted. "Now I have to sit down and figure out who this guy is because you obviously don't even know."

Sylvia was silent. She said, "Do you want me to get you out of there or not?"

"Yeah," Tabitha answered. "Please . . . get me the hell out of here."

"That's what I'm trying to do," Sylvia told her. "I'll get right back to you on it."

All the King's Horses . . .

Tabitha sat breathing heavily on the edge of her hotel bed while thinking.

A wealthy banker? Who do I know who's a banker?

She had been with successful men of every trade, but the banker drew a blank. Would she even be attracted to a banker? What kind of men were bankers?

Before long, her cell phone rang again. She looked at the screen and read Wallace's number.

She answered it with concern. "Wallace, are you okay?"

"Yeah, I'm cool. I was more concerned about *you*," he told her. "Have you talked to Angela?"

"I got her message like I got yours, but I haven't spoken to her yet."

He said, "I just tried to call her and didn't get an answer. I talked to her a couple of times last night, while we were both trying to find you. She was talking about getting to the bottom of things after they sent those crews after us last night."

"You think it was Isaac's people?" Tabitha quizzed. She didn't think so anymore.

Wallace said, "Yeah. Who else could it be?"

"Who did Angela think it was?"

"Isaac's B- or C-team," he answered. "He has a whole lot of people connected to him who you never even *see* half the time. Money draws peculiar crowds, you know."

Tabitha kept her thoughts to herself on that.

She said, "I'll try and call her after I hang up with you."

"Oh, so now you rushing me off the phone. Well, where were you last night?" he asked her.

"I was minding my own. Now let me try to call her."

"Aw, it's like that?"

"It has to be," she snapped. She was not in the mood for playfulness. Under the present circumstances, she figured Wallace should not have been in a playful mood himself.

"Well, be safe, because they're still after you," he told her.

Angela's cell phone went off in a parked car somewhere in New York. An apprehensive henchman looked at it and frowned.

"Aw'ight, now answer the phone this time," his larger partner piped at him from the driver's seat. They sat in an ordinary gray sedan.

"And say what? You know I ain't in'na all that talking. *You* do it."

The larger man twisted his face in irritation. "Give it here to me then."

The smaller man gave the cell phone to the larger man, who answered the ring in silence.

"Hello . . . hello," a young woman's voice asked over the line.

The larger man nodded his head to his smaller partner. It sounded like their mark.

"Is this Teresa?" he asked her.

There was a pregnant pause.

"Who wants to know?"

"Your friend Angela wants to know. She needs your help," the man told her. He and his partner both wore the dark, oversize, nondescript clothing of many urban New Yorkers.

"Where is she?"

He ignored her. He said, "She needs you to give us what we need, so we can *end* this thing."

There was another pause.

"Where do you want me to leave it?" the young woman asked.

The man looked at the phone screen to read the number where she was calling from. He said, "Someone will call you back in five minutes and tell you."

"Let me speak to Angela," she repeated.

"You'll speak to her after we get what we need."

"No, I'll speak to her before I give you *anything*," she contested.

The man hung up the line on her. He shook his head at his partner and said, "Women."

His partner chuckled. The man then took out his own cell phone and called another number.

"Yeah, it's us. She's back at the hotel."

"Did you talk to her?"

"Yeah."

"Does she know what we want?"

"Yup."

"Is she gonna give it to us?"

He hesitated. "She wanted to speak to the girl. That can't happen now. So dodge that question."

"Where is the girl?" the man on the other line asked.

The man behind the wheel of the gray sedan took a breath to explain the situation.

"She wanted to fight us, so she didn't make the car ride."

His partner held in his laugh from the passenger seat.

"You're not saying what I *think* you're saying," the man on the line questioned.

"Take it how you wanna take it."

"Got'*dammit*! That was *stupid*!"

"Look, man, accidents happen. Deal with it."

"That's not a damn *accident*! That's a major *fuck up*!"

The big man looked at his partner and whispered, "Fuck he think he talkin' to?"

He said, "Aw'ight, whatever, do what you need to do," and hung up.

He looked again to his partner in the passenger seat. "Aw'ight, Scrap. Our job is done. Let's hit the road."

He started up the gray sedan and drove off.

His partner asked him, "They didn't want the girl killed?"

"Naw," the driver answered. "They want this other girl's diaries."

The partner looked confused. "Why?"

"Fuck if I know, man. She must'a wrote some shit they don't like. I would just kill her ass, too. But these other muthafuckas are softies, I guess."

"What's up with the guy who hired us? He just wants to bring down Isaac Abraham, hunh?"

The driver grinned and nodded. "Yup. He's a crazy muthafucka wit' money. But I don't ask that many questions, man, just *pay me.*"

"That's kind of fucked up, though, that he's after Isaac Abraham like that. I *like* his movies," the partner commented.

"Yeah, I like his movies, too, man. But fuck it, he ain't helping *us* to eat."

"And you think this whole thing'll bring him down?"

"Well, his boy *Teddy*'s in trouble after they find this girl dead. She did us a *big* favor by arguing wit' his ass out in public last night. That shit was *perfect,*" the driver stated with a laugh.

"Yeah, and we just snatched her ass up right afterward," the partner added with a sinister grin of his own.

"So if the other girl did her job and wrote the shit in her diary, then it's all *gravy*. All the fingers'll point back to them," the driver concluded.

They were impressed with all the details. It was a well-crafted job.

"So when you wanna get something to eat, man?" the partner asked.

The driver looked irritated again. "Shit, nigga, let's get out of New York first. I don't even wanna stop in New Jersey. Let's eat in Pennsylvania some-where."

"*Pennsylvania?* Aw, man, that's an *hour* from here," the partner com-plained.

The driver snapped, "Nigga, don't you even *try'da* act like you ain't went an hour without *food* before. 'Cause I *know* ya' ass used to starvin'."

They shared a laugh while they headed southwest, out of New York.

Out in Las Vegas, an older man wearing a brown velour sweat suit received another call on his cell phone. It had been ringing incessantly that morning. Nevertheless, he remained calm as he walked The Strip in the early morning for fresh air and exercise.

"Yes," he answered.

"They offed the girl," his New York contacts informed him.

The man stopped walking. "What?"

"Not our girl, the other one. The one from New York," they explained further.

"Oh," the man responded. He started walking again. He said, "That wasn't part of the plan."

"We know that."

"Well, did you get it?"

"Not yet, but she's willing to give it to us. But now she wants to speak to the other girl first. How'd they do out there?"

"They found her place full of moving boxes packed with everything but the diaries," the man answered. "This girl sure knows how to hide her private things. But I doubt if she took them all to New York. They have to be around *here* somewhere. So we can actually back off her in New York now. We just wanted them to suspect you know who."

He said, "We'll allow her to come home *untouched,* and then we'll find out where she hid them once she gets here. Have our P.I. out there escort her to the airport. In the meantime, I have to deal with this P.I. out here before our girl gets back," he told them. "We don't need any more helpers on her side."

"So, we don't even call her back?" the New York contact asked.

"You don't even call her back," the older man in Vegas responded. "You just let her catch her flight back home."

The man hung up on his call from New York and took out a second cell phone to call Atlanta.

In Atlanta, Henry Anderson, a striking older man in a tailored suit and a designer tie, sat at his desk in his downtown office. He was viewing a competitor's website in the field of venture capitalism. A picture of his family sat out on the desk. There was also a solo picture of his oldest daughter. She looked captivating with spirit and sparkle in her eyes.

Henry answered the phone on the third ring. "Yeah."

"Your friend in New York still wants to play by his own rules," his Las Vegas contact informed him.

"I wouldn't exactly call him a friend," Henry commented. "What did he do now?"

"They silenced the New York girl. *Permanently.*"

Henry gave his full attention to the conversation.

"We need to cut us a deal out of this thing. He's gone too far."

"You just tell me the deal, and I'll cut it," his Las Vegas man told him.

Henry said, "You get to the girl, and you offer her what she needs for the diaries. Otherwise, we could be left holding the bag on this thing."

"All right. I'm on it as soon as she touches down in the plane."

When they hung up, Henry Anderson sat and thought for a minute. He looked over at his daughter's picture on his desk and felt for her. She was heartbroken by the dream of possessing an older man, one more powerful, popular, attractive, and loved than he. And although he felt inspired to mend her broken heart, he realized now that it was a hasty decision to get involved with a desperate New Yorker. After his embarrassing fallout with the A-team, Walt Nesbitt, the former celebrity lawyer, had obviously grown *reckless* to exact his revenge. How far was he willing to go?

Henry took a breath and took out his cell phone to call White Plains, New York.

Walt Nesbitt watched the local news in the plush office in the basement of his White Plains home. He leaned back in his black leather office chair wearing silk pajamas and a house robe with nowhere to go. He had lost much over the past three years: his client list, his family, his dignity, but he had managed to survive it all by investing well. However, his *latest* investment was of particular and personal interest to him—to take down the man who had left him out to dry.

"Here comes another lucky call," he told himself as his cell phone went off. He expected updates all morning long. "Yup," he answered his cell phone jovially.

"You've turned up the heat a little too much for comfort."

It was Henry Anderson calling him from Atlanta.

Walt responded, "No-o-o, not at all. It feels *nice* and warm to *me*. And it's about to get even *hotter*. Your Las Vegas girl was damned good. I gotta give it to you. I'm *excited* now."

Henry said, "We didn't need that kind of, ah . . . excitement. Everything was going along fine as it was."

"Maybe for you. But just like you have ties to sever with these diaries, I have mine. But my girl didn't have any diaries, she had her mouth. So we had to close it."

Henry paused to think that over a minute.

He said, "It's not fair on my end of this thing for you to have ulterior motives that you didn't explain. I explained everything that *I* needed going in to this."

"And I got you back in *business,* didn't I?" Walt huffed at him. "Now, as far as this diary thing goes, that's just something you're gonna have to work out. I gave you enough *help* on it. Just *take* the damn things from her," he advised. "Stop fucking around with it. You want *me* to do it?"

"No," Henry told him immediately. "I'll handle it."

"Well, handle it then, because things are *definitely* about to get *hot.*"

When they hung up, Walt was pumped with adrenaline. He stood up from his leather office chair and paced the dark room. He had all of his plaques and achievement awards there from years of great work. A career that had gone down the drain.

"Fuck Isaac Abraham!" he spat into the air. "He's gonna find out what a *real* grand performance is."

He got on his phone and made a call to his contact at the New York newspaper.

"*The Post,*" his guy answered.

"It's about to go down," Walt told him. "So keep your pen ready and call the cameramen."

"Will do."

Private investigator Keith Calvins paced his office on the lower end of the Bronx while smoking his third cigarette in an hour. He was nervously awaiting a phone call with his new orders.

"This is crazy," he told himself. "Never again will I get involved in something like this. I'm just gon' take this money, go on a long vacation somewhere, and set up a new office in Florida."

He finally got his phone call.

"Calvins," he answered.

"You can take the girl to the airport now. When you come back, we'll have you pay the guy to keep his mouth shut. And then you'll get *your* last payment."

"Okay," he told them. He hung up the phone and waited for a minute, before he called back out to Las Vegas.

"Hello," Sylvia Green answered. She had been his friend for years. He had even talked her into trying the private investigator business after years on the police force.

Calvins told her, "I'm on my way to take her to the airport now."

"Thank God," she told him. "I'll call her and let her know. But have you heard anything from the Angela girl today? Tabitha just called me and said that they had her held captive or something. I was just about to call you back on that. She said some men answered the girl's phone when she called."

Calvins answered, "I didn't hear anything about that." And he hadn't. He wondered if his New York contacts had grabbed her. But they hadn't mentioned anything about it.

"I'll call her while I'm on my way," he told Sylvia.

She said, "And call me right back so I can tell her something at the hotel. This is really getting crazy, but what did I expect," she commented.

"Who you tellin'?" Calvins agreed with her. He hung up the phone and was hesitant to call Angela. He knew in his gut that something was wrong. He had gut feelings on a lot of things. He now wished he hadn't ignored his gut on turning down this job, despite the money.

He called Angela's cell phone anyway.

"Hello," someone answered. It was another woman.

"Who is this?" Calvins asked her.

"Oh, I just found this phone in the trash. I figured it must belong to somebody. So I just picked it up and waited for someone to call."

"Where are you right now?" he asked her.

"In Harlem."

Calvins told her, "Hold onto that phone, and I'll call you back." He hung up and immediately called his contacts. They were the same two guys who reported to Henry Anderson's man in Las Vegas.

"Yeah," they answered.

"What happened to Angela?" he asked them.

"We don't know. Isaac's people must have gotten her. We heard she was arguing with Teddy last night. Things are working faster than we expected."

Calvins didn't trust their explanation. It sounded rehearsed. But what else could he do?

He said, "You're right. This thing is really speeding up."

He ended the call with them and called Sylvia back.

"There's no word on Angela," he told her. "I just called her cell phone and a woman in Harlem answered it. She said she picked it up out the trash can."

Sylvia froze, thinking the worst. "What do you think they did with her?"

"I don't know what the hell is going on right now," he admitted. "They're trying to blame it all on Isaac's team. So the best thing we can do now is get your girl on a plane out of here."

He felt guilty about putting the girls in harm's way, as did Sylvia. However, everyone was in agreement to get paid. It was the root of all their hasty decisions.

Sylvia said, "I'll just call her back and keep her calm. We have to get her on that plane."

Calvins responded, "Yeah, let's do that."

. . . And All the King's Men

Sylvia called Tabitha back at the hotel.

"Okay, they obviously have Angela to get to you. But *you're* who they really want, so we have to get you out of there," she told her. "Private investigator Keith Calvins is on his way to get you safely to the airport."

"Is he the one who contacted Angela and Wallace?" Tabitha asked her.

"Yes," Sylvia answered. She could no longer hide information from her. The cat was out of the bag. Sylvia was much more concerned about Tabitha's welfare now.

"How well do you two know each other?"

Tabitha had been thinking a mile a minute while waiting there at the hotel. She was determined to piece things together for herself.

Sylvia answered, "We've known each other for a few years."

"And who was contacted for this job first, him or you?"

Sylvia became hesitant again. She answered the question anyway.

"He called me on it. Then I had a meeting with my contact in Las Vegas."

"So *he* sold you on this job *first*," Tabitha stated.

"Yeah, you can say that," Sylvia agreed.

"Okay. And he's coming to get me now?"

"Yes he is."

≈

When Calvins called from the hotel lobby, Tabitha was all packed up and ready for him with a million questions on her mind.

"I'm just letting you know that I'm coming up," he told her.

"I'm ready," was all she said at the moment.

She hung up and mumbled, "I'm gonna get to the bottom of this. They wanna play games."

Once he arrived, Calvins took a breath and knocked on her door.

Tabitha looked through the peephole at a slim, brown man with a trimmed mustache and beard, wearing a black leather jacket.

She opened the door and said, "Okay, you grab those two bags, and I'll take this one."

He smiled. "You got it all organized, hunh?"

Tabitha didn't have a response for him. What was the use? They had a plane to catch. She figured she'd ask him all of her questions once they got in his car.

She hustled up the hallway beside him to catch the elevators.

"I know this has been shocking for you, but it's been an adventure for *all* of us," he told her.

"An *adventure*?" she asked him.

"What else would you call it? We all got ourselves involved, right?" he responded.

They both went silent while surrounded by other passengers on the elevator.

Once they walked out at the lobby level, Tabitha said, "There are plenty of things I would call this, but *'an adventure'* is not one of them."

Calvins was already impressed by her self-control. He was testing her emotional willpower. A less tactful woman would have let him have it while still inside the elevators.

They made it to the front door of the hotel and paused.

Calvins said, "You stay right on my hip. Once we make it to the car, we should be okay."

She nodded to him.

They walked out with her luggage and made it up the street to his car without any altercations. They then placed her luggage in his trunk.

"All right, so far, so good," he told her.

He shut the passenger door behind her and climbed in on the driver's side for the trip to the airport.

"You know I'm flying from Newark now, right?" she told him as soon as they hit the road.

Calvins snapped his fingers. "That's right. New Jersey."

She asked him, "How much did you know about me before I got here?"

He looked at her and answered, "Not much."

"How much did you know about Angela?"

"I knew a little bit more about her. You know, she gets around."

He smiled and looked away when he said it.

"What does that mean?" Tabitha quizzed him.

Calvins didn't want to say what he was thinking.

"What, she's *hot*? Is that what you knew about her? And you think the same about me?"

He was trying not to engage in an argument with her.

He said, "You were hired to do a job that, ah . . . well, everyday girls wouldn't be able to do."

"And what is an everyday girl?"

"A girl who doesn't live to be in the nightlife circles," he answered.

"Well, somebody wanted to pay me new *house* money to get inside this *New York* circle. Why is that?" she asked him.

She caught Calvins off guard with it. He had to look away again. She was increasing his feelings of guilt.

He mumbled, "We figured it was for a good cause."

"Bullshit!" she snapped at him. "The cause was good *money*. Even *I* had to admit to that. So we're all *pawns* to these big money spenders who are playing the real game here. And I wanna know who *hired* me."

Calvins refused to meet her eyes.

She asked him, "Who approached *you* about this?"

He said, "Look here, when this is all over, we can all take what we learned from it and move on as smarter individuals."

"*If* we move on from it. It's not over with *yet*," she stated. "What happens when Isaac Abraham's people catch on to what we're doing? You think they're gonna take it lying down?"

Calvins became suspect of how much she knew at that point.

"What do you mean?" he quizzed her.

She said, "Pawns are sacrificed for the bigger pieces, aren't they? That's what the men in the *circles* taught me. So even *you* can be sacrificed. How much do they value *you*? They obviously don't value me or Angela."

He didn't respond. They were already out of New York City and on their way to the Newark airport exits from the New Jersey Turnpike.

"So *bankers* have that much money to pay for everyone's *silence,* hunh?" Tabitha questioned.

Calvins looked stunned. He said, "How much do you know?" He was ready to pull over on the side of the road and have a private talk with her about keeping her mouth shut.

"I know I must have dated the man and written about him in my diary, since they want it so badly," she told him. She was showing too much trust in a virtual stranger. He even told her so.

"I would watch who you talk to about how much you know. My advice to you would be to think this thing through while you're on the plane, and find a way to walk away from it. But if you're out here trying to solve mysteries . . . things can get real dangerous," he warned her.

Tabitha took the hint and found her cool again. She had to make her flight, and she couldn't allow her mouth to stop her. The man obviously had his own ass to protect, whether he was trying to help her or not.

They made it to the airport gates without further conversation. Tabitha realized by then that Calvins wasn't on her side. He was simply doing what he needed to do to move his assignment along.

"Be careful," he told her at the departure drop-off. "And remember, you *need* to think this thing through. Are those diaries worth your life?"

It was a final warning. She could expect to trust no one.

As soon as Tabitha checked her bags and made it through the security gates, she got on her cell phone and called home to Marisol. She could kick herself for not deciding to make the call earlier. Marisol was not safe.

"Hello."

"Mari, you need to get out of the apartment," Tabby told her sister in a rush.

"What?"

"Look, I found out more about these break-ins, and you're not safe out there, so just do what I *tell you*!" she shouted into the phone. Other travelers at the airport began to look in her direction.

Mari said, "Where am I supposed to go? I don't even have any—"

"Go back to your *friend*'s house!" Tabitha yelled at her. "Call Patrice from there, and I'll get back to you that way. But you need to get away from the apartment *right now*!

"I'll try and get you on a flight back out to Seattle as soon as I can, but my plane's ready to leave for a connection in Chicago now," she explained.

It was definitely the wrong time for Marisol's attitude problems. Fortunately, she caught on to Tabby's urgency.

"All right, I'll see where I can go."

"And don't go *back* to the apartment," she was warned. "Don't worry about packing up all your clothes or anything, just *leave.*"

"Are you serious?" Marisol asked to make sure.

"*Yes,* I'm serious!"

"All right. I'm leaving now."

By the time Tabitha boarded her plane at three o'clock, Teddy Liggins was walking out of a New York precinct, free on bail. He had been arrested and held for over an hour as a suspect in the murder of Angela Simmons, who was found strangled to death in a Harlem alleyway. At least a dozen people had spotted Teddy in a heated argument with the young woman the night before. Evidently, Angela had never made it back home that night. She was found wearing the same clothes.

J.J. bailed Teddy out as fast as the law would allow him. News cameras and reporters were on the scene faster than ants to an opened bag of cookies.

They were jamming their cameras and microphones in his direction.

"Teddy, you've had a known history of womanizing. Has it finally caught up with you?"

"The majority of the so-called A-team has had run-ins with underage girls. Is there a competition going on between you guys?"

"Is it true that you were loaded from the bar last night? You didn't know what you were doing when you strangled her?"

"Why did you have to kill her, *asshole*?! You need some *therapy!*"

Several bodyguards pushed and shoved the cameras and microphones back as Teddy made it to the awaiting stretch limo, with J.J. leading the way.

Once inside, Teddy and J.J. joined Derrick, Charles, Rafael, Michael Bent, and Isaac.

The driver took off as soon as the doors were closed and locked shut.

Teddy looked down the line inside the limo and into the steely eyes of Isaac and Michael Bent, who sat at the opposite end near the driver's seat.

No one said a word until Isaac spoke.

"Teddy . . . what the hell is going on here?" He asked, "Do you know how embarrassing it was for you to get arrested right in the middle of a press conference? I mean, who wrote this shit?"

"It *had* to be written," Michael Bent spoke up in his wire-rimmed glasses. "You couldn't *beat* the timing."

"No bullshit," Rafael agreed.

Isaac held up his hand for silence.

He said, "All right. What's your side of the story, Teddy?"

Teddy shook his head. He said, "All I know is that she came running at me last night, talking about I sent some guys after her. I didn't know what the hell she was talking about."

"You sent some guys after her for what?" Isaac asked him.

Teddy stuttered, "Man, I—, I don't know. I don't know what she was talking about."

"Because you were drunk," Rafael interjected.

"I had a few, but I wasn't drunk. Naw."

"Do you remember anything that she said, *specifically*?" J.J. asked him.

Teddy stopped and thought about it.

"Come on now, you're the publicist. You gotta know what she said. Spit it out," Isaac instigated.

"She said she knows it was me . . . who sent two guys to hassle her . . . about her girlfriend or something."

Teddy was trying to piece it all back together in his mind.

"What girlfriend?" Isaac asked him.

"I don't know. She said something about . . . the girlfriend being at the premiere party . . . as if I knew who she was talking about."

For a second, Charles creased his brow. The premiere party rang a bell for him.

Isaac said, "Okay, you know what *I* know, Teddy. I know that somebody put Angela on the guest list for the premiere party, and then you took her back to the Marriott and laid your wood on her ass. Now are you gonna tell me that that didn't happen?"

All eyes were on Teddy inside the limo.

He answered, "I'm not gon' tell you that."

Rafael began to snicker.

Isaac held up his hand for silence again.

He said, "You not gon' tell me what?"

"That I didn't do that."

"So you admit it then?" Michael Bent asked him.

Teddy shrugged his shoulders. "It ain't nothing but a thing, man. We all do that."

"We all don't go to jail for murder," Isaac stated.

"Isaac, you know I didn't murder that girl."

"Yeah, we all know you're not a murderer. But what *I'm* more interested in is why this girl was *allowed* back around us in the first place," Isaac questioned. "Isn't this the same girl who was around you and *Walt* years ago?" he alluded.

All of them realized how taboo it was in their circle to mention Walt Nesbitt's name, the lawyer who grew to think he was bigger than his star client. J.J. knew his place and allowed Isaac to call the shots.

"Have you been in contact with her recently?" Isaac asked Teddy of the girl.

Teddy shook his head.

"Naw, she just popped up out of nowhere, talking about she had been thinking about me."

Isaac smiled. "And you *believed* that shit?"

"Why can't she be thinking about me?"

Charles remembered that his mystery girl, Tonya Kennedy, didn't show up until *after* Teddy had left the party with Angela. Maybe they needed Teddy out of the way. Then Charles went ahead and introduced Tonya to Isaac, two nights after Teddy had first met her. The girl was also spotted at the theater for the film premiere. However, Charles kept all of his knowledge to himself. He figured he would handle it on his own. Things would be done a lot cleaner that way.

Isaac said, "We're now on media alert, and we're supposed to be heading to Atlanta tonight."

Charles spoke up, "You wanna cancel that and handle business here?"

Isaac shook his head and answered, "No. If *you're* thinking about it, then *you* handle it here; you, J.J., and Teddy. I'm heading to Atlanta," he told them. "One monkey don't stop no show."

Teddy heard that and dropped his head into his lap.

Charles nodded to Isaac, eye to eye on the situation. "That's what we'll do then," he said. "We'll straighten this out, and you head to Atlanta as planned."

On the way back from taking the girl to the Newark airport, Keith Calvins became nervous. What if she ran her mouth about what she knew anyway? He knew *he* hadn't told her anything. But what would *they* think? Would they think he was lying about it?

After thinking it all over, he decided that the girl was right; he was a mere pawn himself.

Calvins immediately jumped on the phone and called Sylvia in Las Vegas.

"Hello."

"Yeah, this is Keith."

"She made it on the plane?" Sylvia asked him.

"Yeah, but . . ."

He stopped and allowed Sylvia to push the buttons.

"But what?" she asked him.

"She, ah . . . started talking about *bankers* and so forth, and people being paid off to be quiet. I tried to tell her to keep things in perspective, because we were *all* doing this under the radar. If you know what I mean."

He said, "Now, I know *I* didn't tell her about this *banker* situation, but if this shit hits the frying pan, I don't think they're gonna *care* who told her."

Sylvia heard his words and realized what he was saying. She had to nip the situation in the bud, or face the firing squad of questions.

"Okay," she told him. "I'll handle it before she even gets out here. She connects planes in Chicago. I'll catch her on her cell phone and talk to her about it then."

Calvins hung up with her and was still unsatisfied. He needed more security. He thought about it further and took a breath before calling his contact in the city.

"Yeah."

"It's Calvins."

"She get on the plane?"

"Safe and sound."

"Good."

Calvins said, "But, ah . . ."

"What?"

"She sounded like she had a whole lot more *coaching* than I thought on this thing. And she was telling me things that *I* didn't even have answers for."

"Things like what?"

"Where the money was coming from," Calvins informed him.

There was a pause.

"Did she know?"

"Sounds like she was smart enough *not* to tell me, but at the same time, she told me enough to let me know that she *knows*."

"What exactly did she say?"

Calvins was forced to be creative.

"She said something to the effect of, ah, 'Somebody has access to a whole lot of money here. Are they just holding it, or can they allocate what they want when they want to?' "

He said, "Now I'm no *Einstein* or anything like that, but it sounds to me like she was telling me something."

There was more silence over the line.

"We'll get back to you," his contact told him.

Calvins hung up the phone and felt miserable and relieved at the same time.

He mumbled to himself as he reached the Lincoln Tunnel back into New York. "I just need to make it through this shit, and then I'll never do this shit again."

Out in Las Vegas, Sylvia received a call from *her* local contact while she drove back to her small office. She had eaten out for lunch to clear her head.

"We need to, ah, reconfigure this deal," she was told by the Las Vegas show runner.

"How do you mean?" she asked him.

"Your girl has access to some documents we need to have, and we're now willing to offer her the *balance* amount of this job for those documents. We also need her to, ah . . . remain in the shadows from here on."

Sylvia read in to it. "So, she's done all she needs to do then?"

"Outside of turning over those documents, yes."

"Well, what kind of documents are these?"

"She knows what they are."

The diaries? Sylvia thought to herself. *This thing is getting more complicated by the minute.*

She said, "So, you want me to offer her the rest, just to turn over these documents, and then disappear?"

"That's what we want."

Sylvia said, "Okay. That should be doable."

"We hope that it is."

Sylvia hung up the phone and went to war with herself.

"All she has to do is give up these *diaries,* and she can start her life back over with *plenty.*"

She didn't see where the problem was with that. But now she realized that the job had nothing to do with young girls and older men.

Sylvia shook her head and mumbled, "I knew this shit was too good to be true. They had ulterior motives with this girl from the start."

It had been a long week of anticipation that she could see stretching into a lot longer, and a gigantic headache. She now wanted to clear the air of the whole case and get back to normal.

"I'll tell you one thing," she told herself, "this Tabitha is *good*. She got them all fetching a bone now."

Charles Grandison made it back to his office in Manhattan to work in privacy. Teddy went to J.J.'s office, where they all agreed to meet later on to discuss resolving the issue. Isaac and the rest of the team prepared to fly to Atlanta in their private jet that early evening.

Charles immediately called the mystery girl, Tonya Kennedy, on her cell phone and got no answer. He left his phone message hoping she would call back. He *trusted* the girl. He just needed to hear what she had to say. He had several hunches about what was going on. However, no one had been right all of the time . . . not even him.

Whom to
Trust?

On the plane ride from Newark to Chicago, Tabitha was able to think long enough to come up with a few leads. She had never dated an actual banker before, but she *had* dated an investor in Atlanta. Henry Anderson. She remembered him most by his passion to buy a percentage of the Atlanta Hawks basketball team.

Does he have a teenage daughter? she thought to herself on the plane ride. She couldn't remember. She *did* remember that Henry had always been eager to see her at the expensive Buckhead hotels where they met for their rendezvous. And she remembered that he had quite the sexual appetite. The man could go all night, and often did, while boasting of his youthful energy.

She smiled to herself and figured it highly unlikely that Henry would have her bring down another man for sleeping with minors. The pot would be calling the kettle black: She was still a teenager herself when she met Henry after a Hawks game. She was also seeing a rookie who played for the Atlanta Hawks at the time. However, an aspiring owner became much more attractive to her than an insecure rookie. So Tabitha dated up in age and in stature.

I guess he would want my diaries if he was the one, she pondered. *But how hypocritical would that be? And how would he know that I kept a diary? Did he go into my personal things? If he did, he could have taken the diaries then.*

Things were still not adding up, but at least she had some ideas.

When she arrived at Chicago O'Hare International Airport after four o'clock central standard time, she immediately checked her cell phone messages.

She had phone messages from Sylvia, Wallace, Patrice, and Charles. She read Charles's number and panicked with a heavy heart. Although it was not

Charles who they were out to defame, she realized that she had betrayed him by working to set up Isaac.

"I'm sorry, Charles," she moaned.

She found a quiet spot in Chicago's busy airport and called Sylvia back first.

"I'm in Chicago," she told her.

"Okay, good. How do you feel?" Sylvia asked.

"I'm just glad to be out of New York. But can you protect me in Las Vegas? I know they're still after my diaries. If they raided my apartment once, they can do it again."

Sylvia paused a minute. She said, "What exactly is in those diaries?"

Tabitha answered, "My life, basically. All the things that I've thought, and most of the people that I've been with."

"How many years have you been keeping them?"

"Thirteen."

"How many different books are there?"

After a while, Tabitha closed up to that line of questioning. She would have never discussed her diaries had she not believed that her life was in danger.

"Did you even try to find out who broke into my place?" she asked Sylvia instead. She added, "I may need you to help get my sister to safety."

"Where is she? Is she still at your apartment?"

"No. I told her to leave and that I would contact her. I can give her your number to call."

"Okay, I'll see what I can do."

"Did you find out anything else about Angela?" Tabitha asked next.

"Not yet," Sylvia answered.

"Well, I hope she's okay. Are they saying anything about that?"

Sylvia took a breath to compose herself and keep her facts in order. She said, "For some reason, they all seem to be concerned about these diaries of yours. The latest that I've heard is that they're now willing to pay you for them."

"For what?" Tabitha snapped. Money was no longer the issue. She needed a *reason* for the drama. *Who* wanted to pay her for the diaries? And *why*?

"They obviously want what you wrote about your life," Sylvia reasoned. "But what's it to you if they're going to give you thousands of dollars for them? You just start a new one. It's as simple as that."

Tabitha was silent inside the airport terminal. She still didn't get it. She was just one lone girl with a book of her thoughts. However, her personal thoughts *did* include her dealings with people who were *not* anonymous. That was the danger of her lifestyle. It was a bomb awaiting detonation. Whoever controlled her diaries controlled pieces of the lives of every person she ever wrote about.

Sylvia realized that she may have gone too hard on her. She backed off a little.

"Just think about it on your plane ride from Chicago," she said softly.

Tabitha mumbled, "All right," just to keep the peace. However, Sylvia seemed insensitive. Tabitha didn't even know what she would say to her once she arrived in Las Vegas. Was it all about the money now? Sylvia had first sold her on the morality of safety for confused girls. But didn't confused girls have a right to privacy? Selling her diaries was a slap in the face to everything that they had discussed.

Tabitha called Wallace back in New York to take her mind off the staleness of her conversation with Sylvia. She wondered if *Wallace* had heard any news on Angela.

He answered the phone frantically. "T, are you all right? I guess you see that they killed Angela," he stated. "It's all over the news."

Tabitha was speechless. "You're lying." She could barely breathe when she said it.

"You didn't see it on the news? Where are you? They arrested Teddy Liggins for it. I'm out of Dodge now," he told her. "So don't even ask me where I am."

Tabitha answered, "I've left New York now."

"Good idea. I'm on my way out, too."

She didn't know what else to say. She was *stunned*!

"Oh my God!" she finally let out. It seemed as if all of the energy in her body had slipped out of her. She didn't know where to turn.

"You think Teddy did it?" she asked Wallace.

Wallace was still *pumped* with energy, the nervous-as-hell kind.

"Naw, man, that dude ain't no killer," he answered. "They said she was *strangled* to death. I can't see him *strangling* nobody. All she had to do was knee him in his nuts. Somebody else did that. Them guys who snatched me up last night."

"What about the private investigator, Keith Calvins? Do you trust him?" *She* didn't trust him.

Wallace said, "Hell no! I just talked to him a minute ago. He didn't even know Angela was *killed* last night until *I* just told him. What kind of private investigator is *that*?"

"How he not gon' know?" he questioned. "Then he tried to tell me he had some money for me to keep quiet. Yeah, I'll be quiet as hell if I'm *dead,* right? I don't trust *nobody* right now."

"Good point," Tabitha agreed. His outrage brought a slight smile to her face, but that was it.

She said, "I'm scared to fly back home now."

"Don't you have *Sylvia* on the other side? She *seems* cool," he reasoned.

"At *first* she did, but now she sounds like the rest of them; they all want what *they* want," Tabby explained.

"So what you gon' do?" he asked her.

Tabitha drew a blank.

"I don't know."

"Well, my phone's about to cut off. I'll call you back in a few," Wallace told her.

"All right."

She hung up with him and prepared to call Patrice to see if she could catch up to Marisol.

"I hope that girl left the damn *house* like I *told* her to," she grumbled.

Before she made the call, someone rang her line. She read the numbers and saw that it was Charles again.

She froze. "Oh, shit! What would I even say to him?"

The line rang a second time. She ignored it and shook her head.

"He's gonna kill me," she told herself.

When it stopped ringing, she found that she was unable to call Patrice. She felt she had unfinished business to address with Charles first.

"He's just gonna curse me the hell out and call me all kinds of names," she imagined. "I know he *knows* by now. It was all a setup . . . but I really *like* him, though," she admitted.

She breathed heavily and stared at the phone.

"I don't believe I'm about to do this."

She went ahead and called him back anyway.

"Was it hard not to call?" he asked her when he answered.

That was all he needed to say to put her back under his spell.

"What do you think?"

"I think I just want to hear what you have to say."

The man used his words like a sword. He cut through all the bullshit with such precision that it left her numb.

She said, "I really like you."

"That's not what I want to hear right now. I think you have something *else* to tell me."

She felt a headache drop from the ceiling and smack her upside the head.

"Mmmph," she moaned. She massaged her temple with her left hand.

He said, "You know I know. I just need to know *why*."

"I, umm . . . don't know why I did it," she told him.

"How much were you paid?" he asked her. He knew she didn't do it for free. That would have made no sense at all. And if other people were involved in it, then what was *her* part?

Tabitha hesitated to come clean.

Charles said, "When you called me back, you *knew* what you had to do. Murder's not something they can just brush under the rug. Do you even *care* about this girl?"

Tabitha didn't answer him immediately. It came out slowly. She had to build up to it.

"Of course I do," she answered.

"Well, you should help me to solve her murder. You *know* that Teddy didn't do it."

"Right," she agreed with him.

"So, what were you paid to do?"

She sighed. "I was paid to get close enough to Isaac . . . to build up some dirt on him . . . so some people could expose his lifestyle with young girls."

She realized that her life was in Charles's hands now. What would he do with it?

"What people?" he asked her calmly.

"I wasn't told."

He paused a minute.

He asked her, "Have you ever heard the name Walt Nesbitt?"

"Yeah. Angela talked about him."

"What did she say?"

"She said that he would never try anything against Isaac."

"Why wouldn't he?"

"She said because he *knows* better."

"Hmmph," Charles grunted. "Sounds like she didn't know who the hell she was dealing with. It was only a matter of *time* before Walt tried something stupid. He's always been a reckless nigga."

Tabitha felt Charles's edge for the first time. She sat silently at the airport and awaited his next question. She wondered if he would press all the right buttons for her full confession. She still felt uneasy about a lot of it.

"What have you found out so far?" he asked her. "Because if they killed *her,* and you're still alive, it must be for a reason."

Tabitha opened her mouth and said, "Raven Johns."

"What about her?"

"I said some real bad things to her in Queens. We got all of her information and followed her to the mall from her school. She was driving a dark blue Lexus, an IS 300," she added.

"What did you say to her?"

Out of nowhere, tears formed in Tabitha's eyes. She needed to release her guilt. She needed somebody to understand. She couldn't understand why she had done it herself. It felt as if someone else had done it. An evil twin.

"I told her that I was one of Isaac's many girls, and that he was in trouble for dealing with minors in his hometown of Detroit. I said that investigators would be looking for more girls to testify in court against him. And I told her that . . . you know . . . she needs to look out for herself because I know that he won't stand by her."

Tears escaped and rolled down her face. She immediately wiped them away while out in public. She felt trapped between two mountains, and was looking for shelter. As Sylvia had stated earlier, they were way out of their league.

Charles responded, "Damn. You made that all up yourself, or did they *tell you* to say that?"

"I made it up," she confessed.

He said, "That was . . . that was *damned good.* I bet that pissed Raven off *real well.*"

Charles could imagine it. He had been around Raven enough to know.

"What else do you know?" he asked Tabby.

She shook her head with her cell phone in hand. "I didn't get to do much else. That was yesterday. Since then, all kinds of things have happened."

"Like what?"

"Some people were after me, and they had it set up to look like it was *your* people, or *Isaac's* people," she corrected herself.

She noticed that it was nearing time to board her plane to Las Vegas.

Charles said, "And then they killed her after sending her out to argue with Teddy in public."

"I guess so," Tabby commented.

"First class only for flight nineteen-forty-five to Las Vegas!"

Her plane was beginning to board.

Charles said, "And you do realize that wasn't *us,* right?"

"Yeah, I know," she admitted.

"And you still *trust* these people?"

It was a perfect question with perfect timing.

Charles followed that up with an even better question, "Do they know where you are right now, or are you running for your life?"

She was stuck. She said, "They need something from me. That's why I'm still alive, I guess."

"Seating passengers in rows twenty-five and higher!"

Tabitha's seat was in row twelve, but she wasn't sure she wanted to get on that plane. New tears of desperation ran down her face.

Charles overheard the second announcement. He couldn't make out all of the words, but he knew it was an airport.

"You're at the airport?" he asked her. "Are you there alone?"

"Yes."

"Do they know where you're going?"

She hesitated. "Yes."

"And you feel *safe* with that?"

The tears ran harder.

"No," she whimpered.

He said, "Don't get on that plane. I don't know where you are, and I don't *wanna* know. But I *will* tell you this: You need to take a bus ride to *any-where; Alaska* if you need to. But not *there* because I told you that. So you take a bus ride to an unknown destination, and you don't answer your phone for *any* of these people. You hear me?"

She nodded, feeling relieved by his orders.

"Okay," she mumbled to him. She stood up and started walking away from the gate with her carry bag. She ignored the final boarding announcements for her flight to Las Vegas.

"Now you said they *need* something from you. Are you gonna trust me?" Charles asked her.

"I *have* to. I know you a lot better than I know them."

"But do you *trust me?*" he pressed her.

What choice did she have? Charles was the straight shooter.

"Yes," she told him.

He said, "Okay . . . now what do they *need* from you? You have to tell me everything."

"My diaries."

That caught him off guard.

"*Diaries*? Did you write about all of this?"

"Of course," she told him. "I didn't add that many *details,* but I still wrote about it."

She was already headed for the airport exits. She planned to call her sisters as soon as she wrapped up her life-saving conversation with Charles.

He paused for a minute and thought about the obvious with her diaries.

"Did you write about me?"

Tabitha hesitated again. She said, "I didn't use your *name* in writing about us. Nor did I use *Isaac's* name."

"Does it have Teddy's name in it, and Angela's?"

"Yeah," she answered.

He said, "And Walt *Nesbitt* wants this diary?"

He was assuming things to get a strong response from her.

"I don't really know much about him," she answered. "I've never met him before or anything, so I don't know why *he* would want my old diaries. They don't have anything about *Isaac* in them either. I never met Isaac before the party. But somebody broke into my apartment at home looking for them."

"In Texas?" Charles asked her.

"I don't live in Texas anymore," she admitted. "But I don't live in New York either."

"Okay, I don't have to know where you live if you're not going there. And you're *not* going there, right?" he quizzed her.

She said, "No, because I don't know what they have in store for me back home. But I *do* need to get my sister to safety. She's at my place, and someone raided it last night."

"And you have no idea who was paying you to do this?"

With her safety established, Tabitha felt more comfortable leveling with Charles about everything. She said, "My contact told me that a wealthy banker had a *daughter* who had an affair with Isaac, and that someone needed to get him to see the evil of his ways. But the only person I could think of who I dated like that was an investor in Atlanta."

Charles said, "Atlanta? What's his name?"

"Henry Anderson," she answered.

Charles thought about it and held his tongue.

"Are you sure about this?"

She answered, "No, I'm just going on hunches from what I was told."

"What else can you tell me to help you?" he asked her.

Tabitha was ready to brave the cold Chicago winds and take a taxi to the train station. The trains were much more comfortable than buses. And she could still get away with a walk-up ticket without being traced there.

She answered, "That's about it. I was contacted by a private investigator where I live, and Angela was contacted by a private investigator in New York."

Charles nodded.

"So they were running the show at the *bottom* level," he told himself. "What are their names?"

Tabitha hesitated again. How *much* did he need to know?

Charles decided, "You know what, I have enough information to start with. I'll start beating the bushes at the *top,* and see what shakes loose.

"You're in good hands," he told her.

"Are you sure?"

She needed confirmation. She had just given him nearly everything.

"What did I tell you before?" he quizzed her.

Tabitha remembered his creed.

"Some men like to talk, but others like the follow-through."

"Which one am *I*?" he asked.

"The follow-through."

He said, "I guess we'll see for real now."

Making Moves

Tabitha called her sister Patrice out in Seattle from inside a Chicago taxi. She was on her way to the train station.

"What is going on, Tabby? I haven't talked to you in *days.*"

"I know, I've been *trying* to call you," Tabitha told her.

"When?"

"Well, I've just been on the run."

"That's what I *thought*. You haven't called *here,*" Patrice huffed at her.

"Well, you were on the *road* the beginning of the week."

Patrice ignored it. "Anyway, Marisol called here *collect* and said that *you* told her to do it after you kicked her out of your apartment."

"I didn't kick her out. I'm not even there. I just told her to *leave* for a while," Tabitha explained. She said, "There's a lot going on right now. I just told her to go somewhere and call you so I could find her later."

"Yeah, she told me somebody broke into your place last night," Patrice informed her. "I'm glad me and the *kids* weren't there when this happened. That would have been all I needed to go over the edge."

Tabitha asked her, "Where is Marisol now? I was just gonna tell her to catch the train back up to Seattle, because I don't really trust her going to the airport alone."

"Well, what's going *on*?" Patrice pressed her.

"It's a long story, too long to explain over the phone right now. I just have to get Marisol home."

"Is somebody after you?" her sister asked her.

"Exactly."

Patrice stopped and thought about it.

"One of those crazy men finally caught up to you," she said. "I *knew it*! It was only a matter of *time*."

Tabitha didn't feel like hearing it.

"Where is Marisol?" she repeated. "Do you have a number for her?"

"She was calling from a casino."

"A *casino*? Shit!" Tabitha piped. "So how do we get back in touch with her?"

"She said she'd call back when she got somewhere stable."

Tabitha calmed down. "We need to tell her to go to the train station. I'm gonna pay for a ticket with a credit card before she gets there."

"Where are you?" Patrice asked her.

"I can't say right now, but I'm safe."

"Why can't you say where you are?"

"It really doesn't make a difference," she commented. "I'm gonna be leaving here soon anyway. I'll just keep calling you back for updates."

"Are you gonna even ask how things are with me?" Patrice questioned.

"*Good,* I hope."

Tabitha didn't have time to be concerned. She had her *own* life to figure out at the moment. Patrice told her anyway.

"Randy and I had a long talk, and we came to some conclusions. And you're right, we both decided that me having some kind of employment outside the house, where I can get my juices going every day, would be good for me.

"I mean, I *did* used to be a lot more active," she admitted. "Randy said he *needs* that in me, seeing me get out and do my own thing instead of waiting around for him with the kids."

Tabitha smiled and never said *I told you so*.

"That's good," she offered instead. "So when do you go job hunting?"

Tabitha had not been job hunting with consistency herself, but she realized that she *needed* to. How long could she continue to depend on the good fortunes of the men she dated?

Patrice answered, "Monday morning at one P.M. *sharp,* right after lunch hour."

"That *is* lunch hour for some people," Tabby told her.

"I'll just sit down and have lunch with them while I fill out my applications then," Patrice joked. She sounded a lot more spirited than before.

She added, "But I *still* let his ass *know* that I won't have him running around with some skinny-ass *white girls*."

Tabitha chuckled at it. She said, "What about skinny-ass *black* girls?"

"*Nobody*," Patrice concluded. "That includes *all* types."

When Tabby hung up with her, she felt guilty all over again. Wasn't Charles Grandison married with children?

She shook her head and blew it off.

"Don't even think about it," she mumbled to herself. "Just leave it alone."

Charles was already on the phone with Isaac. He had plenty of ideas to run past him from his office.

"I found out some things and came up with some plans that can give us some automatic answers."

"Go 'head and spit it," Isaac told him from his hotel room at New York's St. Regis. He had Charles on speaker phone while he packed his things for his trip to Atlanta.

Charles said, "As we already suspected, Walt Nesbitt's name popped up in this thing. He still has lackeys at the papers and the networks who would jump at any smoke screen that he creates."

"Okay, and?" Isaac asked.

"Well, *you're* the target, we all realize that," Charles explained. "But for now, *Teddy's* the one who got hit. So since Walt has had falling outs with Teddy in the past, we can spin our side of the story toward *Nesbitt* going after *Liggins.*"

Isaac followed his logic. "Okay, and then we let Walt tell on himself. That's good. That nigga's always had a big mouth. What else you got?" he asked while packing up his shoes. He knew Charles had more details for him.

"We have quite a *few* things on the menu," Charles answered.

Isaac stopped what he was doing for a minute.

"You found out that many details on this thing?"

"I found the girl."

"Who is she?" Isaac asked him.

"She's new. They flew her in from somewhere. And she got to Raven."

Isaac was pensive. "You sent somebody to get her?"

"Already done," Charles told him. "That was the *first* thing I did. They'll call me as soon as they pick Raven up."

"You think I need to talk to her?" Isaac questioned.

"Not really. We just need to keep her away from Walt's people. Once she realizes what's going on, she'll settle down. She's a smart girl. She probably already suspects something."

Isaac took a seat and picked up the phone. He realized now that the situation was a lot more intricate than he first thought.

"Is that as deep as this thing goes?" he asked his thorough manager.

"No," Charles answered. "This girl has also been involved with Henry Anderson."

"From Atlanta?"

"Zula's daddy."

Zula Anderson had fallen head over heels for Isaac like thousands of other young women. She became one of the select few to make it inside his circle. However, Zula never respected her place. She wanted more of what she couldn't have.

Isaac creased his brow with intensity. "I knew that damn girl was gon' cause me problems. So what's the deal with that?"

"From what the girl was told, Daddy wants the man who hurt his baby to be punished for the evil of his ways."

Isaac snapped, "That muthafucka's *hotter* than me *and* older. How the hell is *he* gon' pull something like this?"

Charles said, "The main thing for me is that we all know one another. We can work it out with him."

Isaac was incensed. "So these two are in bed together like *faggots* trying to bring *us* down!"

Charles kept his poise. "Anderson's not the man to throw the first punch," he commented. "He's an investor. He likes to wage bets from outside the ring. But from what I understand, he's being used as the front man on this thing."

"You think Walt bought him off?" Isaac asked.

"I think you can find that out when you touch down in Atlanta," Charles answered. "This trip is perfect timing. I can set up a meeting for you to pick his brains in person."

"Yeah, 'cause he's a *punk*. He's a *bitch* for money. Even his daughter knows," Isaac snapped. "He probably went broke on one of those bullshit investments of his, and Walt bailed him out and got him involved in this nonsense."

"That's what we got going," Charles concluded. "So let's get out there and clean this mess up."

≋

Walt Nesbitt was reading the *Wall Street Journal* at his office when he received another urgent call on his private cell phone.

"Yeah," he answered.

"They got the girl," his contact told him. Walt had his own contact in the city, separate from Henry's men. There were several teams all in on the job. Big money drew the crowd.

"*They* got the girl? *You* were supposed to talk to her," Walt responded. "What are you telling me? Who are *they*?"

"Isaac's people got to her before we did."

"The high school girl?"

"Yeah."

"Shit!" Walt cursed. "That means they're *on* to us."

"That's what it looks like. We saw them pick her up in the limo a few minutes ago."

"Somebody must have told. What happened to that boy?"

"They can't find him."

"They can't *find him*? Did they give him his money?"

"I heard he didn't want it."

Walt thought it over and snapped, "Got'damnit! Well, what happened to the other girl?"

"She's on her flight back to Las Vegas."

"Did they get those diaries yet?"

"I don't believe so."

Walt started thinking again. He said, "We need our own contacts out in Vegas. We need to get to that girl's diaries before Henry does. That damn Henry'll punk out on us," he stated. "We'll use that girl's diaries to keep him honest."

"All right, I'm on it. I have a few people out in Las Vegas who could help us."

"Good. And if we can't get to these diaries, then maybe an accident should happen with this girl."

There was a pause of contemplation.

"Are you sure?" his contact asked him.

"I said *maybe*, didn't I?" Walt reiterated. "Let's just try and get these diaries first."

"All right, I'm making the call right now."

Walt hung up the phone and felt more desperate. He realized that his ship was sinking before reaching its destination. All he could do now was save his valuables and escape for another mission another day. He hadn't climbed to his position of power without knowing when to pull the plug on things.

He mumbled, "Henry still needs my generous investment, but just in case he doesn't want it anymore, I'll have to find a way to make sure he stays dedicated to me."

The Art
of the Deal

By the time Tabitha arrived at the Chicago train station, she had decided to call the Memphis Grizzlies basketball player Terrence Matthews back. On a whim, she figured she could stay with Terrence in Memphis for a few days, if he would allow it.

However, he answered his cell phone sourly.

"Hel–low." He was driving a black Cadillac Escalade toward the Pyramid Arena in downtown Memphis. He had his first home basketball game there with his new team that evening.

Tabitha read the irritation in his voice and asked him, "Dang, who's been bothering you?"

"Who's this?" he quizzed her. He changed his tone, anticipating.

She answered, "Just some girl you met in Las Vegas at the Mayweather fight. You probably don't even remember me."

Terrence smiled. He knew who it was, and he was glad that she had finally called him back.

He joked, "Yeah, you're right. I meet so many girls now that I forget all their names. Was your name Tonya, Toni, or Tammy?"

Under the circumstances, the joke was no longer funny to Tabby. Terrence had no idea how close he was to the reality of her life. She had already begun to reevaluate things. But how many men could she trust with the truth after living the lie for so long? The illusion was always more soluble.

She responded, "What if I was *all* of them?"

Terrence was only confused by her statement. "What?"

"Never mind," she told him. "I got the message that you called. I'm in Chicago now."

She waited for his response. It would be a slow, meticulous grind to take the conversation where she needed it to go. However, pacing was important for successful impact. If she rushed it, she could end up out of a place to stay.

"What are you doing in Chicago?" he asked her. Her plans were like clockwork.

"I was waiting for my plane back to Las Vegas," she answered.

"Back to Las Vegas from where?"

"I was in New York for a couple of days."

There was no room for hesitation. She had to display her full confidence in him.

Terrence sounded excited by her answer.

He said, "New York? I just got back from New York. We beat the Knicks at Madison Square Garden last night. I had twenty points in thirty-four minutes. Did you see the game? We beat the Clippers in L.A. in my first game for the Grizzlies. I had sixteen points in twenty-eight minutes."

"See that? So this trade *was* good for you," she told him. She didn't mention anything about the game that she had obviously missed in New York.

"So far so good," he responded. "But we still won't be making no playoffs."

"Yeah, but you'll be penciled in as a *starter* soon. How about that?" She perked.

"I mean, that's aw'ight, but I'd rather be playing for a *ring.*"

"Well, you've only been in the league now for what, two, three years? You've already been to the playoffs with Minnesota. How many young guys around the league don't get to play on a playoff team at all? Some guys have been playing without getting rings for *years* now.

"Look at those New York guys for instance," she stated. "How many years have *they* been playing without any rings?"

Terrence broke out laughing. He said, "Yeah, you're right. But shit, at least New York got to go to the *dance.*"

"Just be patient," Tabitha told him. She had to be patient with *him* herself.

"When is your first game in Memphis?" she asked him.

"Tonight. I'm heading to the locker room now. I have to organize my gear."

"It's *tonight?*" It was already after five o'clock. Tabitha realized she would never make it to Memphis in time to see it. "Mmmph, I just missed you then," she grunted.

"What, to see the game?"

"Yeah. I don't really feel like going back home yet. It's nothing there for me."

"What about your sister?" he asked. "Is she still out there?"

"Yeah, but she's a big girl. She can take care of herself."

"Well, what about work?"

She said, "I already have money saved up for two months so I can find the job that I really want out there."

"Yeah? Well, what do you do?"

It was all practiced for Tabby. She answered, "Do you realize how many *events* go on in Las Vegas every night? So I went out there to get my feet wet in event coordination. Then I want to take my skills to other places, because I really like to travel."

"Oh, that's cool," he told her. "So, you're not trying to go back there tonight?"

It was the golden question. However, Tabitha no longer felt good about all of her lies. She was lying more out of necessity now, to escape from harm's way.

"I don't wanna cramp your style in Memphis," she hinted.

"Cramp my *style*? I don't even know anybody from here yet."

"Are you sure?"

"Shit, this is my first day here," he told her. "I was just checking the place out today, gettin' lost and shit. They got me staying at a hotel right near the Arena."

"Oh," she responded. She had to wait again to allow him to make the next move.

"So, you wanna fly down here to see me?"

"More like, take the train," she informed him.

"Take the *train*? For what?"

"Because that's where I am right now, at the train station."

"I thought you *flew* into Chicago."

"I did. Then I left the airport. I was thinking about just hanging out in Chicago for a few days, then I remembered that you had called me. So since the train station was right near me, I decided to see what the times and fares were if I came your way. Of course, I had to call you back first," she added. "Because if you say no, then I'll just have to stay in Chicago."

He said, "Naw, you can come down here. But how long would the train take?"

"If I take the seven o'clock train, I'll arrive in Memphis in the morning, after you're all sore from the basketball game tonight."

"Yeah," he mumbled. "Do you know how to give a good massage?"

"Yeah," she told him.

"I mean, a *good one,* though, not one of them 'this what my grandmom taught me' massages," he teased her.

"You can *find out,*" she hinted.

"Aw'ight then, I guess I'll find out tomorrow morning. They got me staying at the Memphis Hotel on Beale Street. Take a taxi and call me from the lobby, and I'll have them give you a key, 'cause I'm *not* gettin' up before noon.

"This has been a busy-ass *week* for me," he told her. "I *need* some rest."

Tabitha grinned. She said, "I know just what you mean."

On the six o'clock news in New York City, Teddy Liggins stood before several cameras and microphones in a beige suit with a white shirt and a conservative tie to make his prepared statements to the media. Charles, J.J., and a couple of bodyguards stood at his sides.

"It has come to my attention that individuals with old vendettas are out to settle the score through a defamation of my character and a plotted murder charge against me. Although my condolences go out to the family and friends of Angela Simmons, I repeat that I had nothing to do with her murder."

One of the reporters asked him, "Would these old vendettas that you speak about also be connected to Isaac Abraham as your superstar client?"

"Right now, Isaac Abraham is not under the gun; I am."

As a publicist himself, Teddy already knew to keep his comments short and sweet.

"Would this plot be an order from Walt Nesbitt, who years ago was kicked out of the group employed by Isaac Abraham, and whom you've had reported battles with in the past?" someone else asked.

Teddy shook his head. "I will give no further speculation as to *who* until I am exonerated from this and the truth hits the light on its own."

"But aren't you dodging the fact that your entire circle, under the employ of Mr. Abraham, is under suspicion regarding relationships with minors?" another reporter asked.

Teddy answered, "That is pure speculation, which is being used, mostly by you guys in the media, to present something to the general public that is not a reality."

J.J. nudged Teddy to move on and end his statements there.

"But weren't you and Walt Nesbitt *both* involved with this same Angela Simmons while she was still underage herself, years ago?" the same reporter asked.

J.J. stood in front of the microphones and cameras. He announced, "There will be no further statements made by my client at this time. We do expect this matter to be settled *shortly,* and his name to be *cleared.*"

Walt Nesbitt watched the orchestrated statements on the New York local news from his office and laughed out loud.

"These muthafuckas must think I'm stupid!" he shouted at the television in his office. "I'm gonna make my *own* statements that I had nothing to do with this shit, and that I wish them all the best. In fact, I consider it a slap in the face that you guys in the media would even insert my name in this case just because Teddy and I have had our differences in the past. I've moved on to new friends and business ventures, and I'm still enough of a successful man in my own right not to stoop to such ridiculousness, especially with something as *serious* as the murder of a young, innocent woman."

Walt made himself a drink from the bar in his office and continued to laugh.

He said, "You must've forgot who the hell you're dealing with! I'm not some got'damned amateur. I *know* what I'm doing. And now that I got everybody's attention, there's no doubt in my mind that there's gonna be another day of *reckoning.* Isaac Abraham will bear the *cross!*"

Teddy, J.J., and Charles made their way to the awaiting limo after the press statements. The bodyguards warded off the cameras and reporters and shut the doors behind them.

Once inside the limo, Teddy turned to Charles and asked him, "What do you think his response will be?"

Charles was straightforward with his answer. "He'll have his own statements ready to deflect everything you just said. And depending on whether he's gonna be patient or not, he'll continue to speak about it, or leave it alone. My guess is that without Raven, he'll decide that it's over with."

J.J. nodded and agreed with Charles's assessment.

"I hate to say it, but there's not gonna be a big uproar about this girl's murder. She's gonna be painted as a power groupie, who chases older men who have the goods," he commented. "And without any concrete evidence as to why Teddy would kill her, or witnesses saying that they saw his hands around her neck, this case has nowhere to go."

"Yeah, well, I just can't wait for this shit to be over with," Teddy complained.

Charles interjected, "I *will* tell you this: we'll *all* have to watch our steps from here on out. That's surely what Walt will bank on. Since he's not in the public eye anymore, he knows that we have a lot more to lose than *he* does."

Teddy said, "Shit, man, you don't have to tell me that. After this bullshit here, I'm ready to put my dick on *ice* for a *year.*"

J.J. laughed. "It's been a long time coming for that, my friend."

"Yeah, well, the time has *come,*" Teddy added. "No pun intended." He looked to Charles again and asked him, "What happened with that number I gave you?"

Charles said, "I didn't get a chance to use it yet."

Teddy asked him with a grin, "Are you still thinking about using it?"

Charles broke out laughing. "I think we all need to hit the icebox for a while."

J.J. said, "Speak for yourselves. I haven't indulged."

Teddy grimaced at him. "Aw, nigga, that's because you're still *new.* We'll have to keep our eye on you the *closest* over the next couple of months. 'Cause you'll be the next one in trouble."

From the privacy of his office that evening, Charles was finally able to get in contact with Henry Anderson in Atlanta. Henry was driving home for the evening in his black, 7 Series BMW.

"Hey Charles, how's things going? How's the family?" Henry asked him over his cell phone. Charles had called three contacts in Atlanta to chase Henry down.

"I don't know how men like us are even able to have a family," Charles answered.

"It's just one day at a time, young brother. One day at a time."

Henry was nearly twenty years Charles's senior. Nevertheless, Charles had some urgent business to discuss with him from an authoritative position.

"So what can I do for you?" Henry asked him.

Charles said, "Well, in the business of filmmaking, you're always looking for creative ways to finance the production and marketing and so forth of new projects. Sometimes you pick up new partners and lose old ones on the way. So we wanted to call and see if you were still in the business of investing in intellectual properties. We think we may have something to perk your interests."

He said, "But I want to add that our ideas are still a little premature. We would love to be able to work it out with you, face to face if we can, and reach agreeable terms for all of us."

Henry realized immediately that Charles wasn't actually referring to filmmaking. They wanted to talk about the recent events in New York. Henry was rather impressed at how fast they moved on the situation, as well as with how tactful Charles was being with him.

On the other side of the coin, tact was not one of Walt Nesbitt's better skills. It was not a hard decision for Henry to make after Nesbitt's blatant order of murder of the young woman. Henry could *use* some new partners.

He answered, "When would you all like to talk about it?"

"Actually, our star performer is on his way to Atlanta now. He would like to meet with you confidentially tonight, if at all possible. We're just trying to roll the ball for the strike."

Henry nodded. He agreed with the idea of settling things quickly himself. It would calm his nerves from all of the confusions.

"Okay. Just have him call when he gets in," he told Charles. "I'll have a place lined up for us to meet."

"By the way," Charles added to him, "some notes on this project are better left alone. While things are still premature, we don't want to attach any *actresses* to the project just yet. So I had a talk with one, whom we're both *familiar* with, and I *firmly* expressed to her that she's to keep her ideas to herself until further notice, *if* we need them at all."

He said, "Maybe I'll even tell her to *burn* those old ideas she may have had, so we can all start this thing out fresh. I happen to know her closely now myself, so some of those ideas would include me," he informed Henry. "However, I'm certain that we'll *both* have her full cooperation after the other actress was killed off in the script."

Henry was stunned. They had found Tabitha Knight. Not only that, but Charles knew about the diaries.

"How sure can you be that she'll comply?" he questioned.

Charles answered, "How sure can *any* of us be when dealing with young actresses? I'm longing for the day when we won't have to use them at all. You follow me? That young actress is able to dazzle the *best* of us. So I wouldn't make much mention about her to our leading man. He hasn't really made her acquaintance and he's still not familiar with her. But as we know, our leading man has been involved with young actresses in the past, when maybe we both had rather he *not* have been.

"Nevertheless, bygones should be resolved within the private room," he suggested. "You two could do it tonight if you like."

Henry took it all in and was amazed by it. He said, "It looks like you're gonna have a long and prosperous career, my friend. I couldn't have lined out things better myself."

Charles told him, "That's what I get paid the big bucks to do."

"Yeah, well, you deserve every *penny* of it."

"Thank you."

Once the meeting between Isaac and Henry had been arranged for that evening in Atlanta, Charles called back his contact to let her know that everything was going as he had planned.

Tabitha read the phone number on her cell phone screen. It was after nine that evening. She was relaxing on her train ride to Memphis.

"Hi," she answered softly.

"Feeling safe and sound?" Charles asked her.

She smiled. "Now I am."

He said, "I know you don't want to disturb the other passengers with cell phone chatter, so I'll do most of the talking, and you just respond. Is that a deal?"

"Deal," she agreed.

"Okay, well, I talked to Henry Anderson a few minutes ago, and he's *definitely* our man," he informed her. "So I have the boss flying to Atlanta to straighten things out with him, face to face."

"He agreed to that?" she asked.

"Henry's not into homicide, so that's a done deal. That leaves Walt all by himself on this thing. But one point I *did* have to negotiate with Henry was the silence on your diaries. He seems to think that those things could be very embarrassing *and* incriminating to him. And I had to *cosign* on that," he told her. "A piece of *my* personal life is in there, *too,* now."

Tabitha said, "I would never do anything—"

"That's not the point," Charles stated, cutting her off. "The fact that you've been with several men of power and actually wrote *details* about yourself in their lives makes it particularly dangerous for you, especially when dealing with desperate men who *know* about it."

"I'm still *confused* about that," she responded. "How did he know? I've never *told* anybody."

Charles explained it to her calmly, "When you deal with certain high rollers, they have employed people to check out every person they're in contact with. Henry happens to be one of those individuals. His life's income is based on *knowing* the people he invests in. So he obviously found something peculiar with you, and he had some of his people tail you."

Tabitha was amazed by it. Exactly how much did they find out about her?

"What else did he tell you?" she asked. She was curious.

Charles said, "Once he decided he could trust me, we went in to more detail. He said they already offered you a couple of arms and legs for them."

"He told you that?"

"After I asked him how much they were worth to him, he *hinted* as much. And I just know how investors *work.* There are price tags attached to everything for them."

"So, you think I should do it?" she asked him. She was testing him to see where his sympathies were. Would he be straight business like the rest, or would he see *her* side of the story? Her private life was *not* for sale . . . nor was *theirs.*

Charles shocked her with his answer. He said, "If you asked me, I would have you *burn* those things. You know what life you've lived. And if anything happened to you, who would end up with them?"

Tabitha was speechless. She couldn't believe he had said that. Maybe he was shooting *too* straight for comfort now. She had all kinds of mental and spiritual history in her diaries. It wasn't just *sex* escapades with men who had something to hide. It was all of her thoughts, dreams, aspirations, tears, assessments, pats on the back, words of encouragement, and her *therapy* for life as one lonely person in a world of many. It was her connection to herself and to those around her. She couldn't *burn* that. And she couldn't *sell it* either. It was *priceless*!

She said, "That's like asking you to burn . . . I don't know." She couldn't even compare it to anything. What could she compare to thirteen *books* of her life?

Charles decided to change the subject for a minute. He could see how much turmoil she was in regarding those diaries of hers.

He said, "You know what you had me thinking about in the middle of all of this?"

"What?" she asked him.

"The ruin of young women," he answered. "We can all try to rationalize it if we want, but you're right. We're like vultures swooping down on rabbits."

She understood where Charles was coming from, but to the contrary, if it had not been for him, she would have been heading back to Las Vegas for who knows what.

She said, "Yeah, but like you said, if that rabbit is out there running around where vultures, eagles, and hawks fly, then *one* of them is gonna get the meal."

"Don't forget that they're *all* predators," he responded.

"That doesn't mean that every situation is necessarily a *kill*," she countered. "Hold on," she told him. She realized their conversation was getting beyond her public comfort level. She made her way to the train's restroom and locked the door for more privacy.

Charles said, "I got you a little too excited?"

She smiled inside the restroom. "I guess so. I'm in the bathroom now."

With more privacy, she was able to level with him.

She said, "Actually, I was told to stay away from you. They told me that you were the *eagle*. And you *are*. But if I hadn't met you . . ."

He cut her off and said, "Shit, I damn near helped them to accomplish their goals with you."

"And now you're giving me a parachute after I've been thrown out of the plane?"

"I was just trying to save my *own* ass, actually."

"Were you? Or do you really care about me?"

Charles was silent for a minute.

"I think you already know the answer to that."

"That's my point," she told him. "I'm not saying that what older men do with young girls is *right,* but it's a lot more complicated sometimes than predator and prey."

Charles said, "Yeah, sometimes the *prey* becomes the predator."

Tabitha smiled again. "Exactly."

He said, "But seriously though . . . what are we gonna do about these diaries?"

Tabitha was still uncompromising.

"You actually expect me to *burn* them?"

Charles didn't say a word.

Finally, he asked her, "What else do you want me to tell you? You wanna sell them to *me?*" he offered her on a whim. He said, "I don't know how many other scenarios I can agree with. You just put me in an awkward situation here."

"How about I just never take them out again?" she suggested.

"Well, where are they now?"

"I can't tell you that. Are you still on *my* side, or on *theirs?*"

He said, "I'm on my *own* damn side right now. I just need some *securities.* Otherwise, you destroy the substance of my *word,* and my word means *everything* in this business."

Tabitha was still wrestling with the idea of losing her most important property. What else did she own?

She thought about it and took a breath. "I've always dreamed about having a big house where my sisters and I could live together in peace," she told him.

Charles nodded. "I can understand that. House and home are important for peace. That can be arranged."

She let the idea sink into her mind.

Through the silence, a whistle blew to slow the train for an oncoming junction.

Tabitha froze and wondered if Charles had heard it.

He chuckled and said, "I'm in total confidence with you. I just want to resolve this matter. I don't want to know where you're going, *or* how you're getting there. All I need for you to do is take my phone calls and ignore theirs."

On Charles's end, his cell phone rang from the other line. He read his wife's number. He realized he needed to call her back once he finished up with his urgent business.

Tabitha realized the incoming call from the sudden pauses in the phone reception.

Charles nodded to himself and said, "I wanna thank you, actually, for getting me back on track to what's really important. I think it was in the cards for *both* of us to turn a new corner in life. Now we can either ignore that, or do what we both need to do.

"So, before we call it a night and I talk to you sometime tomorrow, I suggest that you think about an ending to an *old* life, and the start of a new one. I mean . . . what did you get involved in this thing to do? If you're going to make moral judgments on someone else, then make one on yourself. I know *I* have to," he concluded.

"Now I have to go. That was my wife calling. I'll talk to you again tomorrow."

"Okay," Tabitha responded softly.

Charles hung up the phone and immediately called his wife.

"How did it go?" she asked him over the line. She knew some of what was going on with Teddy's situation, but a lot less of what was going on with the rest of them. Things were more sane that way. The lifestyles of the powerful were never simple math. There were always complex equations involved. However, trying to solve them usually caused more *confusion* than understanding. So the wives and significant others learned how to accept enough of the equation to maintain their individual sanity.

Charles answered, "We'll have everything wrapped up in another day or two."

"Will you be home any time soon?"

It was a loaded question delivered with passivity. Charles realized its subtle impact.

He said, "After this *new* development is all over with, maybe we should take the kids and get away to Argentina or something."

His wife paused. It was all about maintaining her patience.

She answered, "That'll work. Until the *next* new thing comes."

Charles sidestepped his business reality and perked. "Well, I have some good *news* for you."

"What's that?" she asked him.

"I'm done for the night. I'm calling for the car now. I'll be home in forty."

Long Island was a much shorter commute at night.

His wife responded, "I'll see you when you get in."

Charles hung up the phone and mumbled, "She'll see me with no bells on. The thrill is gone. But this is my life. . . . Deal with it."

He stood up to shut down his office. Before he clicked off the lights and locked the doors, he called his driver to meet him down at the front entrance. It had been a long day for all of them . . . like always.

Game Over

S ylvia Green waited at McCarran International Airport in Las Vegas for no one. It was past six o'clock western standard time, and there was no sight of Tabitha, nor was there any response to the phone calls Sylvia made to her cell phone.

"This girl needs to get an answering service where I can leave more than these phone messages," she snapped in frustration.

The confused private investigator finally decided to call her contact.

"Well, I'm here, but she's not, and I'm not getting any response from her cell phone," she expressed to her Las Vegas point man.

"Yeah, there was another last minute change in the plans," he informed her. Henry's Las Vegas man was still out enjoying the sights and scenes of The Strip. What better way in life was there to cut the edge than by watching people win, lose, and flaunt fortunes? That was the American way.

Sylvia said, "Another change in *plans*? So, what's going on now?"

"Well, I guess this girl's running *scared* now. I can't blame her, though. How would *you* feel in this situation?"

Sylvia asked, "Are there any new plans, or is she just running?"

"Well, her job is done," he told the private investigator. "There are some other developments going on that have our attention now."

Sylvia hesitated to ask her next question, but she *had* to.

"So, what happens with the rest of the money?"

"Ahh . . . nothing," he answered. It was fairly obvious to him. No more job, no more money.

"We don't get it?" Sylvia asked him anyway.

"Let me put it to you this way," he explained to her. "If you were at the craps tables, and you backed out on your bet, do you still win any money?

"Hey, how are you two doing?" he commented to a couple of exotically dressed call girls.

Sylvia mumbled away from her phone receiver, "Ain't this a *bitch*?!" Fif-

teen thousand additional dollars were spinning down the drain. At least she
had gotten the first *five* thousand.

*I wonder if they planned to follow through on paying everyone the money they
had promised in the first place. This seems all too convenient,* she thought to herself.

"It's over with, just like that, hunh?" she asked him to make sure.

He said, "We'll call you if anything else comes up."

That was it. Sylvia decided to drop the issue herself.

"Aw'ight, well, I'm out of here," she told him.

"Nice doing business with you."

"Sure, any time," she responded sarcastically.

She hung up her cell phone and headed briskly for her car at the parking
garage.

She had been so consumed by her lookout for Tabitha that she failed to
inspect the two white men who watched her. Once she left the airport terminal for her car, empty-handed, they made a call to Walt Nesbitt's contact in
New York.

"Yeah, we're on to her, but she didn't pick anybody up. . . . Nobody
showed. . . . She made a phone call, and it looked like she was pretty pissed
off about it. Then she walked out to her car. You want us to follow her?"

"Yeah, follow her," Walt's point man told them from New York.

And they did.

Sylvia drove her sedan out of the parking garage and toward the airport exits,
still unaware of the two white men who tailed her.

As soon as she hit I-15 heading north toward her office, her cell phone
rang. She read the screen and recognized Tabitha's cell phone number.

"Where the hell are you?" she asked herself before she answered.

"Hello."

Tabitha composed herself before she spoke. She was back inside of the
restroom of the train for privacy.

"I don't know if I can even trust you," she stated.

Sylvia composed herself as well.

"I understand that," she answered.

"So I guess you know now that Angela was found strangled to death in
Harlem."

Tabitha wanted to see how Sylvia would respond to it before she asked her for help.

"No one told me that," Sylvia responded.

"What did Calvins tell you after he dropped me off at the airport? I know you talked to him."

"Actually, he said that you were looking for answers and turning over a lot of stones. But he didn't mention anything about Angela."

Tabitha said, "I bet he *didn't*. Everybody's covering for themselves now. Nobody's looking out for anyone," she hinted.

She put Sylvia on a guilt trip.

"I understand how you feel," Sylvia repeated. She didn't know what else to say. She was in the wrong. Point blank.

"Do you?" Tabitha questioned. "I still need your help. But I'm wondering how long your next knife will be when you stab me in the back again."

Sylvia took a breath and was already tired of the guilt game that Tabby was trying to pull.

She said, "Look, I've already told you more than what I was supposed to. And I can't express to you *enough* how bad I feel about this whole situation. It's all given me an even lower opinion of *men, including* Calvins. But at this point, I'm not gonna continue to beat myself over the head about it. So if you need my help, I'm here for you. I *am* in your *debt*. But save me the extra *theatrics,* because I already understand my *wrongs*."

With that, Tabitha calmed down. She had to take a chance on her.

She said, "My sister still needs to get out of Las Vegas safely. And I don't know if I wanna put her life in your hands."

Sylvia was speechless for a moment. If Tabitha didn't need her, she wouldn't have brought it up, *twice* now.

She said, "All I can give you is my word. You're not dealing with anyone else now . . . it's just me. They've already called and told me that we're both off the job now. They told me that once you didn't show up at the airport," she added.

Tabitha paused. "Is that right?" she asked. Evidently, Charles had quickly turned the tables into a win for Isaac's team. However, she still held that information from Sylvia. She didn't need to know.

"I need you to get my sister out of there," she stated instead.

Sylvia said, "You give her my number and have her call me."

"You know what she looks like?"

"I know she's a Latina."

"Right," Tabitha confirmed. She paused again.

Sylvia read the hesitation and said, "I put my life on it. Now, I got you involved in this mess, and it's on me to get you out."

She said, "Your sister had nothing to do with this . . . nor did you." She added, "*I* pulled you into it."

Tabitha nodded her head on the other side. Sylvia did pull her into it. Tabby was minding her own business.

"Thank you," she uttered. "I'll have her call you then."

Sylvia hung up her cell phone and took another breath.

"So Angela was killed in New York, and Keith didn't even tell me," she told herself. "He's probably cutting himself a side deal right now."

She didn't even bother to call him back on it. She just wanted to help Tabitha and her loved ones in any way that she could to soothe her own conscious.

She received the phone call from Tabitha's sister a minute later.

"Hello, can I speak to Sylvia?"

"This is Sylvia."

"Hi, this is Marisol. I don't know what's going on, but Tabby said that I need to trust you."

"Right," Sylvia told her. "Where do you want me to meet you?"

"Tabby told me to walk over to the MGM Grand and meet you at the front entrance."

Sylvia looked up at the exit to Main Street in three more miles.

"I'll be there in five minutes. I'm a dark brown woman in a midnight blue sedan. I'll wait right outside for you."

"Okay. I'm on my way there now," Marisol told her.

By the time Sylvia picked up Tabitha's foster sister in front of the casino, she had finally made the two white men who followed her in a tan Toyota.

I'll know for sure in a minute, she told herself.

Marisol hopped in the passenger seat with one loaded bag that Sylvia tossed into the back.

Mari put on her seat belt and said, "Tabitha told me I have a ticket waiting in my name at the train station. But can I ask you what's going on? She won't tell me."

Sylvia looked at her with a grin. She answered, "She's embarrassed. But this is for *her* to tell you. It's none of my business anymore. I'm just here to get you where you need to go."

Marisol read the stern black woman's demeanor and mumbled, "O-kay." She wanted to get to that train station as quickly as possible.

Tabitha called them back on Sylvia's cell phone.

"You have her?" she asked the private investigator.

Sylvia handed the phone over to Marisol without speaking.

"Hello," Mari answered.

"Good," Tabitha told her. "You have her call me back when you get on the train."

"Yeah, all right," Mari stated. She was particularly *short* with Tabby. Marisol was still pissed about the whole rush job. She failed to see what the big deal was. Nevertheless, she *did* want to get back home to Seattle.

She handed the phone back to the stern black woman at the wheel.

Sylvia was busy watching the two white men who were indeed tailing her in a tan Toyota, two cars back.

She took the phone and answered, "Yes."

"Call me back when she's safe on the train," Tabitha ordered.

"Will do," Sylvia told her.

As soon as they hung up, she called her friends on the Las Vegas police force.

"Yeah, this is P.I. Sylvia Green calling. I have a tan Toyota tailing me with two white male passengers. I'm headed south on I-Fifteen, and I just got on at Main Street. Could you guys check this Toyota out for me? Intercept them before I hit the airport."

"All right. We'll check it out."

Mari overheard her conversation and was anxious to look behind them.

"Don't do it," Sylvia warned her. "You'll tip them off. Just remain calm and I'll get you where you're going."

Mari was ready to freak out.

"Aw, she got some explaining to do *now*," she commented. "Some guys are actually following us?"

Sylvia smiled. "You ask your sister all about it. But I still doubt that she'll tell you everything."

"Oh, she *better*," Mari stated. "This here is *waaay* extra." She was actually nervous now. It was all a game before, but now she realized that it was serious.

"So what do they want with *me*?" she asked the stern woman.

Sylvia told her, "Don't you even think about it. You just get back home safely . . . and make sure you tell *Tabitha* what's on your mind," she added. She wanted to set Tabby up for some of her own guilty medicine.

In a flash, two Las Vegas police cruisers ran their sirens on the Toyota and pulled the white men over.

Sylvia smiled, watching it all in her rearview mirror. She continued to head on her way.

"I guess they got them," Mari commented. She was slightly relieved, but she still planned to sock it to Tabitha.

Sylvia expected as much. She said, "I guess so. But I wonder what they wanted."

Walt Nesbitt received the word back in New York after ten o'clock eastern standard time. He wasn't going to sleep that night until he knew where things were headed with his plans.

"So the girl never showed up at the airport?" he repeated to his point man. He couldn't believe it. Isaac's A-team was kicking his ass.

"They said the P.I. looked confused herself," his man told him. "So I told them to follow her, but she made them out after picking up a Mexican girl outside the MGM Grand. She had them pulled over on the highway by her friends on the police force out there."

Walt said, "A Mexican girl, hunh? Where was she taking her?"

"They were headed to the airport."

Walt shook his head and decided to throw in the towel. There was no longer any use in forcing things. He had been soundly beaten.

"All right, that's it. Let's call it a day," he told his man.

"You don't want to still try and get those diaries?"

"For what? If they got the girl, then they're already working a deal for them. The party's over with, Jack. Go on back home."

After Walt hung up the line, he immediately called Henry in Atlanta. However, he got nothing but Henry's answering service, which he swiftly hung up on.

"Ahhh shit!" he snapped. "Go on and bitch out now, Henry. I know your MO. You're gonna make a deal with the enemy to save your ass. But at least *I'm* still my own man."

Walt poured himself another drink of vodka and orange juice from his office bar. He took a sip and mumbled, "I got my *own* A-team; me, myself, and *I*. And I don't need nobody else."

Henry Anderson prepared himself to meet Isaac Abraham at a dark sports bar in the Atlanta suburbs. He had already noticed his daughter's increased energy that morning when he met her briefly before her classes. She was fully aware that Isaac and his team were coming to town for a second premiere showing of his new film, *All the Way,* at another Magic Johnson Theatre. She obviously still had strong feelings for the man.

Henry took a sip of his rum and Coke and continued to think about their shared dilemma. What made them all crave vibrant young women and power games so much? Sometimes he even wondered about the simple satisfactions of a nine-to-five slave, with little risk and small-time glory, where he could cheer for his kids in their high school and college sports activities. Henry had been so driven to stay ahead of the pack that he barely became a father at all. He had spent far too much time pampering young women to start from scratch. So what a bitter pill it was for his oldest daughter, now a sophomore at Georgia Tech, to fall for a much older man herself.

When Isaac arrived at the sports bar to join him, only his personal bodyguard, Derrick, was with him. Isaac strolled in with his usual flair of confidence, wearing a full-length, black leather coat and a gray turtleneck.

"Hey Henry," he said. He handed his leather coat to Derrick to hold or to hang at the coatrack at the front. He took a seat at the bar stool that sat across the elevated table from Henry.

Henry greeted him with a handshake and a controlled grin.

"It's been a long time," he commented.

"Too long, or not long enough?" Isaac hinted.

"How do you think I feel about it?" Henry quizzed him.

Isaac answered, "You never really know how someone feels about you until you look him in his eyes and ask him."

Henry nodded. "That's true."

Isaac said, "As much acting as I've done over the past twenty years, I still haven't learned how to lie with the eyes. The eyes are still the window to the soul, Henry."

Henry eyed him softly as he listened. He continued to nod and spoke few words in return. It was Isaac's show. He was a performer anyway. Henry was a businessman.

Isaac continued with his lead.

"Your eyes tell me that you would never want to harm a young woman, Henry. But maybe you *would* want to harm a man who has found a way to harm you."

Henry said, "We've all had our share of doing wrong; the key is knowing when to do *right*."

"Is it that time now for you?" Isaac quizzed him.

The waiter stopped by for his first drink order.

"Give me a martini," Isaac told him.

When the waiter walked away, Henry stated, "There comes a time for *all* of us to know our shortcomings. You don't agree?"

Isaac paused to contemplate the question.

He nodded and said, "I do. But the harder question is *how* to make it right?"

Henry answered, "Sometimes you get pointed in the right direction from outside sources. Then it becomes a decision on *you* to take those cues and *act* upon them."

He held up his drink in a mock toast.

"Is that what this is, acting out on your cues?" Isaac asked him.

"What is it for you?" Henry countered.

"I look at it as a search for understanding," Isaac answered. "I'm still trying to understand how a man allows himself to be led into coldheartedness by the intentions of another man. Is it to fortify the welfare of his *family,* or is it about personal vendettas?"

Henry looked Isaac straight in his eyes. He said, "I strive to understand things myself. How is it that some men desire to walk on water without getting wet? Can *you* answer that question for *me*?"

Henry looked pissed off. He said, "When it's time to *quit,* it's time to *quit,* Isaac."

Isaac blew him off. He said, "So, how do we settle this thing, Henry? You need a new partner to invest in? How much are we talking about? You know I haven't walked on water in Atlanta in *years,*" he hinted in reference to the man's daughter.

Isaac's martini arrived before Henry could answer.

"Thank you," he told the waiter.

"No problem."

When the waiter was out of earshot, Isaac repeated, "So, how much are we talking?"

Henry took another sip of his drink. He said, "You can keep your money, Isaac. I can't go down that road no more. Buying it don't make it right. So it don't make no sense to keep spending on it. And it don't make no sense for me to put myself further in debt."

Isaac grinned at him. "Are you serious, Henry? I mean, your family still gotta *eat,* right? That's why you got involved in this mess, ain't it?"

Henry said, "Yeah, well . . . now it's time for me to get out."

He caught Isaac off guard. He was used to writing checks and alleviating problems. Few people turned down money no matter what the situation was.

"So, you're telling me that everything is squashed, right here, right now, and it won't cost me a *dime*?" Isaac clarified with him.

Henry dug deeper and said, "Let me ask you something, Isaac. Do you still have a conscience in that slithering body of yours? When are you gonna stand up and walk upright like a man instead of slippin' and slidin', and making backdoor deals for people's souls?

"What makes you so different from all the rest of the crooked wheelers and dealers out here?" he asked him. "What, because you got a public audience and people like to look at you? They like to look at the local drug dealers, *too,* Isaac. Does that make *them* right? Think about it. What role are you playing now?"

Isaac couldn't believe his ears. He said, "Henry, you got yourself in *much* deeper shit than what you're trying to accuse *me* of. So you point that loaded gun back at yourself before you take aim at *my* shit."

Henry shook his head as the other patrons began to peek in their direction. It was a long time coming for him to make a stand, not really against Isaac Abraham, but against himself. He *was* pointing the loaded gun in his own direction, Isaac just couldn't see it.

Henry took a breath and told him, "It's good for a man to change his *hobbies* when they become too *expensive* for him. Hopefully, an *intelligent* man can see that before he goes bankrupt."

He wasn't planning on staying much longer. He stood up to begin making his way to the door.

"Strong warnings are not bad to be *heeded* sometimes," he concluded.

Isaac was pissed off himself, now. He said, "Oh, so now you wanna *leave,* right? Well, let's talk about *homicide.* Are you ready to talk about that?"

Henry shook his head and continued to move toward the door.

He said, "I think *you* need to deal with *suicide,* because you're killing yourself. And I'm no longer gonna participate in that. So just like you told me about the eyes, what do you see when you look in the mirror at your *damn self?*"

The worst punishment in the world for a proud man was to leave him injured in battle with no way to win or heal.

Isaac thought about how silly it would be for him to chase Henry out of the bar, so he decided against it. Besides, Henry had a point.

Isaac sat there alone for a minute and nodded to himself while finishing his drink.

He mumbled to himself, "It's the third act, Isaac. Time for resolution. So what are you gonna do?"

And there was no fanfare to buffer his lonely decisions.

Final Entry

Tuesday, August 6, 2002
New Home Deck
Oakland Hills, California
Tabitha Knight

Today I was given the keys to a four-bedroom home in the hills of Oakland, California. I'm standing here on the deck right now, with a clear skyline view of San Francisco. It's a beautiful, sunny day out. And I should feel great about how things turned out, but I don't.

My sisters are still down on me for living the lifestyle that got me this house. So here I am with my dream house and no family to share it with. Inviting them over now would only intensify the argument. Of course, they don't believe I deserve it. I can't say that I do myself. So what do I do now? Do I give my dream house back and start over to earn it? What if I'm never able to?

I know one thing. It was heart wrenching for me to burn my old diaries to get this place. I cried my ass off for days, but that was the deal. Charles had a man stand right beside me while I showed him the dated pages and tossed book after book into the incinerator. Nobody wanted them popping up on them down the road. They let me keep my first diary, though. Thank God!

I started a new diary collection in April with no names or revealing details, but what fun was that after the suspense of my first collection? That's like driving a stripped-down go-cart after having a Mercedes. It's just not the same.

I wonder if anyone would ever believe how I got caught up in the middle of more than a hundred million dollars worth of men. That's the truth, though. A girl even lost her life over it. That whole situation made me think again about the lifestyles of the rich and famous. Those folks have a lot more to lose than everyday people, and they'll do whatever they have to do to protect it. Now I feel like I want to protect this house, earned or not.

I still date Terrence Matthews off and on, but I don't pressure him to be my steady or anything. He's just fun to be with. And I still have to decide how to reveal my real identity and age to people. I need to come clean with a lot of things. I guess it's gonna be a long process for me. But I'll never overdo things again. It's good to keep my feet on solid ground.

I'm re-enrolling in school now, actually. I want to be a psychologist. I still believe I have a gift of understanding people and what they need out of life. I've been helping out my sisters and the high-post men that I've been involved with for years. Why not make it a profession to help everyone? Or as many people who would come to me. Life can be real lonely without having someone who gets where you're coming from. I feel that more than ever now.

I cut off most of the men that I was dealing with. I needed a break from running around, basically. And as much as my sisters like to complain about me, they're still as confused about life as they'll always be. Patrice is still married to Randy and they're working things out. Marisol had a false alarm on her suspected pregnancy. She now has a new boyfriend who treats her a little better than the last. And Janet is still doing her thing in Frisco. I do believe that Janet will visit me. I'm less than an hour away.

As for all of the high rollers that I got into trouble with, Charles Grandison turned out to be a real angel. I still would like to know more about Isaac Abraham, though. He's still the center of attention, and he's always making new movies. But now I know that Charles follows through on most of the business. I also appreciate how Sylvia Green helped me out with getting Marisol home.

And me? I guess I'll always have a mystery about myself that will never be written about or understood. Everybody's not understood on this earth anyway. I just wish more people could be who they are. Maybe I was meant to be many people instead of just one. I don't know. My life seems to make more sense when I can break it down into different parts. Tabby needs this. Teresa needs that. Tonya needs this and that. Toni needs that and this. And Tamarra needs a little bit of everything.

Isn't everybody's life like that anyway? We all need different things. I'm just able to find those different things from different people. Why hate me and call me names for that?

I just find a way to live on, diary or not. It's still my life. I want to be able to do what I want with it. Maybe I'll start another diary when or if I get married. That one will just be about me, my husband, and our babies.

Charles said I should never feel guilty about wanting to start a regular American family, no matter what kind of life I've lived. Since I can't keep any more references to anything that went on between us, I'll have to burn these pages, too. But you know what? I don't mind having to erase it all anymore. I never wrote everything down in my diaries anyway. I still have my memories. Those are forever. And now I have my dream house. Although, I still feel guilty about keeping it.

I don't know if my sisters will ever feel at peace here while knowing how I got it. But you know what? I just might have to live with that, because no one is promised anything in this world. So I have to continue being optimistic that they'll get over it and just accept things for what they are.

However, I did promise myself that I'll never get involved in a fiasco like that again. But who knows what'll come tomorrow? You can never predict it. One day you're a nobody, the next day you're on television and in all the newspapers for whatever. Who can control that? When it happens . . . it just happens, and you live to deal with it.

ABOUT THE AUTHOR

Omar Tyree is a *New York Times* bestselling author and winner of the 2001 NAACP Image Award for Literary Fiction. His books include *Leslie, Just Say No!, For the Love of Money, Sweet St. Louis, Single Mom, A Do Right Man. Flyy Girl,* and The Urban Griot series. He lives in Charlotte, North Carolina.

To learn more about Omar Tyree, visit his website at www.omartyree.com.